The Prince
of
Beverly Hills

*Also by Stuart Woods
in Large Print:*

Blood Orchid
Capital Crimes
Cold Paradise
Dirty Work
Orchid Blues
Reckless Abandon
Chiefs
Dead Eyes
Deep Lie
Grass Roots
Heat
L.A. Times
Santa Fe Rules
Under the Lake

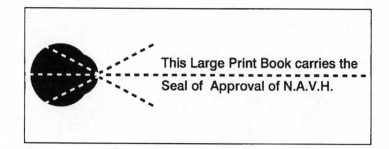

This Large Print Book carries the
Seal of Approval of N.A.V.H.

The Prince
of
Beverly Hills

Stuart Woods

This is a work of fiction. Names, characters, places, and incidents either are the product of the author's imagination or are used fictitiously, and any resemblance to actual persons, living or dead, businesses, companies, events, or locales is entirely coincidental.

Published in 2004 by arrangement with G. P. Putnam's Sons, a division of Penguin Group (USA) Inc.

Wheeler Large Print Hardcover.

The text of this Large Print edition is unabridged.
Other aspects of the book may vary from the original edition.

Set in 16 pt. Plantin by Elena Picard.

Printed in the United States on permanent paper.

Library of Congress Cataloging-in-Publication Data

Woods, Stuart.
    The prince of Beverly Hills / Stuart Woods.
        p. cm.
    ISBN 1-58724-798-4 (lg. print : hc : alk. paper)
    1. Police — California — Los Angeles — Fiction. 2. Hollywood (Los Angeles, Calif.) — Fiction. 3. Motion picture industry — Fiction. 4. Large type books. I. Title.
PS3573.O642P75 2004b
813'.54—dc22
                                                    2004057174

This book is for Suzanne Jones Maas.

National Association for Visually Handicapped
----------------------- serving the partially seeing

As the Founder/CEO of NAVH, the only national health agency solely devoted to those who, although not totally blind, have an eye disease which could lead to serious visual impairment, I am pleased to recognize Thorndike Press* as one of the leading publishers in the large print field.

Founded in 1954 in San Francisco to prepare large print textbooks for partially seeing children, NAVH became the pioneer and standard setting agency in the preparation of large type.

Today, those publishers who meet our standards carry the prestigious "Seal of Approval" indicating high quality large print. We are delighted that Thorndike Press is one of the publishers whose titles meet these standards. We are also pleased to recognize the significant contribution Thorndike Press is making in this important and growing field.

Lorraine H. Marchi, L.H.D.
Founder/CEO
NAVH

* Thorndike Press encompasses the following imprints: Thorndike, Wheeler, Walker and Large Print Press.

1

Rick Barron heard the howl of the engine from
at least a block away. He was not happy to be
sitting in a patrol car at the corner of Sunset and
Camden at two a.m. on a summer evening in
1939; he was not happy to be wearing a badge
with the rank designation of Police Officer, instead of the detective's badge he had worn until
the day before; and he was not happy to be in a
uniform, instead of a suit. The stiff, new cloth
itched.

He looked to his right, toward Ciro's and the
Mocambo and the rest of the clubs on the Strip.
At this hour, Sunset was devoid of traffic, except
for one set of large headlights rushing toward
him at a high rate of speed. Rick started the patrol car. This might be fun, he thought.

Then he saw the other car. It was a Model A
Ford coupe, and it was across the boulevard,
coming toward him down Camden, about to
stop at Sunset. Only it didn't stop. The little car
drove right through the stop sign, moving
slowly, toward the safety of Camden on the

7

other side of Sunset. Rick's mouth dropped open; this couldn't be happening. He looked at the oncoming speeder and had just enough time to identify it as a Mercedes-Benz SSK, top down, before it struck the little coupe broadside. The powerful sports car had been doing at least sixty, Rick thought, and it had never even braked.

The coupe collapsed as if it had been made of tinfoil, absorbing nearly the entire force of the crash, then spun toward the side of the road and came to rest, hard, against a telephone pole. The Mercedes was not stopped, only deflected. It skidded sideways toward the opposite side of the street, struck the curb and rolled over, flinging its driver into a high oleander hedge before coming to rest in an upright position. Rick picked up the microphone.

"This is car 102. I've got a serious car accident at Sunset and Camden. Request an ambulance and another patrol car immediately."

The radio crackled. "Roger, 102, they're on their way."

Rick switched on the flashing light on top of his Chevrolet patrol car, drove across Sunset and stopped at the curb, next to what was left of the coupe. The street was still perfectly clear, with a wreck on each side. He jumped out of the car and started for the coupe.

Sheets of paper littered Sunset, and Rick picked up one. There was a picture of Paul Whiteman on the front: sheet music. He dropped it as he reached the coupe and looked inside. The car was a third of its former width, and the woman inside was barely distinguishable from a pile of cubed beef on a butcher's counter. Rick had never seen such gore. He reached into the car and picked up her left wrist, feeling for a pulse, but felt none. Nothing more to be done here.

The road was still empty of traffic. He ran across Sunset to the hedge and found the other driver lying facedown in the hedge. Rick turned over the unconscious man and saw that he was wearing a tuxedo. And he wasn't unconscious. The man coughed and sat up, leaning on his elbows. "Jesus H. Christ," he muttered. "What the fuck happened?" He had the makings of a fine shiner around his left eye.

Rick got a snootful of alcohol fumes. "You hit another car," he replied. "Are you hurt?"

The man shook his head. "I don't think so," he said. He was handsome, tanned, with thick blond hair and a well-trimmed mustache. "You've got to get me out of here," he said, grimacing. His beautifully even teeth gleamed under the streetlamp. His accent was British.

Then Rick recognized him. Sirens could be heard in the distance, and his mind worked at a furious pace, weighing options, considering gain against punishment. He decided. "Can you stand up?" he asked.

"I guess so," the man replied.

Rick helped him to his feet, took hold of a

9

wrist and slung the man's arm around his neck. Rick was six-two, and the man was as tall. "Come on," Rick said, "we've got to move fast." He scurried across Sunset, half walking, half dragging, and got the man into the rear seat of the patrol car. "Lie down there, so nobody can see you," he commanded. He was about to get behind the wheel, when he had another thought. He ran back across Sunset to the wreck of the Mercedes, found his pocketknife and quickly unscrewed the license plates. Then he went to the driver's side, groped around the steering column and ripped off the registration certificate that had been secured there. As he stuffed it into his pocket, another patrol car arrived, siren dying.

"I've got one of 'em in my car," he said to the driver. "He doesn't seem to be hurt too bad. I'll take him to the hospital. You wait for the ambulance. The other one is hamburger."

"Okay," the other cop replied.

Rick ran for his car and got behind the wheel. "Where can I take you?" he asked.

"Find a phone," the man replied from the depths of the rear seat.

Rick started the car, made a U-turn and swung down Camden, driving fast. After two blocks he saw a pay phone on a corner. "Who do you want me to call?" he asked.

A hand came up from the backseat with a small, black address book. "Call Eddie Harris," his passenger said. "Tell him what's happened.

He'll know what to do."

Rick ran to the phone booth and closed himself inside it. The light came on, and he riffled through the book, looking for the number. The names there made a roster of Hollywood celebrities, most of them women; Lana Turner and Hedy Lamarr were there. He found a home number for Harris, dropped a nickel into the phone and dialed. Harris was something at Centurion Studios; Rick wasn't sure just what.

"What?" an angry, sleepy voice barked into the phone.

"Mr. Harris, my name is Barron. I'm a Beverly Hills Police officer."

"Go on," Harris replied. His voice was calm now.

"I've got Clete Barrow in my patrol car. He's been in a bad accident; a woman is dead."

"How badly is Barrow hurt?" Harris demanded.

"He seems to be okay. He should be checked out at a hospital, though."

"No. Take him to Centurion, to his bungalow. I'll meet you there. What was your name again?"

"Barron." Rick spelled it for him.

"Hurry up," Harris said.

"Yessir." Rick hung up and ran for the car.

It took him less than ten minutes to reach the film studio, no flashing light, no siren. He slid to a stop at the gate. A guard, apparently warned he was coming, waved him on.

"First left, second right," the man in the backseat said. "Number 104."

Rick followed the directions.

"Right here," Barrow said from the rear seat. He was sitting up now.

Rick parked the car, slid across the seat, opened the rear door and helped his passenger out. He looked around. He was on what looked like a street of bungalows. He steered Barrow up the front walk of a pretty cottage with window boxes and a swing on the front porch. Barrow fumbled with a key and let them into the house.

Rick found himself in a beautifully decorated living room, furnished with every comfort. Barrow opened a door and switched on some lights in an adjoining room. Rick blinked in the glare. Barrow sat down at a wide dressing table with a big mirror surrounded by little lightbulbs. He looked carefully at his face in the mirror. "No real damage," he said, with some satisfaction. He felt his body. "Maybe some bruised ribs, and they'll have to shoot my right side only, but I can work." He got up and went back into the living room, to a bar. "You want a drink?" he asked.

"No, and you're not going to have one either," Rick said, removing a decanter of scotch from the actor's hand. "You're going to need to be as sober as possible."

The door opened and a sturdy-looking, balding man in his forties walked into the room.

"Clete," he said, "are you all right?"

"Sure, Eddie," Barrow replied. "Thanks for coming."

"That's some shiner. We're going to have to shoot around it tomorrow. The doctor will be here in a minute. I want you checked out thoroughly. Get out of that tux and into a robe."

"Sure, Eddie. You want a drink? The cop won't let me have one."

"No," Harris replied. He turned to Rick and stuck out his hand. "I'm Eddie Harris," he said.

"Hello, Mr. Harris."

"Call me Eddie; everybody does. What's your first name?"

"Rick."

"Frederick?"

"Richard, but nobody has ever called me that, except my mother, when she was angry with me."

"Rick, is Barrow under arrest?"

"Not unless you want him to be," Rick replied.

"Good man. Come and sit down for a minute, and let's talk."

Rick followed Harris to a pair of leather armchairs before a fireplace and sat down in one, removing his uniform cap.

"That uniform looks brand-new," Harris said, "but you don't look like a rookie."

"I'm not. It's just my first day back in uniform. I seem to have put on a little weight since the last time I wore one."

"How'd you get busted? What was the beef?"

"I was seeing a young lady who turned out to be my commanding officer's niece," Rick said. "The captain and I didn't see eye to eye about it."

"I'll bet," Harris said. "Is she pregnant?"

"Not anymore."

"What was your job before?"

"Detective, assigned to Homicide and Robbery."

"That's a plum assignment, isn't it?"

"It was."

"Now you're a patrolman. It's a long way to fall."

"You're telling me."

"Sounds like you don't have much of a future with the Beverly Hills Police Department."

"Let's say Chief Blair doesn't have to worry about his job."

"I've seen you somewhere before, but I can't place you."

"I get around, I guess. Probably a restaurant or a club."

"That's it: at the bar at Ciro's, more than once."

"I've been there more than once."

Harris nodded. "Tell me what happened tonight. I want it straight — everything."

"I was sitting in my patrol car at Sunset and Camden. Barrow came from the direction of the Strip, doing at least sixty. He struck a Model A coupe that ran a stop sign. The woman driver was killed instantly. Barrow's car rolled, and he was thrown into a hedge."

"What did you do?"

"I called for an ambulance and a patrol car to deal with traffic, checked the woman, then checked on Barrow. When I recognized him, I got him out of there. The car's license plates are on the bar." He reached into his pocket. "Here's the registration."

"Good man. Let me give you a little lesson in Hollywood damage control: The woman drove right out in front of Barrow, so she was at fault. He was driving the speed limit; he didn't smell of liquor; he asked to be brought here, instead of a hospital. Got that?"

Rick nodded. "If you can, you ought to send a tow truck over to Sunset and Camden to get Barrow's car out of there. You don't want those two cars compared in newspaper photographs. The coupe got much the worst of it."

Harris picked up a phone next to his chair, dialed a number, barked some orders and hung up. "It'll be out of there in half an hour."

Simultaneously, Barrow came out of his dressing room in a robe, and a man came in the front door, carrying a satchel.

"Doc," Harris said, turning toward the man, "Mr. Barrow's been in a car accident. I want him checked out thoroughly, and get some ice on that eye, will you?"

"Right," the doctor said. "Mr. Barrow, let's go in the other room." He turned back to Harris.

15

"You want a blood sample taken?"

"Yeah," Harris said, turning to Rick. "You been drinking at all tonight?"

"No."

"Roll up your sleeve."

Rick did as he was told, and the doctor removed a syringe from his bag, swabbed the arm with alcohol and drew some blood.

Harris stood up and held out a business card to Rick. "You may not have much of a future with the police," he said, "but you just might have a future with Centurion. Call me tomorrow morning."

"All right," Rick replied, pocketing the card.

"What's your captain's name?"

"Lawrence O'Connell."

"Don't speak to him unless you have to. If you have to, stick to the story. I'll call him first thing in the morning."

Rick was back at the accident site before the ambulance left. A fire engine was present, and two firemen were working on the wrecked coupe with crowbars, while two patrol cars stood by. The Mercedes was nowhere in sight.

A sergeant got out of a car and walked over. "Where the hell have you been?" he demanded.

"I took the passenger who was still alive to a doctor," Rick said.

"Is he all right?"

"He seems fine."

"Was he drunk?"

"I observed nothing that would make me think so." He took a glass tube from his pocket and handed it to the sergeant. "I witnessed the doctor take a blood sample," he said, but he didn't say whose. "I'd like you to take custody of it."

"All right," the sergeant said. "You said you took him to a doctor. Not a hospital?"

"He didn't seem badly injured, and he insisted on seeing his own doctor."

"Was this guy somebody . . . I ought to know about?"

"He was Clete Barrow. A Mr. Eddie Harris at Centurion Studios said he would speak to the captain."

The sergeant nodded. "I'll tell the captain about this. You stay away from him. Write an accident report and have it on my desk before you go off duty."

"Right," Rick said. "Can I go back to the station and do it now? Tomorrow's my day off."

"Go ahead. And I don't want you talking to the press, you understand? If they track you down, refer them to the captain."

Rick nodded. The sergeant walked away, and Rick looked over at the remains of the Ford coupe. Two firemen had done their work, and now the ambulance men were loading the mangled remains of the woman onto a stretcher. He felt for the woman, but she shouldn't have run that stop sign. His conscience, such as it was, was clear.

2

Rick was wakened by the ringing telephone at nine a.m. He let it ring three times, then picked it up. "Barron," he groaned.

"I saw your report," the captain's voice said. "Is that the way it happened?"

"That's the way I saw it, Captain."

"It better be correct in all respects."

Rick didn't reply to that.

"Where is the Mercedes?"

"I don't know. It was gone when I got back to the scene. A Mr. Eddie Harris said he'd call you."

The captain hung up without another word.

"Miserable son of a bitch," Rick said aloud. He reached for his cigarettes before he remembered he had quit smoking some weeks before. He swung his feet over the side of the bed and stood up, stretching. He'd had only three or four hours of sleep — he'd have had more, if the captain hadn't called — but he felt pretty well. At twenty-nine, he could stand the strain. He showered, then fixed himself some breakfast.

He retrieved the LA *Times* from outside his door and scanned it as he ate. There it was, on page four:

PIANIST KILLED IN SUNSET BLVD ACCIDENT

Somebody got it in the paper at the last minute, he figured. That way, there was no time for anybody at the paper to investigate before they went to press.

> Lillian Talbot, a professional musician, was killed in a traffic accident on Sunset Boulevard early this morning. Police say Miss Talbot, who was on her way home from a party at which she had played the piano, ran a stop sign at the corner of Sunset Boulevard and Camden Drive and drove into the path of an oncoming car, the resulting crash killing her instantly. The other driver was examined by a doctor and pronounced unhurt. The Beverly Hills Police Department released a statement that said, in part, "The accident was witnessed by one of our officers on patrol, and a thorough investigation indicates that Miss Talbot was at fault. A test of the other driver's blood found no trace of alcohol, and no charges will be brought against him.

Well, that wrapped it up neatly, Rick thought. He washed the dishes and put them away. Rick was neat by nature, and, as a result, the little apartment in West Hollywood seemed a better place than it really was. He got dressed, and in changing the contents of his pockets from the uniform to his civilian clothes, he came across Eddie Harris's card. "Edward R. Harris, Executive Vice President," it read. Rick picked up the phone and called the number, which turned out to be a direct line.

"Mr. Harris's office," a woman's voice said.

"My name is Rick Barron. Mr. Harris asked me to call him this morning."

"Oh, yes, Mr. Barron," she replied. "Mr. Harris would like it if you could come to see him at four o'clock this afternoon. Would that be convenient?"

"Yes, it would."

"There'll be a pass for you at the main gate. Come to the administration building. The guard will direct you."

"I'll be there at four." Rick hung up. A future for him at Centurion? It was nice to know there might be a future for him *somewhere*.

Rick dressed in his best suit, drove his Chevrolet coupe down to the Beverly Hills Hotel and went to the barbershop. He had a shave, a haircut and a manicure and, feeling fresher, had a club sandwich in the garden of the Polo Lounge. He couldn't really afford all this anymore, in his reduced circumstances, but he felt like keeping up appearances. Word had already gotten around about his being busted, and he wanted to be seen doing the usual things. He didn't want people feeling sorry for him. He spoke to a few people he knew, left a generous tip and went back to his car. He didn't have anything to do until four, so he drove out to Santa Monica, to Clover Field, and parked at the tin hangar that was Barron Flying Service. He looked into the office and found only the bookkeeper.

"He's in the hangar," she said, barely looking up from her ledgers.

Rick strolled into the hangar to find his father changing the oil in the smaller of his two airplanes. He was dressed in his suit trousers, a white shirt and a tie. Rick grabbed two sets of coveralls from a shelf, got into one and handed the other to his father. "Put these on, Dad. You'll ruin your clothes."

"You sound just like your mother," Jack Barron said, struggling into the coveralls. "What brings you out here?"

Rick walked around the airplane and peered at the other side of the engine. "It's my day off. I thought I'd see how you're doing." He picked up a wrench and tightened a fuel line fitting, then began looking for other anomalies.

"I'm doing fine," Jack said. "You want to fly a party down to San Diego for me this afternoon?"

"Sorry, Dad, I've got an appointment at Centurion Studios at four."

"They making you a movie star?"

"I don't think that's what they've got in mind," Rick said, laughing, "but a guy named Eddie Harris seems to have something in mind."

"I heard of him," Jack said. "I could use some business from those people, if you get a chance to mention it."

"I'll do that at the first opportunity."

Rick noticed an airplane he hadn't seen before — a Lockheed Vega — parked in a corner of the hangar. "Who belongs to the bush plane?" he asked.

"New customer. I'm leasing it from him."

The two men worked on quietly for a while.

"I heard you're back in uniform," Jack said.

"Afraid so," Rick replied.

"Heard it was something to do with a girl."

"It was."

"Figures."

"You want to hear about it?"

"Only if you want to tell it."

"I was seeing this girl, and she turned out to be Captain O'Connell's niece."

"Wouldn't think that would upset anybody all that much, unless you got her in trouble."

Rick blushed, in spite of himself. "Well, yeah."

"She still in trouble?"

"Don't worry, you're not going to be a grandfather."

"Not ever?"

"Never say never."

"Well, I guess you can handle it. You always land on your feet, you do."

"I try."

"You ever want to fly for me, come into the business, it's here."

"Thanks, Dad, I appreciate that."

"So how long's it going to take for you to get the gold badge back?"

"I don't know. I don't know if I want it back." That was a lie.

"What do you want? I've always wondered."

"Me, too," Rick replied.

The two men continued working on the airplane.

3

The guard at the Centurion main gate wrote down Rick's name and issued him a visitor's pass, then gave him directions to the administration building. Rick put the pass on the dashboard of his '32 Chevy coupe and drove onto the studio lot. The night before had been his first visit to a movie studio, and he was interested to see it in daylight. He drove down a street that looked like New York, with neat brownstones lined up, curtains in their windows. When he turned a corner, he saw that they were only facades, propped up by scaffolding.

He found the administration building and parked in a visitor's spot. There was an array of expensive cars in the lot — sedans, convertibles and roadsters — with people's names lettered in gilt on little signs. In Eddie Harris's spot was parked a black Lincoln Continental convertible, very new. Rick entered the building and came to a desk where a uniformed studio guard took his name and directed him to an elevator to the third floor.

A receptionist greeted him and asked him to take a seat. The waiting room was lushly furnished, with movie posters on the walls and an array of trade publications arranged on a coffee table. He had been seated for only a moment when a handsome woman in her forties appeared.

"Mr. Barron? I'm Celia Warren, Mr. Harris's assistant. Would you come with me, please?"

Rick followed her through another, smaller reception room, where two secretaries worked at desks, and into a large, sunny office furnished in dark mahogany furniture and paneling, with a conference table at one end and a group of sofas at the other. Eddie Harris was seated at his desk, his feet up, talking on the telephone. He waved Rick to a chair, and the assistant left them. A moment later, Harris hung up the phone.

"How you doing?"

"I'm fine, thanks."

"Get any sleep last night?"

"Nearly enough."

Harris laughed, something he seemed to do easily. "What do you know about Centurion Studios?" he asked.

"You're the new kid on the block, and you're growing fast," Rick replied. "That's about it." He read *Variety* once in a while.

"That's it in a nutshell," Harris said. "Sol Weinman and I were at MGM, until a couple of years ago. Sol had his own unit, and I was his production manager. When Irving Thalberg

25

died, Sol didn't want to work directly for Louis B. Mayer, so he rounded up some investors, including me, and with some of their money and a lot of his wife's, he bought this property, which had been a poverty row studio with a lot of real estate. He got it at Depression prices. It originally had two soundstages. We've built another two, and there are two more under construction. We're already making two pictures a month, and by this time next year we expect to be making one a week. We're hot, and the whole town knows it. Being new, we've had to borrow a lot of stars for productions, which puts our costs up, but we're building a stable, and since we stole Clete Barrow from Metro, it's getting easier. What Clark Gable is to Metro, Clete Barrow is to us."

"Sounds wonderful," Rick said.

"It is. Now, enough about us, let's talk about you." Harris opened a manila file folder on his desk and consulted the contents. "You know what I found out about you that really surprised me?"

Uh-oh, Rick thought.

"You and I were born sixteen miles apart."

Rick relaxed. "Where were you born?"

"In Greenville, Georgia, right near Delano, where you were born."

"Well, we left there when I was a kid and came out here, so, apart from a couple of visits to my grandparents there, my only claim to Delano is my birth certificate. What happened to your Southern accent?"

26

"It comes back when I've had a couple of bourbons. You know who else is from Greenville?"

"Nope."

"Y. Frank Freeman, who's head of production over at Paramount. Frank and I grew up together, came out here together, but we were too close to work together, if you know what I mean."

"I can see how that could be tough in business," Rick said. He had no idea what he was talking about.

"How did you come to be born in Georgia?" Harris asked.

"My old man is from Minnesota, but he was a barnstorming pilot in the old days, and he met my mother when he blew through Meriwether County. It was a whirlwind courtship, and I'm the result. My mother and I stayed on for a while in Delano while he barnstormed and saved his money, then he joined the Lafayette Escadrille during the first war and flew over there for two years. When he came back, he moved us out here. He was planning a solo flight across the Atlantic, but his friend Lindbergh beat him to it."

"Your folks still alive?"

"My mother died when I was ten. Dad has an FBO over at Clover Field in Santa Monica."

"What's an FBO?"

"Fixed Base Operation, as opposed to barnstorming. He has two airplanes — a Beech

27

Staggerwing and a Lockheed Electra — for air taxi work, and he gives flying lessons and maintains a few airplanes for private owners."

"What's the FBO called?"

"Barron Flying Service."

Harris made a note of it. "Maybe I can throw some business his way."

"He'd like that, and you'd like him."

"You fly, too, it says here." Harris consulted his folder again.

"Yeah, I've got a commercial license and a few thousand hours."

"Why did you become a cop? Didn't you have any interest in the family business?"

"Not really. I enjoy flying for recreation and as a means of travel, but if you're doing it for a living, you're just a glorified taxi driver, and on somebody else's schedule. I intended to become a lawyer, but after UCLA and a year of law school I found it pretty dry stuff. Torts were not for me. The practical application of the law on the street seemed a lot more interesting."

"You were with the LAPD first?"

"Yes, for three years. I've been with the Beverly Hills Department for five. I switched to get a detective's badge quicker."

"You ever expect to get it back?"

Rick shrugged. "Not while Larry O'Connell can still draw a breath."

"I talked with him about you," Harris said.

"Then you must have a low opinion of me."

"Nah. I can read between the lines. He

couldn't find anything bad to say about you as a cop. I talked to a few other people, too — cops, headwaiters, bartenders. You and I have the same barber."

"I'm beginning to wonder if we're kinfolks," Rick said. "So what did you find out?"

"You're unmarried, smart, good at your job, cool under pressure, discreet, reasonably honest, for a cop. You can hold your liquor and you get your hair cut twice a month."

Rick laughed. "What else is there to know?"

"Not a hell of a lot," Harris said. "I'm a good judge of character, and last night I made you for a fellow of some substance. You handled a difficult situation well, you were calm, thorough, and you wouldn't let Clete Barrow have another drink. You saved this studio one hell of a lot of money. Barrow is in the middle of the most expensive production we've ever filmed on this lot, and if you'd arrested him it would have been very difficult to keep him out of jail. You can't recast the lead in the middle of a picture, you have to start over. I like it that you didn't try to put the arm on me, either." Harris opened a desk drawer, took out an envelope and tossed it to Rick. "That's a week of Clete's salary," he said. "You deserve it more than he does."

The envelope felt thick, and Rick slipped it into his inside pocket without looking at it. "Thank you," he said.

A buzzer sounded, and Harris pressed an intercom button. "Yes?"

"Mrs. Harris is here," a voice said.

"Send her in." He turned back to Rick. "My wife. This'll just take a minute."

A tall, blond woman in her mid-thirties swept into the room and gave Harris a big kiss. "Hey, honey," she said.

Rick was on his feet.

"Rick, this is my wife, Suzanne," Harris said.

She offered her hand, and Rick took it. "I've heard a lot about you," she said.

"So has your husband, apparently," Rick replied. "I'm very pleased to meet you."

"Eddie is naturally nosy," she said. "You'll have to forgive him."

"Would it do any good?"

"No." She laughed. "I guess not." She turned to her husband. "I need some money, sweetie."

Harris reached into the desk drawer and came out with a check. "Put that in your account," he said. "I hope it'll last you a while."

"Probably not," she said. "Rick, it's very nice meeting you. I have to run, dear. See you at dinner." She whispered something in her husband's ear, kissed him again and left.

"She's lovely," Rick said.

"Thanks. She is, isn't she? I love it that she was never an actress. She was an agent, if you can believe it." Harris walked around the desk. "Come on, let me show you the lot, and I'll tell you what I have in mind."

Rick followed along like a puppy. He was dying to find out what Harris had in mind.

30

4

Outside the administration building, they got into a small, open electric vehicle with a fringed canvas top, and Harris drove down the nearest street.

"You ever visited a movie studio before?" Harris asked.

"Not until last night."

"Well, the big, hangar-like buildings are soundstages, where the interior shots of movies get shot, and sometimes exteriors, too. Over there is the props warehouse, and next door is costumes and makeup. The stars all have bungalows. All the other actors get made up en masse over there. Remember where the wardrobe department is."

"Okay."

"Let me tell you about my problem, Rick," Harris said. "You remember hearing about a murder-suicide in town last month?"

"Up in the Hollywood Hills somewhere?"

"That's the one."

"I read about it in the paper. It wasn't in my jurisdiction."

"Fellow named John Kean shot his wife — she was twenty years younger than he was, and the thinking is he thought she was screwing around. Then he shot himself. Kean was chief of the studio police here, and he was good at his job."

"I see." Now Rick began to get the point of his visit.

"I've already replaced Kean with his deputy, Cal Herman."

Now Rick was back to square one. If he'd already replaced the guy, why was Harris talking to him?

"Cal's a good cop, very competent," Harris said, "but there were a lot of things that Kean took care of that Cal isn't really suited for, if you get my meaning."

"I'm not sure that I do," Rick replied.

"As our chief of police, Kean was in charge of more than just studio security. He handled a lot of more delicate matters having to do with the press, the public's perception of the studio, and . . . well, the sort of thing you handled last night."

"I see," Rick replied.

"Have I explained what I do here?"

"No, you haven't. Your card says 'executive vice president.' "

"Right. I'm the number-two man at the studio. Sol Weinman is my only boss. As such, I do a lot of things. I produce movies; I hire and fire administrative and financial personnel, as well as producers and directors; I approve the casting of every movie we shoot; the head of production reports to me, and so do the studio police. I've got a public relations director, but I still spend a lot of time seeing that what gets into the press about the studio is favorable."

"Sounds like a big job," Rick said.

"It is, and it's getting bigger. I'm trying to delegate more work, and with that in mind I've decided to create a new position at the studio. Let's call it director of security. Instead of reporting directly to me, the chief of studio police will report to this man. I wouldn't expect the new man to spend a whole lot of time overseeing the studio cops, because Cal Herman can do that. The principal job of the new man will be to protect the studio and its people from scandal, from the press, and, if necessary, protect it from the unwarranted attention of the police — sometimes even protect it from its own employees."

"You mean, embezzlement, that sort of thing?"

"Yes, but more than that, I mean the behavior of some employees."

"What kind of behavior?"

"The movie business attracts kids from all over the country — all over the world, even. They arrive here with nothing more than ambition and talent, and sometimes not even talent. If they find work, then they're making more money than they would as secretaries and gas-pump jockeys, and sometimes it goes to their heads. They get into trouble, and it can reflect badly on the studio, unless these situations are handled. Often, we can do more to straighten out difficulties than the police can, and we can do it a lot more quietly and with less harm to everybody concerned."

"I understand," Rick said.

Harris was now driving through the main street of an Old West town. "We're on the back lot now. We've got several hundred acres with various sets and open ground where we shoot war movies and Westerns and other outdoor situations." He made a turn, and they drove into a street of neat houses, shaded by large trees. "Here's our American small town," Harris said.

"This is all amazing," Rick replied, looking around. "A lot of it looks familiar from movies I've seen."

"You go to the movies much?"

"A couple of times a week, I guess. I enjoy them."

"That's good. Back to business: Rick, you know when you called me last night? I don't want to get calls like that. I want you to get them. I want you to be my new director of security at the studio. What would you think about that?"

Rick took a deep breath and tried to remain calm. "That sounds very appealing."

"The movie business is very big, and it's getting bigger, and Centurion is getting bigger, faster than almost anybody else. There are going to be a lot of opportunities here over the next few years. There might come a time when you'd want to do something else with us. I like to promote my own people, when I can. You do a good job for me, and I'll be appreciative. I want you to remember that."

"I certainly will."

Harris had headed back toward the administration building now. "Here's my offer," he said. "Three hundred a week to start. When you're worth it, you'll get more. There are the usual perks — a pension plan, et cetera. You'll have an office, but you'll spend a lot of time out of it. I warn you, this is a twenty-four-hour-a-day job."

"I'm accustomed to that," Rick said.

Harris turned a corner and pulled into a large building that Rick had thought was a soundstage. It was filled with all sorts of vehicles — sedans, convertibles, police cars, ambulances, wagons and buggies, even stagecoaches. "This is our motor pool," Harris said.

"That's my car," Rick said, pointing at a Chevrolet.

"It is." Harris waved a man over. "Hey, Hiram, how you doing?" he asked.

"Pretty good, Eddie. This the guy?"

"Rick, this is Hiram Jones. He runs the transportation department."

Rick shook the man's hand.

"What do you reckon his car is worth?" Harris asked the man.

"I'll give him three hundred for it."

"Sell the man your car, Rick. We'll find you something else to drive."

"Done," Rick said, grateful to be rid of his old crate.

Harris climbed out of the cart. "Let's see what you've got, Hiram."

Jones led them down a row of parked cars, and Harris stopped in front of a cream-colored 1938 Ford convertible. "This looks like you, Rick," he said. "What do you think?"

"I'll defer to your judgment," Rick said, smiling.

"Put it in the admin parking lot, Hiram," Harris said. "Come on, Rick, let's get back. It's getting late."

Rick looked farther back into the building and saw Clete Barrow's Mercedes. It looked a total wreck to him. "What are you going to do with that?" he asked Hiram Jones.

"Repair it," Jones replied. "It's impossible to replace."

They got back into the cart and drove back to the administration building.

"One thing I didn't ask you," Harris said.

"What's that?"

"How do you feel about Jews?"

"Just fine. I have no problem with anybody."

"Good, because Jews invented this business, and most of the people who run it are Jewish. They're great people, and I don't like it when

36

people call them yids or tell kike jokes."

"I understand."

"I've got some poker buddies; we're all gentiles. We call ourselves the 'goy scouts.' "

Rick laughed.

"You'll have to play poker with us sometime."

"Thanks," Rick said, "but I don't play poker with people who are richer or smarter than I am."

Harris grinned. "I think you're going to work out just fine." He led Rick through a door at one end of the administration building, past the reception desk and through a glass door marked "Studio Police." Harris went to an open office door. "Cal," he said, "come out here. I want you to meet your new boss."

Cal Herman, in uniform, came toward Rick with his hand out. "You must be Rick Barron," he said. "Glad to have you aboard."

"Thanks, Cal," Rick replied, surprised that Herman was expecting him.

"Come on, I'll show you your office," Harris said.

"See you later, Cal."

"Sure thing, Rick. I'm available when you want to talk."

Harris led Rick out of the police office and across the reception room to another door. A sign painter was lettering "Director of Security" in gilt, and below it, "R. Barron." Harris opened the door and a secretary stood up at her desk. "Rick, this is Jenny Baker. She'll be your secretary, if that turns out to be all right with both of you."

"Hello, Jenny," Rick said, shaking the girl's hand.

"How do you do, Mr. Barron?"

"Rick, please." She looked like the Central Casting all-American girl, he thought.

Harris led him into the adjoining office. It was a quarter the size of Harris's, but still spacious, with a handsome desk, a leather sofa and chairs, a bathroom with a shower to one side and Centurion movie posters on the walls. There was a safe in one corner. "Will this do?" Harris asked.

"It certainly will," Rick replied. "This is all a little overwhelming."

Harris went to the desk and picked up a stack of cards from a silver tray. "Put these in your pocket," he said.

Rick looked at the cards. "Richard Barron, Director of Security, Centurion Studios." Below that were two phone numbers, one office and one home. "Very nice," Rick said, "but this isn't my home number."

"We'll talk about that tonight," Harris said. "I want you to come to dinner at my house."

"I'd be delighted," Rick said.

Harris handed him a card with the address and phone number. "Seven o'clock, black tie."

"I'm afraid I don't own a tux, and it's a little late to rent one," Rick said.

"Go back to wardrobe and ask for Marge. She's waiting to fix you up." Harris steered Rick

38

back to the reception area, where Celia Warren, Harris's assistant, was waiting for them. "Celia, Rick is joining us as of this moment."

"I'm delighted to hear it," she said. "Here's a check for your car, Rick." She handed him an envelope.

"I hope you've no problem with leaving the police department immediately," Harris said.

"None whatsoever," Rick replied, and he meant it. He walked out to the parking lot and saw the cream-colored convertible parked in a spot, which was reserved by a neatly lettered sign with his name on it. Harris had been very confident that he would accept the job.

He drove over to the wardrobe department. Marge was a motherly woman in her fifties, and she had a handsome tuxedo waiting for him.

"We made this for Clete Barrow," she said, "and you're about his size. Try it on."

It fit as if it had been made for him. She found him a pleated shirt, a black tie, shoes and some cuff links and studs, too. "You'll look very elegant," Marge said as she showed him out.

On the way home, with his studio tuxedo on the backseat of the convertible, Rick stopped at the Beverly Hills City Hall, went into the police department squad room, borrowed a typewriter and wrote out his resignation. He took it to his captain's office, knocked once and opened the door without being invited in.

"What do you want?" O'Connell said, glaring at him.

"To resign, Captain," Rick replied, handing him the letter and placing his badge and Smith & Wesson revolver on the desk. "Effective immediately."

O'Connell nearly smiled. "And good fucking riddance," he said.

Rick closed the door behind him, walked out of the building and to his new car, seeming to float. As he tucked a copy of his resignation letter into his inside pocket, he felt the envelope that Harris had handed him earlier. He opened it, looked inside and quickly counted. Apparently, Clete Barrow made five thousand bucks a week. "My God, what a day!" he said aloud.

5

Clad in borrowed elegance — a finely tailored mohair tuxedo, silk shirt and waistcoat and gleaming alligator shoes — Rick arrived at the Bel-Air address of Eddie and Suzanne Harris at ten minutes past the hour. He hoped he was only fashionably late.

His car was parked by an attendant, and he was greeted at the door by an English butler who was dressed as well as he. Rick had been in houses as impressive as this Greek Revival mansion, with its marble entryway and sweeping staircase, but usually when the owner had either been robbed or was lying facedown, bleeding into the Aubusson carpet. He tried to adopt the mind-set of a guest, instead of an official intruder.

The butler showed him into the living room, where the Harrises and another couple were standing before a cheerful fire.

"Ah, Rick," Harris said, coming toward him, a martini glass in his hand, "good to see you." He drew Rick toward the fire. "You met Suzanne earlier, of course."

"I'm so happy you could come, Rick," she said, offering her hand.

"So am I," Rick replied.

"Rick," Harris said, "I'd like you to meet our boss — or God, as we sometimes call him. This is Sol Weinman and his wife, Rebecca."

"How do you do, Mr. Weinman, Mrs. Weinman," he said, shaking hands with both.

"I've heard much about you from Eddie," Weinman said. He was short and plump, with a fringe of white hair circling a hairless dome. "He's needed someone like you for some time now, and I'm glad you're coming aboard. You must drop by my office for a chat soon."

"Thank you, Mr. Weinman, I'd like that," Rick replied.

"And you must call me Sol. Everybody at Centurion is on a first-name basis. We don't stand on ceremony like Metro and some others I could mention."

"Thank you, Sol."

A waiter appeared at Rick's elbow with a tray of martinis, and he took one. As he did, two other couples were being shown in, and Rick found himself being introduced to Sam Goldwyn and William Wyler and their wives. The party was completed when Clark Gable and Carole Lombard arrived, accompanied by an attractive older woman, who turned out to be Sol Weinman's sister, Adele Mannheim. He was in illustrious company, and he was finding it easy to get used to the idea.

After another half hour of chat, they were called to dinner, twelve around a table of glistening china, silver and crystal. Rick sent a silent prayer of thanks to his mother, who, when he was a boy, had drilled him in his table manners and which fork to use. He was seated between Carole Lombard and Adele Mannheim, and as dazzled as he was by Lombard, he was smart enough to pay a lot of attention to Mrs. Mannheim, since he had clearly been invited as her dinner partner.

"I was widowed earlier this year," she confided, "and the Harrises have made a point of inviting me over regularly." She leaned over and whispered, "I must say, I'm having more fun than when my husband was alive; he didn't like going out."

Rick listened closely to her every word and tried to charm without flattering too much. When she excused herself for a moment, he turned to Lombard, and was disappointed to find her engrossed in conversation with Wyler, who sat on her other side.

When dinner was concluded, the ladies went somewhere with Suzanne Harris, while the men remained at the table over coffee, port and cigars. Rick declined a cigar; he despised them.

"Sam," Sol Weinman said to Goldwyn, "what do you think about this television thing? Do we have anything to worry about?"

"I don't think so," Goldwyn replied, in accented English. "A fuzzy little picture of base-

43

ball games and puppet shows is not going to take anybody away from a big screen in Technicolor, and you can say I didn't say so."

"Clark," Wyler said, "would you act on television?"

"In what?" Gable replied, "a baseball game or a puppet show? And you can say I didn't say so."

Goldwyn wrinkled his brow. "That didn't sound right, Clark."

Everybody laughed except Goldwyn, who seemed surprised to find himself funny.

Rick took it all in, speaking only when he was spoken to, which wasn't often.

They eventually joined the ladies in the library for coffee, and as ten o'clock chimed on a large clock in a corner, people began to leave. In five minutes, they were all gone. Harris had indicated that Rick should stay. They said good night to Suzanne, and she left them.

"Let's take a walk," Harris said, taking Rick's arm. They left the rear of the house through French doors and followed a path around a high hedge until they came to a large swimming pool, lit from underneath. A cabana was at one end, and another building across the pool. "That's one of the guest houses," Harris said. He led the way around the pool and down another path, and shortly they came to a cottage, ablaze with light. "This used to be the gardener's cottage before we bought the place, when the grounds were twice as large. Suzanne has done it up as another guest house, but we don't really need

44

it." Harris opened the front door with a key and they walked through the cottage. There was a living room with a dining table at one end, a kitchen, a bedroom and a small room that had been done up as a study, with a desk and bookcases. "You like?" Harris asked.

"It's beautiful," Rick said.

"How would you like to live here?"

"I don't understand."

"I travel to New York on business now and then, and Suzanne wants somebody on the place besides the servants, who live in an apartment over the garage, and she likes the idea of an ex-cop being here. There's a little garage out back, and another drive that goes directly to the street. You can come and go as you please, and we promise you privacy. I'll charge you, say, a hundred a month? You'll pay the utilities and the phone, of course."

Rick turned to him. "Is this place the home number on my new business card?"

"I thought you'd like it," Harris said, grinning.

"Like you say, Eddie, you're a good judge of character."

Harris handed him the keys. "And don't even think of fooling around with my wife. She's got a gun in her bedside drawer, and she's a hell of a shot."

Rick laughed, but he took it seriously.

"Come on, I'll walk you back to the house. You can move in tomorrow."

They strolled back up the path, arm in arm. "Let me tell you a couple of things about this business," Harris said. "It's a candy store, where women are concerned, and nobody expects you to be a priest, but try and be discreet. Sol doesn't approve of his people getting blow jobs in their offices, and he'd like to think that every starlet who gets a walk-on part didn't get it on the casting couch with one of his executives, and you're one of his executives now."

"I'll keep that in mind," Rick said.

"By the way, you were smart to talk a lot to Adele tonight. She has Sol's ear, and he respects her opinion about just about everything."

"That was easy. She's a charming woman."

"I want you to take tomorrow to get moved in, and I want you to buy some clothes with some of that money I gave you. You'll need to dress better than you did when you were a cop. If you didn't, Sol would notice."

"Thanks, I'll do that, and thank you again for the money. You're very generous, Eddie, and I appreciate it."

"You earned it. The day after tomorrow you take on your first assignment from me."

"And what is that?"

"Clete Barrow. He's got another three weeks on this picture, and last night scared the hell out of me. I want you to become his friend, which is easy; he's a nice guy. You don't have to keep him sober, which is impossible, but I want him in

46

one piece and at work on time every day. Understood?"

"Understood."

"I don't mean to turn you into a babysitter, but this is probably the most important picture we've made so far, and we have hopes for a few Academy Awards. A lot depends on Clete, and that means a lot depends on you."

"I'll take care of it."

"That's what I like to hear. Say, the tux looks great on you! Keep it. I'll square it with wardrobe."

"Thanks again," Rick said as they reached the front of the house. His car was waiting. "And thank Suzanne again for such a wonderful evening."

"Don't worry, there'll be more. Now she'll have a bachelor on the premises, an odd man for dinner parties."

"I'll look forward to it," Rick said. He drove away into the cool California night, the top down, inhaling the fragrant Beverly Hills air. He had a new job, a new home, a new car and five grand in his pocket. Tomorrow, he'd have a new wardrobe. Life was looking good.

Then he began to think about Clete Barrow. How the hell was he going to handle that problem?

6

Rick took most of the following morning to clean out his furnished apartment, amazed at how much junk he had collected in the two years he had lived there. He threw away everything he would not need in his new life, and when he was done, there were only a few items of sports clothing, some files, a few personal effects and his new evening clothes. He left a large pile of cardboard boxes filled with his old things for trash pickup. Everything he took with him fitted into the convertible. He wrote the landlady a generous check and left it in her mailbox with a note.

An hour later, he had moved into his new cottage, had everything put away and had been confronted by his empty closets. He went down to Rodeo Drive and into an old-line Beverly Hills men's shop and, inside of an hour, had chosen suits, jackets and odd trousers, two dozen shirts — dress and sport — half a dozen pairs of shoes, plus ties, socks, underwear. While the shop's tailors worked like beavers to cuff his trousers — the only alterations needed, since he was a perfect 42 long — he chose tennis whites, golf shoes, three hats and a trench coat for chilly evenings. It was an orgy of shopping, and he had never enjoyed anything more that hadn't involved sex. He paid in cash, which took a big bite out of his five thousand dollars. At a hundred and fifty bucks for a suit, it added up. He put on a new outfit and ordered everything else delivered to the cottage before the day was out. Then he went grocery shopping. That night, he grilled himself a steak, had a swim in the Harrises' pool, listened to the radio for a while and turned in early.

Next morning, he was at Centurion bright and early. He waited while the gate guard affixed a sticker to his car window — artwork of a Roman centurion — then drove to the administration building and entered his new office. Jenny was already at work.

"Good morning, Rick," she said brightly. "Your office is ready. I've cleaned everything out."

A cardboard box sat on her desk with what had apparently been John Kean's desk contents. Rick picked up a framed photograph of a couple, beaming at the camera. "Is this Kean and his wife?"

"Yes," Jenny said. "Her name was Helen. Pretty, isn't she?"

Rick nodded.

"Oh, one thing," Jenny said. "I spent all day yesterday trying to get the safe opened, but our usual lock and safe people couldn't do it. It's a Schneider, a German model, and, apparently it's impossible to open without the combination. I looked all over the office, thinking John might have hidden the combination somewhere, but I found nothing. You want me to have it hauled away?"

"Leave it," Rick said. "I think I may know somebody who can open it."

"Good luck," she said. "Oh, Eddie Harris said to let him know when you came in. Shall I call him?"

"Sure." Rick went into his office and arranged his desk, placing an old photograph of his parents on the desktop. They were wearing flying clothes and standing in front of an old World War I Jenny. Then he looked up a number in his address book and dialed it.

"Jah?" a gutteral voice said.

"Hans, it's Rick Barron. I've got a safe I want opened."

"Rick," the man replied plaintively, "you know I'm not doing dis no more. I'm an honest man now."

"Don't worry, it's strictly legit," Rick said. He gave him the address.

"All right," Hans sighed. "I'll be there in an hour."

"It's a Schneider," Rick said. "Can you handle it?"

"Please, Rick, not to be insulting me. You vant a new combination?"

"Yes."

"Give me some numbers."

"Okay. Ten, fifteen, twenty."

"You are having no imagination, Rick, you know dis?"

"I'll leave twenty bucks with my secretary." Rick hung up in time to greet Eddie Harris, who was walking through the door, followed by a middle-aged man in a business suit. Rick recognized his old boss from the LAPD immediately.

"Welcome aboard, pal," Harris said, pumping his hand. "I want you to meet somebody. Rick, this is Chief Davidson of the LAPD."

"Chief, how are you?" Rick knew the man had held the job for less than a year, and rumor had it he was already on his way out.

"Pretty good, Rick. Raise your right hand."

"What?"

"Do it, Rick," Harris said.

"Do you swear to uphold the laws of the city of Los Angeles and the state of California and to protect and defend the people of this city?"

"I guess I do," Rick replied.

"You're now a lieutenant on the LAPD," Davidson said, handing him a gold badge in a wallet. "If you'll excuse me, Eddie, I've gotta run."

"See you around, Brian." Davidson left.

51

"I thought the badge might come in handy," Harris said to Rick. "The chief sells them to the right people for a hundred and fifty bucks. You ready to go to work?"

"You bet."

"Come on, then."

Rick paused at Jenny's desk. "A little German man is going to show up to open the safe. Watch him and see that he doesn't take anything out of it."

"He's a thief?"

"He used to be. Don't worry, he's harmless." He handed her twenty dollars. "Give him this when he's finished."

Harris grabbed the money and handed it back to Rick. "Get that from petty cash," he said to Jenny.

She handed him a pad of chits, and he signed one.

"You'll be able to sign, yourself, after today," Harris said. "Don't spend your own money on studio stuff. Now come on."

"Where will you be?" Jenny asked.

"I've no idea," Rick replied.

Harris led him to the electric cart and began driving. "Sleep well last night?"

"You bet."

"I saw you in the pool. You're pretty athletic."

"I swam at Santa Monica High," Rick replied, "and I played on the tennis and golf teams at UCLA."

"Useful sports," Harris replied. He pulled up

52

in front of Clete Barrow's cottage. "Here we go."

Barrow was sitting in a barber's chair while a woman lightly applied makeup to his tanned face. The shiner was hardly noticeable.

"Hey, Clete," Harris said. "Remember this guy?"

"Indeed," Barrow replied. "I never got your name, chappie."

"It's Rick Barron." They shook hands.

"Ah, yes. I hear you're our new top copper around here."

"You heard right," Harris said. "Listen, I've got someplace to be. I'll leave you guys to chat."

Rick walked him to the door.

"You've just started work," Harris said as he left. "Good luck."

Rick turned and went back into the dressing room.

Barrow stood and stretched. He was wearing a handsome military uniform with a red jacket. "So you're the new nursemaid, eh?"

Rick laughed. "I guess I am."

"Think you can keep up with me?"

"I'll do my best."

"Is it your job to keep me sober?"

"I was told that's impossible. Eddie just wants you to show up for work every day."

"Not an unreasonable request," Barrow said, checking his hair in a mirror. "Well, come on then, let's do it." He led the way to his own electric cart, and they set off.

"Where you from, Rick?" Barrow asked.

"Born in Georgia, came out here as a boy, grew up in Santa Monica. How about you?"

"England, old boy; a village in Kent, south of London. I was meant for the Navy, but after Dartmouth I opted for the Royal Marines. Served out my obligation, then was attracted to the stage. A scout from Metro saw me in a play in the West End, and the rest, as they say, is history. How long were you a cop?"

"Eight years."

"That's long enough, surely."

"Long enough."

"Eddie is a good chap. Give him what he wants and he'll always be your friend. He's certainly been mine."

Rick nodded. "What's this picture you're shooting?"

"A Khyber Pass horse opera, with pretensions of quality," Barrow drawled. "Nothing special, except for the money they're spending on it. We did the exteriors last month out in some godforsaken part of the desert. Now we're doing the interiors." He stopped at a soundstage door and swept inside, with Rick in his wake, introducing him to the director, the assistant director, the producer and a dozen other people.

"We're ready for you, Clete," a woman with a clipboard said. "Take my chair," Barrow said to Rick, pointing to one with his name printed on the canvas back.

Rick sat down and watched as Barrow strode

onto the set, that of the commanding officer's office at an Indian Army outpost. The scene was shot over and over, from different angles, with close-ups for the various actors. It went smoothly, and Rick thought that Barrow made a commanding figure in the gorgeous uniform.

The shooting occupied the morning, then Barrow took Rick to the studio commissary for lunch, where he was introduced to another dozen people, mostly actors that Rick had seen in movies. After lunch, they returned to the soundstage, and a scene was shot on another set, this one a moonlit terrace with a very realistic painting of mountains in the distance.

During a break, Rick approached Barrow. "I should get back to the office for a while. What are you doing for dinner?"

"Joining you, I should think," Barrow replied. "Pick me up at my bungalow at six?"

"Will do." Rick left the soundstage, and an assistant drove him back to the administration building in Barrow's cart.

"The safe's open," Jenny said as he entered his office. "What a funny little man."

"He's the best safecracker on the West Coast," Rick replied.

She handed him a key. "He made this for a lockable compartment inside the safe," she said. "He said you'd be interested in its contents."

Rick went into his office and, using the new combination, opened the safe. There was nothing in sight. He used the key to open the interior compartment and was stunned at what he found. Bundles of twenty-, fifty- and one-hundred-dollar bills were stacked in the compartment. Rick did a quick count and came up with an approximate figure of twenty-two thousand dollars. There was also a manila envelope in the compartment and a Colt Model 1911 .45-caliber semiautomatic pistol. He took the clip out of the weapon and worked the action. It had been loaded, cocked and locked. He replaced it in the safe and opened the manila envelope.

Inside was an eight-by-ten glossy photograph of John and Helen Kean in bed with another couple, caught in various sex acts. The other woman was even more beautiful than Helen Kean, and the other man was a handsome Mediterranean-looking man who Rick thought looked familiar, but he couldn't place the face. He checked the envelope, but the negative was not present.

He looked at the photograph again. There was nothing arty or posed about it, and it left nothing whatever to the imagination.

Rick locked the photograph and the money in the safe and went out to Jenny's desk. "Do you know if John Kean had any family?"

"Just his wife, I think. There was a lot of talk about it after the . . . incident, and from what I heard, nobody had any idea what to do with his personal effects or any estate he might have had. I guess it all goes to the state, or something, not that he had any money. My impression was that he spent everything he made. Word was, he and Helen lived pretty high on the hog."

"Thanks," Rick said. He went back into his office and sat down. He took the photograph from the safe and looked at it again. None of the four participants seemed aware of a camera. The whole thing smacked of blackmail, and judging from the amount of money in the safe, it seemed that Kean was on the collecting end.

But Kean's being a blackmailer didn't square with his suicide, let alone his murder of his wife. Unless somebody had staged the event. Rick's first impulse was to call Eddie Harris and tell him about this, but he hesitated. Harris had hired him to take the load off, not to add to it. He locked the safe. He'd think about it for a while, see what he could come up with.

Later, Rick left his office, picked up his car and went to have his second successive dinner with a movie star.

7

Rick drove to Clete Barrow's bungalow, enjoying his new car. He loved the Ford's V8, and the transmission was smooth as silk. Obviously the motor department at Centurion had done a lot of work on the car, above and beyond the cream paint job. The upholstery was cream leather with red piping, and the original dashboard had been replaced with beautifully varnished burled walnut. He had a feeling he had seen the car in a movie, but he couldn't quite place it.

The front door of the cottage was open. "Hello?" he shouted through the screen door.

"Come on in, old boy!" Barrow shouted back. "Be with you in a minute." Barrow came out of his dressing room, wet, clad in a terry robe. "Fix yourself a drink. Be right with you."

Rick went to the bar and opened a Coca-Cola. He figured the best way to deal with Barrow's drinking was not to let the man get him drunk. He strolled around the living room, looking at the pictures. There were no framed glossies of movie stars, or scenes from Barrow's films; instead there was a collection of small oils and watercolors, mostly landscapes of what Rick assumed was the English countryside.

Barrow came out of his dressing room clad in a double-breasted blue blazer and white trousers. His thick, blond hair was slicked back, still wet. "Shall we, then? We'll have to take your car, since mine is, well, incapable."

"It's right outside."

Barrow closed the door behind him but did not lock it. "Hey, that's a beauty," he said, looking over Rick's car. "I've seen it in a film, haven't I?"

"That's what I thought, but I can't place the film."

"No matter." Barrow settled himself into the passenger seat.

Rick turned the car around and drove out the front gate, accepting a salute from the guard with a wave. "Where to?"

"Where do you live?"

"Bel-Air."

Barrow whistled. "That's quite an address for so recent a copper."

"I'm renting Eddie Harris's guest house, or one of them."

"You own a dinner jacket?"

"Since yesterday."

"Let's go pick it up, then we'll go to my place and I'll get mine. I think we should go out on the town to celebrate."

"Celebrate what?"

"My new minder, old bean."

"Look, Mr. Barrow, let's get something straight."

"Clete," he replied. "Let's get that straight first."

"Clete, I don't really give a shit what you do with your evenings or how much you drink, as long as you show up on time until this picture is done. You don't have to have dinner with me or be my pal, or take me out on the town, all right?"

"May I call you Rick?" Barrow asked politely.

"Of course."

"Rick, if I wanted to stay drunk for a month and never show up at the studio again, there wouldn't be a damned thing you could do about it. I, like all drunks, am sneaky and resourceful."

"I don't doubt it," Rick replied, turning toward Bel-Air.

Barrow laughed. "All I'm saying is, I'm happy to have the pleasure of your company. Most of my friends are married or living with women. I don't have many single mates to tie one on with, you see?"

"In that case, let's go out on the town."

"Righto."

Rick turned down his secret drive and pulled up in front of the cottage.

"Well, what a fine hideaway," Barrow said, opening the front door and walking in. "I see you've just moved in."

"Yeah, I haven't got all my books put away yet. I'm going to grab a shower. Can I get you anything?"

"Just point me at the bar."

Rick rolled his eyes.

"Relax, chappie," Barrow said, chuckling. "Unlike most drunks, I can control it, if I want to."

"Suit yourself," Rick said. "There's a bottle of bourbon in the cabinet, there. I haven't had time to lay in a stock of anything else."

"Bourbon is not my idea of whiskey," Barrow said, "but if it's all that's going . . ." He headed for the cabinet.

Rick showered and dressed in his new tuxedo. When he came out, Barrow was sitting on the couch, a drink in his hand, listening to the news on the radio.

"We're going to be at war soon," Barrow said sadly.

"You really think so?"

"Hitler's not going to stop until somebody stops him, and who but us? The French are useless."

"You really think Roosevelt would take us into a war?"

"Not you — us. The Brits."

"Oh."

"Churchill is right, you know, but nobody will listen to him."

"If you say so. Shall we go?"

Barrow left half his drink in the glass and

headed for the car. "Say, that's my dinner suit you're wearing."

"It is?"

"They made it for me to wear in *Hilyard's Choice*, last year."

"Centurion wardrobe supplied, and Eddie told me to keep it."

"Fits you perfectly, old chap. Savile Row couldn't have done better."

They got into Rick's car, and following Barrow's directions, Rick drove up Sunset and turned into the Hollywood Hills, climbing more and more until they turned into a narrow dirt lane at the top of a ridge. They stopped in front of a Spanish-style house built into the hillside and hidden from the road by trees and rhododendrons.

Rick followed Barrow up the steps and into the house. They entered a foyer and emerged into a large living room, comfortably furnished. Two sets of French doors opened out onto a terrace and pool, and in the dusk, the lights of the city were beginning to show. The view was spectacular.

"Won't be a moment, old boy," Barrow said. "The bar's over there." He pointed at a bookcase.

Rick walked over to the shelves, puzzled, but on closer inspection the books turned out to be spines glued to the paneling. He found a handle and pulled. The "bookshelves" swung open, revealing a beautifully designed bar, complete with crystal glasses.

"A far cry from my cabinet," Rick muttered to himself. He drank another Coke and watched the lights of LA come on.

8

They coasted down to Sunset in the gathering night.

"Ciro's?" Clete asked.

"Why not?" Rick replied, turning onto Sunset. As they approached the nightclub, he began automatically looking for a parking spot, then realized he didn't have to save money on tips anymore. He pulled up front and gave the car to the valet, and they walked inside. The Latin strains of the Xavier Cugat Orchestra wafted across the room from the dance floor.

Rick was a few paces behind Clete, and he was glad, because the man knew how to make an entrance, and Rick wasn't accustomed to the attendant glad-handing. While Clete received admirers, Rick went over to the bar and found a stool.

"Your usual bourbon, Rick?" the bartender asked.

Rick had spent a fair number of evenings at this bar, though not in a tuxedo in the company of a movie star. "Not yet, Charley," he said.

"Heard you had a little trouble with the Beverly Hills PD," Charley said. "Sorry to hear it."

Rick put one of his new cards on the bar. "Let's just say I left for better things."

Charley perused the card and tucked it into his shirt pocket. "Congratulations," he said, obviously impressed. "I'm buying. What'll it be?"

The house had never bought him a drink before. "Oh, all right, an Old Crow on the rocks."

Charley produced a different bottle. "Try the Wild Turkey," he said, pouring a more-generous-than-usual slug of the bourbon.

Clete shook hands with his admirers and walked over. "Evening, Charley." He turned to Rick. "Bring it with you to the table." He turned and walked toward the maître d'.

Rick was still playing catch-up. He had never sat at a table at Ciro's, and there wouldn't have been one available if he'd asked.

"Evening, Mario," Clete said, shaking the man's hand. "We'll be two, but we might get lucky, so you'd better make it four."

"Of course, Mr. Barrow," the man said.

"Oh, and let me introduce Rick Barron. He's the new head of security at Centurion."

Mario, who had never let his gaze fall upon Rick during his days at the bar, was wreathed in smiles. "It's a great pleasure to meet you, Mr. Barron," he said. "Please follow me."

They descended to the dance floor level and

were given a front-row table, discreetly to one side.

"I see you're drinking that awful colonial brown stuff," Clete said as the captain scurried over, carrying a glass of another brown liquor.

"Johnny Walker Black, Mr. Barrow," the captain said. He bowed in Rick's direction. "Good evening, sir."

"Pino, this is Mr. Barron, Centurion's head of security."

"Very pleased to make your acquaintance, Mr. Barron," the waiter said. "I see you already have a drink. May I offer you a menu?"

"What are you feeling like, Rick? Hungry?"

"You bet I am," Rick said.

"Let's split a porterhouse, all right?"

"All right."

"Medium rare?"

"Fine."

"Pino, the porterhouse medium rare and a couple of your Caesar salads. And let's have some champers."

"The Krug, of course, Mr. Barrow."

"Of course."

The man went away, leaving the two to sip their drinks. Cugat stood in front of his orchestra, a violin in one hand and a tiny Chihuahua in the other, while a buxom woman in a long, low-cut evening gown began to sing something in Spanish, surrounded by men in big-sleeved costumes playing conga drums and maracas.

66

"I love this Latin stuff," Clete said. "You?"

"I prefer jazz and swing," Rick said, "but the lady is easy to look at."

"She's Cugat's wife," Clete said. "You don't want to mess with a Latino's wife."

"I wasn't considering it," Rick replied, "just admiring."

"And admirable she is."

Several couples occupied the dance floor now.

"I'd ask you to dance," Clete said, "but people might talk."

Rick laughed.

"Oh, now, what have we here?" Clete asked, nodding toward the maître d', who was leading a man and two very beautiful young women toward the next table.

"Very nice," Rick said appreciatively. "Pity they're with the guy."

"The guy is a studio flack," Clete said, waving them over to the table. "He's making sure they get seen." They both stood up.

"Evening, Clete," the young man said. "May I introduce Carla and Marla?"

"Carla and Marla?" Clete laughed. "How absolutely charming. Why don't you all join us?" He introduced Rick, and a waiter rushed over with another chair.

They had hardly sat down when the young man looked at his watch. "Will you excuse me? I have to make a phone call." He got up and walked toward the bar.

"He won't be back," Clete said in an aside to

Rick. "He's done his work." He told the captain to adjust their dinner order, then turned to the two young women. "Now tell me again, which one is Carla, and which one is Marla?"

But Rick's attention had been drawn to the other side of the room, where the maître d' was seating a man and a woman.

Clete followed his gaze. "You know who that is, don't you?"

"No, do you?"

"It's Lara Taylor, the new hot young thing at Metro," Clete said.

"Oh, yes." He'd seen her in a picture, but she wasn't who interested him. "Who's the man?"

"The latter-day Valentino? His name is Chick Stampano. Word has it he works for Bugsy Siegel."

Rick didn't have to ask who Bugsy Siegel was; everybody knew he ran the LA branch of the mob. He looked carefully at Stampano, who was wearing a white dinner jacket with a red carnation in the lapel. He was as sleek as an otter, flashing white teeth at other patrons nearby.

"Why are you so interested in Stampano?" Clete asked.

"I saw a photograph of him once," Rick said, "but I didn't know who he was." The photograph was in his safe at the office.

9

The girls were pretty and fun, and they were thrilled to be having dinner with Clete Barrow, peppering him with questions about his next film. Finally, one of them — Marla or Carla, Rick wasn't sure which — turned to Rick.

"Are you an actor, too?" she asked.

"No."

"Well, you're good-looking enough to be an actor," she said. "I thought you were on the Centurion roster, too."

"Well, I am, in a way," Rick replied, "but not as an actor. I'm the head of security at the studio."

She seemed impressed. "And what does the head of security do?"

"That remains to be seen," Rick replied. "I just started today, and I sort of have to invent the job. If you ever get into trouble, I'm the guy who'll try to get you out of it."

"Well, I must get into trouble right away," she said, batting her eyes.

Their salads came and went, and Rick excused himself to go to the men's room. He was standing at a urinal when he heard the door open behind him. He zipped up and was washing his hands when he looked into the mirror and saw Stampano leave another urinal and approach the sink. The attendant was not there, so they were alone.

Stampano looked at him in the mirror. "So, why were you staring at me?" he asked.

"Sorry, I wasn't aware that I was," Rick replied.

"You weren't aware?" Stampano said, and suddenly he was seething.

Rick paused a moment to figure out what was happening. "No, I wasn't aware that I was staring at you. In fact, I was staring at Miss Taylor. You're not my type."

Stampano turned to face him, and Rick heard a metallic snap. Switchblade, he thought, and took a step back.

"Maybe I ought to teach you something about staring at other men's women," Stampano said. His right hand was slightly behind him.

Rick was drying his hands, and he wrapped the towel around his left hand, while reaching into his coat pocket with his right. He flashed his brand-new LAPD detective's badge. "Back off, greaseball," he said. He did not ordinarily indulge in such epithets, but he wanted to insult Stampano.

Stampano looked at the badge, then back at Rick. "Maybe I'll meet you sometime when

70

you're not carrying the badge."

"I doubt it."

"Then we'll meet sometime when the badge don't matter."

"Put the knife away or I'll cuff you and take you down to headquarters, and Miss Taylor will have to find another ride home."

Stampano thought about it for a moment, then his hand went to a pocket, and he held up the empty hand. "What knife?" he asked.

"After you," Rick said, ushering him toward the door. He wasn't going to turn his back on this guy.

Stampano turned and walked out of the men's room.

Rick followed a moment later. Stampano was standing at the bar, watching him pass. When Rick got back to the table he glanced back toward the bar. Stampano was saying something to the bartender. Charley reached into his shirt pocket and handed him a card. So now Chick Stampano knew who Rick was, and Rick didn't much like that.

"You were a long time for a boy," Marla/Carla said.

"Someone struck up a conversation," Rick replied.

"Someone interesting?"

"Not as interesting as you," Rick said.

Their steaks arrived, and Rick watched as Stampano returned to his table and the waiting actress. He said something brusque to her, and

71

she shook her head. He repeated himself and threw some money on the table. She got up, annoyed, and followed him out of the place.

"Is that who you had the conversation with in the men's room?" Clete asked.

"Yes, and it wasn't very pleasant."

"I wouldn't want to meet that guy in a dark alley," Clete said.

"Neither would I."

"I'd watch him, if I were you."

"I don't want to watch him or even know him."

"Good."

The four of them drove back to Clete's house. Clete mixed them a drink, then disappeared with Carla/Marla into what Rick assumed was the bedroom, leaving him on a sofa with the other girl.

"I'm sorry," Rick said, "tell me again, are you Marla or Carla?"

"I'm Carla," she said, "and I have a last name — Travis."

"You're a very beautiful girl, Miss Travis," he said.

"Well, we don't have to be so formal," she said. She nodded toward the bedroom. "Marla told me they'd like us to join them in there."

"Where are you from, Carla?"

"Omaha, Nebraska."

"Is that what girls do in Omaha?"

"If we had a movie star to do it with."

72

"Well, you do. You can go in there and have a threesome, if you like."

She frowned. "Don't you find me attractive?"

"I just told you so, didn't I?"

"Finding me beautiful isn't the same as finding me attractive."

"It is to me."

"Well, I guess this sofa is big enough."

"Carla, let me tell you something: You might advance your career a little by sleeping with a movie star or a producer, but not by sleeping with the studio cop. I'm just an employee, and I can't do a thing for you."

"You must be more than a studio cop if you're hanging around with the studio's biggest star."

"I'm here to make sure he makes it to work sober tomorrow morning, that's all."

"Oh." She sounded disappointed. She looked at her watch. "Well, it looks as though they're going to be in there for a while. Would you mind taking me home?"

"I'd be glad to," Rick said, rising. He walked her out to his car and opened the door for her.

"Wasn't this the girl's car in *Bank Job*?" she asked as he got in.

"That's it!" Rick said. "I'd been trying to remember which movie I saw it in. Where do you live?"

"On Doheny, the other side of Sunset."

Rick started the car and headed down the hillside. They had gone less than a quarter of a mile when, in his headlights, he saw a man and a woman standing in the street, arguing. The man was wearing a white dinner jacket. As the car got closer to them, Rick saw the man slap the woman, hard, and then she staggered back against a parked car, a black Cadillac.

Rick stopped the car, put on the hand brake and got out. "Do you need help, Miss Taylor?" he asked.

"No, it's all right," she said shakily, sounding frightened.

"Would you like me to escort you to your door?"

Stampano wheeled on Rick, the knife in his hand.

Rick didn't wait even a split second. He kicked Stampano in one knee, which brought him down on the other. Rick grabbed the wrist of the knife hand and twisted. He took the knife and closed it against his thigh.

"Is this your home, Miss Taylor?" Rick asked, keeping the pressure on the wrist.

"Yes."

"Why don't you go inside. I'll see that this . . . gentleman . . . doesn't follow you."

"Thank you," she said, then ran into the house.

Rick dragged Stampano closer to the Cadillac, then he opened a door, snapped open the switchblade, kicked the door shut on the blade and snapped it off. He tucked the broken knife into Stampano's pocket. "Now," he said, "I want you to get into your car and drive away.

I'm going to have a patrol car here in a minute, so you'd better not come back. Got that?" He twisted the wrist for effect.

Stampano nodded.

"Now, I'm going to let you go, and if you give me any more trouble, I'm going to put a bullet in you." Rick let go of the wrist and stepped back.

Stampano hobbled into his car, started it and drove away.

Rick got back into his own car.

"You did that very well," Carla said, "as if you've done it before."

"I used to be a cop," Rick said. He drove Carla home and saw her to the door of her apartment building.

"Would you like to come up?" she asked.

"Thanks, but I'm tired, and I have to work tomorrow." He shook her hand and left.

10

It was past one a.m. when Rick got to bed, but he woke up at six, with one thought in his head. He had to get Clete to the studio and the girl home, since Clete didn't have a car. He showered and shaved and was at the actor's house at seven-thirty. To his surprise, the couple were having breakfast on the terrace beside the pool, attended by a Filipino houseman, and they were both stark naked.

"Morning, old chap," Clete said. "Join us for some breakfast?"

"Don't mind if I do," Rick said, sitting down and trying not to stare at Marla.

"Manuel, this is Mr. Barron. Please get him whatever he wishes."

"What time are you due on the set?" Rick asked.

"Not until eleven," Clete said. "Lucky day."

Rick cursed himself for not having asked the night before; he could still be asleep. "In that case," he said to Manuel, "I'll have two eggs over easy, bacon, toast, and orange juice; coffee later."

"Yes, Mr. Barron," Manuel said, then disappeared.

"Lovely evening, wasn't it?" Clete asked.

"Yes, indeed."

"Pity you and Carla didn't join us."

Rick glanced at Marla. She didn't seem in the least embarrassed. "I was tired. Big day yesterday."

"How about today?"

"I've no idea," Rick said honestly.

Clete thought that very funny and laughed heartily. "That's right, you have to make up the job as you go along, don't you?"

"Maybe I should just go around the studio checking the locks, the way I did when I was an LAPD rookie."

"Oh, no," Clete replied, "you must think of yourself as a studio executive. No one really knows what they do, so no one will question you."

"Then that's what I'll do," Rick said. His eggs arrived and he fell upon them, while Marla excused herself to go and find her clothes.

"Marla's not working today," Clete said. "We can drop her at home on the way to the studio."

"There's a stop I'd like to make after that," Rick said. "Shouldn't take long."

"I'll come along for the ride, then," Clete said, "after I've put on a few duds." He got up and went to join Marla.

After Rick had finished his breakfast and had sat for a while, wishing he could smoke a cigarette, the couple still didn't appear, and he figured they were doing again whatever they had done the night before. He sipped his coffee and watched the view change as the sun climbed.

They dropped Marla off at the same apartment building where Rick had taken Carla, and he wondered if they were roommates.

"Where to now, old bean?" Clete asked, turning his face to seek the morning sun.

"A place on Melrose," Rick said, driving away. Ten minutes later, they sat in front of Al's Armory, waiting for the shop to open.

"You're gun shopping?" Clete asked.

"Yeah. When I left the force, I gave them back their gun, and I sold two of my own a while back, when I needed a few bucks."

"Some special reason why you need one?"

Rick shrugged. "Seems like a good idea, since I'm in the security business."

"You're in the movie business, my friend. You're worried about Chick Stampano, aren't you?"

"He pulled a knife on me in the men's room," Rick said, "and again later, when I found him in the street about to beat up Lara Taylor."

"Are you joshing me?"

"He hit her only once, before I could get out of the car."

"I'm sure Metro will thank you. I happen to know she's in the middle of a big production right now. You're lucky Mr. Stampano's knife didn't end up in your gizzard."

"I took it away from him and broke the blade."

"Do you often get into street fights?"

"No, but I stopped a lot of them when I was a cop, before I made detective."

"So you humiliated Chick Stampano in front of his girl?" Clete patted him on the shoulder. "I think you ought to be very careful, old sport. Stampano may not have many friends, but he has a lot of associates, so to speak. I wouldn't be at all surprised if he sent a couple of them to call on you."

"That's why we're here," Rick said. "And here's Al." He nodded toward a man unlocking the door of the shop. They got out of the car and walked in.

Al was just turning on the lights. "Well, Rick," he said, "I hear you're in the movie business."

"God, word gets around," Rick replied. "I only started yesterday."

"Your German safecracker friend was in yesterday, sold me a gun. Come to think of it, last time I saw you, you were selling, not buying. What can I do for you today?"

"I want something to carry, something light but with plenty of stopping power."

Al opened a case and took out a small semiautomatic. "Colt Model 1908," he said. "It's a .380, but with hollowpoints, it ought to do you."

"That's a little light, Al. I like autos, but I'd

like a bigger slug, something that will knock a man down and stop him from shooting me back."

Al scratched his chin. "I do some gunsmithing," he said, "some custom work."

"I've seen a few examples, Al. You do beautiful work."

"I've got something I did for myself, actually, but I don't carry very often. Let me get it." Al walked to the rear of the store, and Rick could see him opening a large safe. He came back a moment later with a walnut box.

"What have you got there?"

Al didn't open the box just yet. "I started with a Colt .45 Officer's Model slide, and I milled a smaller frame out of a block of aircraft-grade aluminum," he said. "I installed a three-and-a-half-inch barrel and a better trigger, shortened the slide half an inch, deburred it, so it doesn't hang on clothing, refinished it, changed the grips. It holds one less round, only six, plus one in the chamber, because I shortened the grip, too." He turned the box around and opened it.

Rick blinked. "It's gorgeous, Al," he said.

"Go ahead, handle it, see what you think."

Rick picked up the gun, dropped the magazine and worked the action to be sure there wasn't a round in the chamber. It was polished to a mirror blue finish, and the grips were ivory. "It may be too beautiful to carry. I'd hate to scratch it."

"I build guns to be used, not displayed."

"I can't believe how light it is."

"Nineteen ounces, unloaded, and it's accurate, too. I can put six rounds in a one-inch circle at twenty-five feet, and you're not likely to use a gun like this beyond that range."

"Are you sure you want to sell it?"

"I've been thinking of building myself another one."

"What do you want for it?"

Al scratched his chin again. "For you, five hundred."

Rick whistled. A couple of days ago that would have been beyond his dreams. "Done," he said.

"You have yourself a very fine piece," Al said. "I've never built anything better. How do you want to carry it?"

"Shoulder holster, I think. Do you have something?"

"I do." Al went back to the safe and returned with a shoulder rig made of glossy mahogany leather. "I had this made for the gun. Let's see, you're a little heavier than I am." He unscrewed a couple of screws and adjusted the length of the straps. "Try it on."

Rick took off his suit jacket and slipped into the rig. It settled on him as if it had always lived on his body. He slipped the gun into the holster and snapped the thumb break closed.

"Wait a minute," Al said, taking two full magazines from the walnut box. He slipped them into the mag holders on the right side of the rig and snapped them shut. "That'll help balance things a bit."

Rick slipped on his jacket and buttoned it.

"Doesn't show," Clete said. It was the first time he'd spoken.

"You need to wear it a lot to get used to it," Al said. "After a while, the leather will soften and conform to your body better, like breaking in a pair of shoes. In a week, you won't feel dressed without it. The shoulder rig is fifty bucks. I'll throw in the walnut box."

Rick took his checkbook from an inside pocket. "I'm going to need some ammo, too."

Al took down four boxes of ammunition. "Two of hardball, to fire at the range, and two of my own loads — hot hollowpoints. You don't want to put too many of them through the gun, but then you'll only fire them when it's really important. Call it five sixty-five for the works."

Rick wrote the check and handed it to him. "Thanks, Al. I feel safer already."

"Before we go," Clete interjected, "I think I'd like something, too."

"What did you have in mind?" Al said.

"I'm sorry, Al," Rick said, "I didn't introduce Clete Barrow."

"It's a familiar face," Al said, smiling and offering his hand.

"I want a Colt .45, new, full-sized, and I want you to do whatever you'd like to it."

"What do you want to use it for? Range? Self-protection?"

"Combat," Clete replied.

Al nodded. "How soon do you need it?"

"Soon."

"Give me a few weeks."

"If I have to. I'll need a holster for it, too — something military-looking."

"I'll postpone some other work, do it as fast as I can."

Clete gave him a card. "I'll look forward to hearing from you."

They all shook hands, and Rick and Clete returned to the car.

"Combat?" Rick asked.

"I hold a commission in the Royal Marines, remember? I served four years before turning to the theater."

"Combat?" Rick asked again.

"We'll talk about that another time," Clete said.

They drove on toward the studio through the bright California morning.

11

Rick delivered Clete to the soundstage at eleven
sharp, costumed, made up and sober. He drove
back to his office, and as he walked in, Jenny
Baker, his secretary, was hanging up the phone.

"That was Eddie Harris's assistant," she said.
"Mr. Harris would like you to call him."

"Thanks." Rick went into his office and called
Harris.

"Good morning," Eddie said.

"Good morning."

"I want to thank you for getting Clete Barrow
to work on time this morning."

"You're welcome. It's what you asked me to
do."

"You free for lunch?"

"Sure. Where and what time?"

"Studio commissary, twelve-thirty."

"See you there." Rick hung up. He went to his
safe, opened it, unlocked the compartment inside and took out the envelope. He sat back
down at his desk and removed the photograph.
He had wanted to study Stampano's face, but

he found himself drawn to all four faces.

John Kean looked fifty, gray around the temples, but in pretty good shape. He wasn't looking into the lens — none of them were — which made Rick think they hadn't known the camera was there. Kean's wife was attractive, dark-haired and had very large breasts. The other girl was slim, but with pretty breasts, hair a little lighter than Mrs. Kean's and the expression on her face could have been either ecstasy or revulsion; Rick guessed the latter, a reaction to what Stampano was doing to her.

Stampano was grinning, really putting it to her, and the expression made Rick like him even less, if that was possible. He picked up the phone and called a detective sergeant he knew who worked organized crime at the LAPD.

"Ben Morrison," a voice said.

"Ben, it's Rick Barron. How are you?"

"I'm fine, Rick, and I hear you're even finer. How's life in Hollywood?"

"Jesus, word gets around in a hurry."

"It's a small town, in its way."

"I guess it is."

"What can I do for you?"

"Ben, I wonder if you'd run a name for me, see if the guy has a sheet?"

"Sure. Who is he?"

"Goes by the name of Chick Stampano."

Morrison laughed. "No need to run the name. Born Ciano Stampano, Palermo, Sicily, thirty-three years ago. Parents emigrated to the

85

U.S. when he was six, settled in New York. Father was a stonemason who, for lack of any other work, became a button man and muscle for the Mob. Mother ran a little restaurant. He was naturalized at eighteen, finished high school, got through two years at the City College of New York before dropping out to help his mother in the restaurant. Didn't help his mother in the restaurant; instead, took up with his father's buddies, but worked occasionally in the restaurant for cover. A favorite of Charlie Luciano, it seems. Charlie sent him out here when he got into some sort of trouble in New York — killed a civilian, rumor has it. He's never been arrested, but everybody knows he works for Ben Siegel and Jack Dragna. No visible means of support, but he's carried on the books of a liquor distributor that Dragna owns as assistant director of sales, which is a laugh. As far as anybody knows, he's never done a day's honest work in his life."

"That's pretty good, for off the top of your head, Ben."

"I've had my eye on him since the day he got off the train, four years ago. I'd love to bust him."

"Well, he pulled a knife on me twice last night, but I don't think I could prove it."

"No kidding? Pity you didn't need a few hundred stitches, then you could have identified him as your assailant, and I could send him to Quentin for a while."

"You may get another shot at him. I'm not sure he's done."

"He still wants to cut you?"

"I humiliated him in front of his movie-star girlfriend. I think he'd like to cut my head off."

"You better watch your back, pal. The guy has a hair-trigger temper, and the goombahs often travel in twos and threes."

"I'll watch myself."

"If he takes another swipe at you, try and dig up a witness or two, and I'll get him out of your hair for a few years."

"I'll sure try, Benny. Thanks, and take care."

"Get me a date with a movie star, will you?"

"What would your wife say?"

"Oh, yeah, forgot about her."

"See you, Benny." Rick hung up. Nothing he had learned about Stampano was encouraging.

Rick found the studio commissary and Eddie Harris at a table for two in a quiet corner. He looked around as he walked across the room. It was a Hollywood zoo — people in all sorts of costumes: cowboys and French aristocrats, sepoys and lumberjacks. He shook Eddie's hand and sat down.

"I already ordered for you," Eddie said. "I don't have much time."

"Thanks."

"I got a call from Eddie Mannix over at Metro this morning. You know who he is?"

"I've heard of him."

"Mannix is at Metro what I am here. He told me what you did for Lara Taylor last night, and he wanted you to know he's grateful to you."

"How the hell did he find out about that?"

"A makeup lady called him, after she had to patch up Miss Taylor for work this morning. Mannix is a good guy to have owing you a favor," Eddie said, "and a bad one to be on the wrong side of. He's tough as nails, and he always gets what he wants."

"Then I hope he wants Chick Stampano's head," Rick replied.

"I think he'd like that, but Eddie won't do anything about Stampano. He wants to stay on the good side of Ben Siegel."

"Why?"

"Because he doesn't want labor problems, and Siegel can make a couple of phone calls and give him plenty of trouble with the extras union, on which he has a grip."

"Oh."

"I don't want any labor problems, either," Harris said, "so I try to stay on Siegel's good side, too."

"I'm sorry if my personal problems are causing you any difficulty, Eddie."

"They're not. Last night's incident is not the sort of thing Stampano would want Siegel to know about, so it's going to stay strictly personal."

Rick nodded.

"Not that that's good news, Rick. Stampano is

not the sort of guy who'd take this and not do something about it. Do you own a gun?"

"I bought one this morning," Rick replied, "and I'm wearing it."

"Good. I don't want you found bleeding in a gutter somewhere."

"Me, either."

Eddie looked around to see that he was not being overheard. "If you have another encounter with Stampano, you'd better make it decisive."

"Beg pardon?" Rick said, surprised.

"If you hurt him, he'll keep coming back. If you should make sure that he can't come back at you, then you'd better do it in such a way that nobody who works for Siegel can figure out it was you. And, it goes without saying, be sure you stay clear of your former colleagues."

Rick was stunned and said nothing.

"I'm just trying to give you some practical advice," Eddie said. He wrote a number on a paper napkin and pushed it across the table. "Memorize that and then eat it, or something," he said. "The guy's name is Al, and he's the sort of fellow who makes problems go away. Tell him that Eduardo sent you, and don't give him any money. I'll take care of that."

"Eduardo?"

"That's what he calls me. I've known him a long time."

"Thank you, Eddie, but I don't really think this is going to be necessary."

"I hope it isn't, but there may come a time when this is the only way to resolve the situation. I just want to be sure that it's resolved in your favor."

A waitress put two minute steaks and two beers on the table and left.

"Eat my steak, too," Eddie said, rising. "I gotta run." He turned and left the commissary.

Rick began to eat his steak, then he glanced at the phone number on the napkin and stopped. He reached in his pocket and found the receipt for the gun he had bought that morning. The phone number on the receipt was the same as that on the napkin.

"You learn something new every day," he said aloud to himself.

12

Rick left the commissary and drove over to the studio motor pool. He found Hiram Jones at a desk in a little glassed-in office in the garage.

"Hey there, Rick," Hiram said. "How's that little Ford treating you?"

"She's a sweet thing, Hiram. I've never owned anything like her."

"Good. We did a lot of work on that baby. You're lucky to have her."

"I know it."

"What can we do you for?"

"Clete Barrow needs something to drive while you're working on his car."

"Yeah, that's going to take a while. We're having to get some parts from Germany. Why doesn't he just buy a car?"

"Hell, I don't know, but I've got to see that he turns up for work every day until his picture is finished, and I don't want to turn into his chauffeur."

"I don't know what I can give him that would be as exciting as that Benz of his."

"Exciting isn't what I'm looking for, believe me. Something sedate will do; just wheels."

"I got a nice Packard that isn't being used right now."

"Great. Can you leave it over at his cottage?"

"You sure this is okay with Eddie Harris?"

"I'll take the responsibility." He wasn't going to start pestering Harris with the small stuff.

"Okay, I'll send it over there."

"Thanks, Hiram."

"That Ford needs anything, you bring it to me. Don't take it to no grease monkey."

"I'll do that." Rick drove over to soundstage two, where Clete was at work on his Khyber Pass horse opera. The red light over the door wasn't on, and he went inside. The set was of an Indian Army officers' club, and it was gorgeous, with every detail taken care of. He worked his way around the floor and found Clete sitting in a canvas chair with his name on it, reading a script.

Clete looked up. "Hello, old chap. What's up?"

"I got you something to drive from the motor pool. It's a Packard, and it'll be parked outside your cottage when you get back."

"Getting tired of driving me, eh?" Clete laughed. "Can't say that I blame you. How about some steaks at my place tonight? I could ring up Marla and Carla."

"Sounds good."

"Seven o'clock?"

"Good."

"Will you pick up the girls?"

"All right."

"See you then."

Rick drove back to his office. Jenny didn't have any messages for him, so he sat at his desk and thought about killing Chick Stampano.

Rick had shot and wounded one man in the line of duty, when he'd happened on a liquor store robbery on the way home from work. He hadn't enjoyed it, and he didn't particularly want to repeat the experience, but he was damned if he was going to let Stampano or any of his hood friends kill him.

He closed his office door, took out the little .45 and looked it over again. It was a thing of beauty. He opened a box of Al's hot hollowpoints and loaded three magazines, then he stuck two of them into the mag pouches of his shoulder rig and slapped the other into the gun. He worked the slide, chambering a round, then he removed the magazine and loaded a replacement. Now he had seven in the gun and twelve more rounds in the magazine pouches. That ought to be enough, he thought.

He flipped up the safety, shoved the gun into its shoulder holster and practiced popping the thumb break and drawing the weapon. It wasn't a very quick draw, and he spent a few minutes working on it until he had it down smooth, if not fast. It was clear that he was going to have to anticipate trouble, if he was going to get the gun clear quickly enough to do some good. He put

93

his coat back on and opened his office door.

"Jenny, who supplies the weapons for the studio?"

"There's an armory," she said, "but I've never been there." She opened her studio directory and looked it up, then got out a map of the property. "It's way over here," she said, pointing to the back lot.

"Can I borrow your map?"

"Sure, keep it. I've got another. You have any work for me to do?"

"Not yet. I'll see what I can scare up. I'm going over to the armory, if you need to reach me." He got into his car and, following the map, drove to the back lot, where he found the armory in a long, low building. He went inside and found a man working on a dismantled rifle at a workbench.

"Can I help you?" the man asked.

Rick handed him a card. "I'm new here."

"Oh, hello, Mr. Barron," the man said. "I've heard about you. I'm Mike Schwartz." He offered his hand.

Rick shook it. "I want to do some shooting," he said. "Where would I best do that?"

"Right through that door," Schwartz said. "We've got a fifty-yard range. You want something to shoot?"

"I brought my own," Rick said, "but I could use a couple of boxes of .45 hardball."

"Sure thing." Schwartz went to a large steel cabinet and unlocked it, revealing boxes of ammo. He took out four boxes and handed them to Rick, along with a set of rubber ear-plugs. "Live it up," he said. "Let me know if you need anything."

Rick went into the range and found a young man firing a Winchester '73. He put in the ear-plugs, unloaded his magazines and reloaded with the hardball ammo. The targets were on a pulley system and he moved one in to about twenty-five feet, figuring that was as far as he was likely to have to shoot. He fired a magazine into the target, then pulled it in for inspection. His group covered a good twelve-inch spread. He was going to have to improve on that.

He spent the rest of the afternoon improving, until he was down to a four-inch group. It wasn't great, but he reckoned he could put seven rounds into a man's chest, if he had to.

13

Rick left his office at six o'clock and departed the studio through the main gate. Immediately, he thought he had made a mistake. A black sedan containing two men in suits and hats pulled away from the curb across the street and fell in behind him.

Rick tried to keep track of the big car in the mirror without turning his head, so they wouldn't know he was on to them. When he sped up, the black car sped up; when he slowed, it slowed. He was approaching a traffic signal, and when it turned red, he plowed through the intersection, narrowly missing a large truck. He checked the mirror and saw the car blocked by crossing traffic, and he took an immediate left, then another, and finally turned back toward his original route. He stopped at a corner, got out of the Ford and looked down the street. The light changed, and he saw the black car drive through the intersection.

He got back into the Ford and made the next left, putting him back on his route, then he stopped the car and waited five minutes by his watch. The men in the black car would be looking for him in the side streets, so he continued on his way home, checking the mirror often for signs of the black car. He did not want Stampano's people to know where he lived.

He made his way to Bel-Air without the attentions of the two men, went home, changed and then drove up Sunset, toward Doheny and the girls' apartment house. He collected Marla and Carla without incident and drove up into the hills toward Clete's place.

"Why are you looking in the mirror all the time?" Marla, who was sitting in the front seat, asked.

"I like to know who's behind me," Rick said. "Do you two girls live together?"

"We do everything together," Marla said.

"Are you related?" he asked.

"We're twins," Marla replied.

"You don't look all that much alike." Marla was a blonde, Carla a redhead.

"We're fraternal twins, not identical," Marla said.

"Oh." Rick turned into Clete's drive and got the girls out of the car and into the house.

Clete greeted them, martini pitcher in hand. "Just in time," he said, stirring furiously. He began pouring the drinks, then looked at Rick. "I know; you're going to want bourbon, aren't you?"

"If you've got it," Rick said. "I never acquired

the taste for martinis."

Clete handed the girls their drinks, then rummaged in a cabinet until he came up with an unopened bottle of Jack Daniel's. "This do?"

"That will do just fine." Clete handed him the bottle, and he poured his own drink.

"Happy days," Clete said, raising his glass.

He led them out onto the terrace, and they took seats. Marla and Clete were being especially affectionate, having broken the ice on the previous occasion.

Carla sat down next to Rick on a sofa and turned to him. "Are you queer?" she asked pleasantly.

"What?"

"I mean, it's all right if you are. I have nothing against pansies; half the men at the studio are pansies."

"I'm not queer," Rick said.

"Then what was the problem last night?"

In fact, he wasn't sure what the problem had been last night. God knew, the girl was lovely, and he wasn't in the habit of avoiding sexual opportunity. "I just broke up with somebody," he said. And that might even have something to do with it, he thought. He missed Kathleen, but she was out of his reach now, probably in a convent somewhere.

"Oh," she cooed, putting her hand on his arm. "I'm sorry, I know how tough that can be. Did you end it, or did she?"

"Her family ended it," Rick said.

"They objected to you? Why? You seem like such a nice boy, handsome and everything, and you certainly have a good job."

"They objected to anybody who wasn't Catholic. And I was a policeman at the time, and I don't think they looked at that as much of a career."

"Oh. Well, there's no accounting for human nature, is there?"

"I guess not."

"Aren't you attracted to me at all?"

"You're very beautiful."

"But you're not attracted."

"Didn't we talk about this last night?"

"I didn't get a satisfactory answer."

Rick hooked a finger under her chin and kissed her.

"Mmmm," she said. "That's better. What's next?"

He reached out a finger and scratched at a nipple through her dress.

"That tickles," she said, drawing back.

"Let's finish our drinks, Carla, then maybe have another, then some dinner, then . . . who knows?"

Manuel came out of the house with a sack of charcoal and began building a fire in the brick barbecue near the pool. A woman followed him with a tray of large steaks. Inside the house, a phone rang, and Manuel went to answer it. He came back a moment later.

"Mr. Barron, there's a telephone call for you."

Rick was taken aback. "Who is it?"

"He didn't give a name, sir."

Clete looked at him. "Did you give anyone my number?"

"I don't have your number," Rick replied. He got up and went into the house with some trepidation and picked up the phone. "Hello?" He fully expected Stampano to be on the other end.

"Rick Barron?"

"Yes?"

"This is Eddie Mannix."

Rick managed to say, "How do you do, Mr. Mannix?"

"I do very goddamned well, thanks. You know who I am?"

"Of course."

"Maybe Eddie Harris mentioned that I appreciate what you did for our girl?"

"Yes, he did. You're very welcome."

"Then why did you try to shake my boys?"

"Your boys?"

"Who did you think was following you from the studio?"

"Oh, of course. I'm sorry, I thought it might be . . ."

"Somebody else?"

"Somebody else."

"They were there to protect you, not hurt you."

"Well, I appreciate that, Mr. Mannix, but —"

"My friends call me Eddie."

"Thank you, Eddie, but —"

"I'm not going to have somebody sticking a shiv into a friend of mine."

"I appreciate your concern — and your help."

"So don't try and shake my boys again."

"How am I going to tell your boys from Stampano's boys?"

"They'll be the ones who ain't shooting at you."

"How did you know where to find me?"

"You didn't shake them; you just thought you did."

"Well, I have to tell you, they did a very fine job of not letting me know they were there."

"They wouldn't be working for me, otherwise."

"I guess not. How did you get this number?"

"Are you kidding? I've got everybody's number."

"Oh."

"I hear you're packing these days."

"Yes, I am."

"Don't shoot my boys," Mannix said, "and don't try to lose them again."

"I won't."

"This will blow over in a few days, and we can get back to normal, and we can get back to shooting Lara from both sides."

"I hope so."

"Count on it. Ben Siegel runs the mob out here, and I'm going to talk to him about this, but he's out of town. When he gets back, I'll straighten this out."

"Thank you, Eddie," Rick said, but Mannix had already hung up.

Rick walked back out onto the terrace, where he was greeted by the aroma of seared meat.

"Who was on the phone?" Clete asked.

"I'll tell you later." Rick picked up his drink and snuggled up to Carla. He felt a lot more relaxed now.

14

Rick woke slowly, at first disoriented, then he realized there was a lump in bed beside him — a lump with red hair. He was about to reach for her when the door opened and somebody pulled the cord on the venetian blinds, flooding the room with sunlight.

"Come on, old chap," Clete said. "I've got an eight o'clock call today, and it's seven-twenty. You're supposed to be the one getting me to work on time, not the other way around. Manuel has made some coffee."

Rick grabbed a quick shower, and Carla joined him.

"You were just swell last night," she said. "I'm sorry I thought you were a pansy." She kissed him and took him in her hand. "My mistake."

"Listen, I hope you won't think I'm a pansy if I tell you I've got to get out of here."

"Why?"

"I've got to get Clete to work."

"What are you, his chauffeur? He's got a car."

Rick grinned. "You've got a point," he said, yielding to her idea.

When they came out of the bedroom, Clete was pacing the floor.

"I've got to get going," he said. "Are you ready?"

"So get going," Rick replied. "You've got the Packard."

"Christ, I forgot. Will you see the girls home?"

"Sure."

Clete ran down the stairs, and Rick had some breakfast with the girls. He wasn't due in early. After he'd dropped them off, he went back to his place for some clothes and was surprised to see the big black car a couple of cars back on Sunset. Mannix was taking care of him. He shaved and changed, then stopped. If this was the kind of life he was leading, he'd better take some clothes to the office. He packed a bag and threw it in the car.

Rick was still new enough at this that he greatly enjoyed the guard's salute at the Centurion main gate. He returned the salute and drove to his office. To his surprise and discomfort, Eddie Harris was sitting on his leather couch, waiting for him. Rick snuck a look at his watch: eight forty-five. "Good morning, Eddie," he said.

"Congratulations. That's two days in a row you've gotten Clete to work on time. You've saved us at least twenty-five grand."

"Clete has been the soul of cooperation." Rick sat down at his desk. "It's strange how he can handle the booze when he wants to. We had dinner with some girls last night, and he had a couple of martinis and some wine, but he never got drunk."

"There are drunks and drunks," Eddie said. "I've known all kinds."

"Is this a social call, Eddie, or is there something I can do for you?"

"I'm going to have to fly somewhere next week," Eddie said. "I want to meet your old man."

"Right now?"

"Why not?"

"Come on, I'll drive you."

"Nah, I'll drive you."

Rick followed Eddie out of his office, stopping to whisper to Jenny, "Call my old man at Barron Flying Service at Clover Field and tell him I'm bringing him a customer and to put on some clean clothes and get the grease from under his fingernails."

She nodded, and Rick followed Eddie into a Lincoln Continental convertible, top down.

"It's beautiful," Rick said.

"It's the 1940 model — delivered this morning. That's half of why we're going to Santa Monica; I want to drive it."

"I don't blame you."

"How's the Ford working out?"

"It's a beauty. I love it."

"I took it off the books. It's yours now. Hiram will send over the pink slip."

"Eddie, that's extraordinarily kind of you."

"I like it when people meet my expectations," he said. "And you're doing just fine."

"To tell you the truth, once I get Clete to work, I'm having a little trouble filling my time. Anything you want done?"

"I'll give it some thought."

They drove out the main gate and headed for Santa Monica. Rick tossed his straw hat in the backseat and enjoyed the sun on his face and the wind in his hair.

"Ah, California, huh?" Eddie laughed.

"You bet. I don't know why anybody lives anywhere else."

"The way the state is filling up with Easterners, pretty soon nobody will live anywhere else. Want some advice? Invest in real estate. If you see something you want and you think it's too expensive, buy it anyway."

"That's good advice. I'll save my money so I can do that."

"Borrow, if you have to," Eddie said. "Money's cheap — one of the few advantages of the Depression. I can send you to the right people."

"Thanks, I'll keep that in mind. You know, a week ago, after some years of doing pretty well, I was back at the bottom in my job, and I had hardly any prospects. I was thinking about quitting the force and going in with my dad. Then, all of a sudden, I meet you, and my life goes off

106

on a completely new tangent."

"You deserved a break," Eddie said, "and I'm happy to have had something to do with it. By the way, I talked to Eddie Mannix last night, and he tells me he's having somebody keep an eye on you."

"I've put myself in his hands," Rick replied. "He says he's going to straighten things out with Ben Siegel."

"That's a good move," Eddie said. "He knows those people better than I do. I try to steer clear of them."

"Good idea," Rick said. "They may be colorful, but dealing with them is dangerous. I saw enough of their handiwork on the force to want to stay away from them. Not everybody did; I knew some cops who took their money, who were in their pocket. They'd do them a few favors, take a few bucks and suddenly they found themselves covering up a murder."

"It's a dirty town," Eddie said, "and it's not our job to clean it up." They drove on toward Santa Monica in silence.

When they were nearly to the airport, Eddie spoke up. "I see Mannix is keeping his word," he said, looking in the rearview mirror.

Rick looked back. "I don't see them."

"Gray Chevy," Eddie said. "They've been behind us almost since we left the studio."

"Earlier this morning, it was something big and black," he said.

"You think . . . ?"

"I don't know, but it can't hurt to lose them. I don't want them following me to my dad's place."

Eddie took a sudden hard left and gunned it.

15

It took Eddie ten minutes to lose the gray Chevy and another five to be sure. "You think we're okay?" he asked.

"I think so," Rick replied. "Let's get back on course."

Ten minutes later, they pulled up at the hangar that housed Barron Flying Service. Rick led Eddie inside, and they found Jack Barron at his desk, in a suit, looking at papers. His dad had gotten the message.

"Morning, Dad," Rick said. "I want you to meet Eddie Harris, who runs things at Centurion. Eddie, this is Jack Barron."

"How are you, Jack?" Eddie said. "I've heard a lot about you."

"Good to meet you, Mr. Harris."

"Please, call me Eddie."

"Thank you."

"Rick has told me about your flying service, and I wanted to see what you've got in the way of airplanes."

"Let me show you my Lockheed Electra,

then," Jack said.

"You two go ahead," Rick said. "I want to use the john." He walked back through the offices and to the back door of the hangar. He stopped, yanked the .45 from the shoulder holster. Then, holding the small gun concealed in his hand, he stepped outside and had a look around. There was a small parking area behind the hangar, and Rick walked through it, checking every car. Every one was empty, and there was no gray Chevrolet.

He circumnavigated the hangar, looking for cars that may have driven onto the field. A Beech Staggerwing took off and turned north, and Rick watched it for a moment, admiring the beautiful airplane. It was one he fantasized about owning. Maybe he would make his dad an offer for his, when he got a little ahead. He continued his walk around the hangar, then went back inside through the back door. He put the gun on safety, holstered it, used the john, then went back to join his dad and Eddie, who were deep in conversation.

"Your dad tells me you're his number one pilot," Eddie said.

"A father's pride; take it with a grain of salt," Rick replied. "He's got half a dozen good guys on his list."

"I don't employ a full-time pilot," Jack said. "It makes more sense to hire them by the hour. I'm not running an airline, after all."

"I see your point," Eddie said. "Jack, I've

bought a house down in Palm Springs, and I expect to spend a lot of weekends there, but it's a two-and-a-half-hour drive. How long would it take you to fly my wife and me and maybe some friends down there in the Electra?"

"Half an hour, forty-five minutes each way, depending on the winds."

"How much?"

Jack scratched his head and named a price.

"Sounds good. How about this weekend?"

"When do you want to take off, and when do you want to come back?"

"Outbound, Friday at three; coming home, pick us up in Palm Springs at four on Sunday."

"You've got yourself a charter. Every weekend, if you like."

"Let's see how Suzanne likes the ride, then we'll talk."

"That's fine with me."

Eddie turned to Rick. "We'd better get back to work," he said. He shook Jack's hand, and they walked back to the car.

"You disappeared for a few minutes," Eddie said. "Looking for the gray Chevy?"

"Just being careful," Rick replied.

They got into the Continental and started back.

"Rick, our executives do a fair amount of flying, so much so that we've been thinking about buying an airplane. I've heard good things about the Electra."

"So did Amelia Earhart. The Electra is a good

airplane, but it might be a little cramped for the studio's purposes. I'm inclined to think you'd be happier with the Douglas DC-3. It's bigger, just as fast and a damned fine machine. It would get you to New York a lot faster than the train."

"How would you like to operate an aviation department for us at the studio, in addition to your security duties?"

"I'm not sure that would be a good use of your money, Eddie," Rick replied. "It might make more sense for my dad to do that for you. He could hangar the airplane, hire another mechanic to see to its maintenance, and find you a regular pilot."

"Suppose we expanded to two or three airplanes — eventually, I mean."

"Dad could handle it for you, and one of these days he's going to retire; he's sixty now. Maybe you could buy him out in a few years and then own the hangar and his equipment. You might defray some of your costs by flying charters."

"That's good thinking," Eddie said. "I'll talk to Sol about it."

They drove back to Centurion, and as they were turning through the front gate, Rick saw the big black car and Mannix's two men sitting outside. They had missed his leaving, since they hadn't expected him to leave in Eddie's Continental. But whoever had been in the gray Chevrolet had not missed him.

16

Rick spent the afternoon reading *Gone with the Wind* in his office. He had somehow not gotten around to it when the book had been published three years before, but it was being filmed at Metro, and he wanted to read it before seeing the movie. He felt guilty about reading at his desk, but his job was turning out to be a little like police work — long periods of boredom, punctuated by occasional, more exciting moments.

Later, he drove over to Clete's cottage and waited for him to come back from the set. He turned up in the same beautiful uniform, with its red tunic, that Rick had seen him in before, but this time it was dirty and torn, and Clete sported a four-inch gash in his forehead. Rick was alarmed, until he realized it was makeup. He had a Coke and waited for Clete to shower.

"Well, old sport, what say we go over to Dave Chasen's place for some chili?"

Rick had passed Chasen's Southern Pit in

West Hollywood, but had never been in. "Sure, why not?"

"Been there?"

"Nope."

They got into Rick's car. "Dave is an old vaudevillian," Clete said, "and he makes a mean bowl of chili."

They walked in without a reservation, and as usual Clete got the welcome treatment from the owner and the best available table. They were about to sit down when a handsome, well-dressed woman in a large hat approached Clete.

"Hedda!" he roared, kissing her hand. "How are you, my darling?"

"I'm very well, Clete, and I hear that *Khyber Uprising* is on schedule — or have you managed to slow it down, as usual?"

Clete laughed as if this were very funny. "You know me, darling, always right on time. Have you met Centurion's new chief of security? This is Richard Barron."

"How do you do, Mr. Barron?" she said.

"I'm very well, Miss Hopper," Rick replied. "And please, call me Rick."

"Of course, my dear. And has the studio assigned you to see that our Clete shows up on time and sober?"

"Miss Hopper, I don't think anyone in the world could make Clete be either on time or sober, unless he really wanted to. He seems to be enjoying himself on this picture."

"I don't know your name," Hopper said. "Where were you before? Metro? RKO?"

"I was with the Beverly Hills Police Department," Rick said.

"I suppose Eddie brought you in to replace that John Kean fellow, yes?"

"Yes."

"I never liked him, and I never understood that murder-suicide business. What really happened?"

"I'm afraid I have no idea. That business was handled by the Los Angeles department, and they didn't confide in me."

"I'd like very much to have that story, when it's solved," she said. "Will you promise to bring it to me first? I'd be very upset if I read about it in Louella's column." There was an edge to her voice.

"I'll certainly be happy to bring you anything I learn," Rick said. Hopper had started her column in the Los Angeles *Times* earlier that year, but she had already earned a reputation as a bitch, and Rick didn't want to get on her bad side.

"Do that, and I'll put in a good word with Eddie Harris for you," she said.

"That's very kind of you."

"Must run, darling," she said, kissing Clete on both cheeks and shaking Rick's hand. "I've all of Hollywood to cover."

"Goodbye, sweetheart," Clete said, waving her off. He sat down. "Whew," he said, "it's hard work being nice to these columnists. You

115

say something innocuous, and it turns up in the papers the next day as entirely another thing."

"I hear she's a bitch," Rick said.

"And proud of it," Clete replied. "She revels in her bitchery. Louella has, at least, an air of sweetness about her, but of course, I wouldn't trust either of them as far as I could throw them."

A waiter brought them a drink and menus, and Rick looked around. Jack Benny and his wife were across the room, in a booth next to Spencer Tracy and a woman Rick assumed to be his wife. "This place must be catching on," he said, nodding toward the two stars.

Clete looked over and waved at Tracy. "Evening, Spence, Louise." He turned back to Rick. "Yes, word does get around when a place is good, and almost everything on the menu is. I do recommend the chili, though."

Rick ordered the chili and sipped his bourbon while he watched the room fill. The headwaiter had just assigned the last remaining table when Rick looked up and saw Chick Stampano at the door with a beautiful young woman.

"Who are you staring at?" Clete asked, looking over his shoulder. "Movie people don't like to be stared at."

"He's not movie people," Rick said, pretending to look somewhere else, but keeping an eye on Stampano.

"Oh, it's your friend, the Eyetie gentleman, isn't it?"

Stampano seemed to be arguing with Dave Chasen, who shrugged and waved an arm around the room, indicating the lack of available tables. Then Stampano's eye fell on Rick, and he seemed to turn to marble, standing and staring.

Rick gave him a little salute, which seemed to annoy him even more. Not only could he not get a table, but Rick had one. Stampano grabbed the girl's arm and hustled her out of the restaurant.

"What is it with you two?" Clete asked.

Rick told him about the conversation with Eddie Mannix and the people following him.

"I see," Clete said. "Tell me, are you carrying that pistol you bought?"

"Yes," Rick said.

"Oh, good. Then at least you'll be able to shoot it out with Stampano when we leave. Try to aim away from me, will you?"

17

Clete had the weekend off, and he invited Rick to play golf at the Bel-Air Country Club. No matter how much he had drunk the night before, Clete never seemed to be hungover, but Rick was.

They stood on the first tee. Clete teed up, took a couple of practice swings and faded the ball down the right side of the fairway.

"That's about two-fifty, Mr. Barrow," the Negro caddie said.

"Not bad," Clete murmured to himself.

Rick teed up and hit a long draw.

"That's a good two-eighty, Mr. Barron," his caddie said, lording it over his co-worker.

"Shit, old boy," Clete said, "where'd you learn to hit it like that?"

"I played for UCLA," Rick replied, "and I had a good coach. You didn't think I was going in the tank for a movie star, did you?"

"What's your handicap?"

"Two," Rick said. "How about you?"

"Six."

"Five bucks a hole?"

"You're on, laddie. I hope you've been practicing."

"I haven't, but I'm going to start. I've got to join a club."

They walked briskly down the fairway toward their balls.

"Eddie Harris is a bigwig in this one," Clete said. "I'll second you, and we'll scare up some supporters."

"Thank you, Clete, I appreciate that. It's a beautiful course."

"And conveniently located. Golf courses always make me think of England — so green."

"Do you miss England?"

"At times. I'm very worried about what's going to happen to the old girl if they don't start listening to Winston Churchill."

"I don't think Hitler really means to go to war," Rick said. "He's got the Rhineland back, he's annexed Austria, and now he's got Czechoslovakia. What more could he want?"

"The whole pie," Clete said.

"What do you mean?"

"Europe, all of it, maybe a lot more than Europe. I think he's thinking in global terms."

"Come on, how many Germans are there? Fifty million? How are they going to take all of Europe, let alone the world?"

"We haven't seen anything like Hitler since Napoleon," Clete said, lining up his shot to the green. "And Hitler's a lot meaner." He swung and lofted the ball onto the green. It stopped four feet from the cup.

Rick walked farther down the fairway to his ball. He had only a sand wedge to the flag, and he put it a foot outside Clete's ball.

"You said you held a commission?" Rick asked.

"I do."

"What will you do if war breaks out in Europe?"

"Not much I can do, legally," Clete replied, accepting his putter from the caddie. "I've got nearly four years to run on a seven-year contract."

"You think Eddie would let you out of the contract if England goes to war?"

"Maybe, but I don't think Sol ever would. And if I jump ship, I'll never make another film, even in England, unless Sol allowed it. I'd have to eke out a living on the stage."

Clete sank his putt, and so did Rick. They played on.

At lunch on the terrace of the clubhouse, Clete continued. "I'm in a tough spot," he said. "My family would expect me to fight, not to mention my regiment."

"How much family do you have?"

"I have a father, a mother and a younger brother. Pater is a clergyman — an Anglican priest — and my brother is in the City."

"The city?"

120

"The City of London — shorthand for the financial world, like Wall Street. He's a partner in a merchant bank, and they expect great things of him. He invests most of my money."

"That's convenient. Now that I'm making good money, I'm going to have to start investing. Eddie has suggested real estate."

"That's what all the smart people seem to be doing," Clete said. "It's too much bother for me. I prefer stocks and bonds. I wouldn't like being a landlord."

"You know, until I started this job, I never had more than a month's pay in the bank, and when I got broken down to patrolman, I didn't expect to ever have more than a week's salary saved. I thought I was going to have to go to work for my old man."

"What does he do?"

"He has a flying service down at Clover Field, in Santa Monica."

"What would you have done for him?"

"Fly charters, help run the place."

"You fly?"

"Since I was twelve."

"Funny, I was thinking of going up to Oregon with a couple of chums, do some trout fishing, when we wrap the film. How'd you like to fly us up there? You fish?"

"Never have, but it sounds like fun. Dad is leasing a Lockheed Vega that would be perfect for the trip. You charter it from him, and I'll throw in the piloting for the loan of some gear."

"Sounds perfect. Book it, will you?"

"Will do."

"You'll like fly-fishing. It's a world of perfect peace and good eating. You'll like my chums, too."

"Sounds wonderful." Rick looked up to see Eddie Harris, dressed in plus fours and kneesocks, making his way across the terrace toward them. "Look who's here," he said.

"He doesn't look all that happy," Clete remarked.

Eddie reached their table. "There you are," he said. "Clete, your houseman told me where to find you."

"What can I do for you, Eddie?" Clete asked.

"Not a thing. I'm looking for Rick." He clapped a hand on Rick's shoulder. "You come with me, pal. You and I have a date. I hope you finished your round."

"Yes, thanks," Rick said. "Do I have time to finish my lunch?"

"Nope," Eddie said, starting back across the terrace.

"Sounds serious," Clete said. "You'd better hurry."

"Sorry about this, Clete."

"Call me when you're free. We'll have dinner."

"Sure." Rick threw down his napkin and started after Eddie, wondering what the hell could be wrong.

18

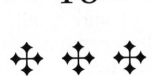

Eddie drove the Continental fast and without saying anything, so Rick didn't either. Eddie's expression was, if not worried, then at least intent. He was ordinarily so relaxed and amiable that it began to worry Rick.

They drove down Stone Canyon to Sunset and turned east. It was a glorious California day, the perfect sort of weather to be driving through Beverly Hills in an open car, but in deference to Eddie's mood, Rick tried not to appear to be enjoying it too much.

They finally stopped, to Rick's complete surprise, in front of the Trocadero, which was probably the hottest nightclub on the Sunset Strip. Eddie left the car at the curb, and they went inside.

The place was dimly lit and smelled slightly of spilled alcohol and disinfectant and strongly of stale cigarette smoke. The chairs in the large main room were all stacked on the tables, and a man was using a noisy vacuum cleaner on the carpet.

"He said to wait here," Eddie said, parking himself on a banquette in the bar.

Rick wanted to ask who but didn't.

Ten or twelve minutes ticked by, then the front door opened and a tall, well-built man, also in golf clothes, came in.

"Eddie," Eddie said.

"Eddie," the man replied.

"Rick, this is Eddie Mannix."

Rick stood up and shook his hand. "How do you do?"

"Pretty good. Are they keeping us waiting?"

"You guessed it," Harris replied.

"I'll be damned if I'm going to be kept waiting by these fucks," Mannix said, and turned toward the door.

A man in a double-breasted suit came through an inside door. "Okay," he said, "you can come in."

Mannix looked nearly disappointed, as if he would have preferred walking out on the meeting. He turned and led the way through the door and down a hallway to a set of double doors. Before he could open them, two men came out, looking annoyed, and brushed past them in the hallway.

Mannix pushed open a door and walked into the room, followed by Harris and Rick.

It was an office, large and well furnished. One man sat behind the desk, another in a leather armchair, and, across the room on a leather sofa sat Chick Stampano. The two Eddies shook

124

hands with the man behind the desk and the one in the armchair. They all seemed well acquainted.

"Siddown, everybody," said the man behind the desk. "How you doin', Eddie, Eddie?" He laughed at his own joke.

The two Eddies murmured their well-being.

"Is this your studio cop?" the man asked.

"Yes," Eddie Harris said. "Rick Barron, Jack Dragna."

"I heard about you," Dragna said to Rick.

"Same here," Rick replied.

"So, what are we going to do about this?" Dragna asked the room at large.

Stampano's glare was fixed on Rick. The man in the armchair, handsome in a linen suit, simply looked bored.

"That's what we want to hear, Jack," Mannix said. "What do you propose?"

"A thing like this shouldn't be worth everybody's time," Dragna said. "What are we doing here?"

"You called the meeting," Mannix said.

"So, what's your beef, Eddie?" Dragna asked Mannix.

Mannix nodded in Stampano's direction. "I don't want your boy, here, beating up on Metro's girls."

Dragna turned and looked at Stampano. "Don't fucking beat up on Metro's girls no more."

Stampano nodded almost imperceptively.

Dragna turned back to Mannix. "Happy?"

"I'll be happy when it doesn't happen," Mannix said.

"It won't happen, will it, Chick?" Dragna asked.

Stampano shook his head slightly.

"Now you, Eddie," Dragna said, turning to Harris. "What do you want?"

"I want your boy to stop pulling knives on my people," Harris said.

Dragna looked at Stampano. "Chick?"

"I never pulled a knife on nobody," Stampano said, glaring at Rick.

Rick spoke for the first time. "Your boy is a liar," he said to Dragna.

Harris made a tamping motion in Rick's direction but didn't say anything.

Stampano was on his feet. "Gimme five minutes alone with him, Jack," he said.

"So you can pull another knife?" Rick asked.

Dragna slammed his palm down on the leather top of the desk. "Everybody shut the fuck up!" he bellowed, turning red.

Harris made the tamping motion again.

Dragna sat back in his chair and sighed. "Young guys," he said, shaking his head. "We were all young once, right?" he asked Mannix and Harris.

"I'm still young," Harris said, and everybody laughed a little, except Stampano.

"What we got here is two young stallions in a great big barn with a lot of fillies," Dragna said.

126

"It's natural that they might bump heads a little. I want both of you to stop doing that, you hear me?"

Rick spoke up again. "I haven't done anything, yet, except stop your boy from beating up a girl and taking a knife from him."

Harris rolled his eyes.

Mannix turned to Dragna. "Fix it, Jack. I'm late for golf."

"Always happy to do you a favor, Mr. Mannix," Dragna replied.

"This isn't a favor," Mannix said. "Let's get that straight. It's only what's right."

Dragna sighed again. "Chick," he said slowly, "I don't want to hear any more about this."

Stampano was still staring at Rick.

"CHICK!" Dragna yelled.

"Awright, awright," Stampano said, holding up his hands in surrender.

Dragna turned to Rick. "That good enough for you? You want his word?"

"I'd rather have your word," Rick said.

Dragna looked at Rick as if he were undecided whether to shoot him or cut his throat.

Rick held his gaze.

"You got my word," Dragna said finally.

"Thanks," Rick replied.

"You hear that, Chick?" Dragna said. "They got my word."

"Yes, Jack," Stampano said, almost contritely.

"Okay, go play golf," Dragna said to Mannix.

The two Eddies shook hands with Dragna,

and the man in the armchair got up and opened the door for them. Both shook his hand as they left.

"Oh, Rick," Harris said, "meet Ben Siegel."

"How are you?" Rick asked, shaking his hand.

"Always good," Siegel replied.

The three men found the front door and stepped out of the gloom of the nightclub into the bright California sun, blinking.

"Gentlemen," Rick said, "I'm sorry you had to do that for me."

"It wasn't just for you," Mannix said. He shook both their hands, then got into a car parked at the curb and drove away.

Eddie and Rick got into the Continental and headed back toward Bel-Air.

"I hate dealing with those people," Eddie said.

"I'll try and see that you don't have to do it again on my account," Rick replied.

"Rick, it's not your fault. You didn't do anything that any other upright fellow wouldn't do. This is just the cost of doing business in this town. I'm glad Mannix made it clear to Dragna that he wasn't doing us any favors."

"As far as I'm concerned," Rick said, "he was doing Stampano a favor. What the hell are they doing in an office at the Trocadero?"

"Jack Dragna and Ben Siegel own the place," Eddie said.

"I thought Bill Wilkerson owned it."

"He did, but Billy's a big gambler, and a bad

one. He got in hock to the boys, and . . ."

"I had no idea. He still owns Ciro's?"

"As far as I know."

"I'm staying out of the Trocadero."

"Good idea."

Rick laughed. "I can't believe I just met Jack Dragna and Bugsy Siegel."

"Don't ever let Siegel hear you call him that."

"Sorry, it's Ben."

"Good. He's hard to stay away from. He's everywhere, all the time, with a beautiful woman on his arm. He's a charming guy, but I hear rumors of bad things. Dragna was running the LA mob until Siegel showed up and elbowed him aside. And Siegel never said a word during our meeting."

They pulled into the parking lot of the Bel-Air Country Club.

"You belong to a golf club?" Eddie asked.

"No. When I played for UCLA, we used to practice here sometimes."

"I'll put you up for the club. Clete can second you, and we'll find a few more guys to write letters."

"Thank you, Eddie, I'd like that."

They got out of the car.

"Something I wanted to ask you about," Rick said.

"What?"

"After Clete's movie wraps, he wants me to fly him and a couple of buddies up to Oregon to do some fly-fishing. Is that all right with you?"

"Sure, I guess so, but don't fly if there's bad weather. I don't want to lose either of you." With a wave, Eddie returned to the club.

Rick got into his car and drove home.

19

Rick was sleeping late on Sunday morning when his phone rang. He groped for it, knocking some things off a side table. "Hello?" he croaked.

"Well, you sound wide awake," a woman's voice said.

Rick cleared his throat. "I'm getting there."

"This is Suzanne Harris. I need another man for tennis this morning. Do you think you can stand upright and hold a racquet?"

"Sure."

"There'll be three couples, so we can trade off and not get too tired."

"What time?"

"Ten. There's lunch afterward."

"See you then."

"We play in whites."

"I have some."

"See you at ten."

Rick hung up and picked up the alarm clock from the floor. Eight forty-five. He had time for breakfast and hangover recovery.

★ ★ ★

At ten sharp, Rick, wearing his new whites, with a sweater draped over his shoulders and carrying his Dunlop Maxply racquet, walked past the pool to the tennis court, which he found empty. He found a basket of balls on a bench and began serving into the fence, to warm up.

At around ten-fifteen he heard female voices and looked back toward the house. Three women were walking down the hill from the house — Suzanne Harris; Adele Mannheim, Sol Weinman's sister, whom he had met at dinner; and — he got a little weak in the knees — Greta Garbo.

Rick tried to breathe normally and not stare. He gave Suzanne and Adele pecks on their cheeks, then turned to shake Garbo's hand, which was larger than he had expected. He managed to keep breathing and smile a little.

Right behind the women were Eddie Harris and George Cukor, the director. After the introductions were made, Suzanne broke them up into mixed pairs, and Rick and Adele Mannheim spent the first set on the bench. He was glad he hadn't been paired with Garbo, because he didn't think he could have spoken many words in her presence, but Adele was an amiable woman, and she looked better in her tennis skirt than he would have imagined.

"So, how's it going for you at the studio?" she asked, keeping her eyes on the players.

132

Rick was happy to keep his eyes on the players, too, since he could watch Garbo move gracefully around the court. "It seems to be going well," Rick replied. "I'm enjoying myself."

"I hear good things from Sol," she said, "which means Sol hears good things from Eddie. I'm glad he got that business with that gangster straightened out."

"Well, I . . ."

"Oh, nobody thinks you were at fault, Rick," she said. "From all I hear, you did exactly the right thing."

"Well . . ."

She patted his hand. "You've taken a load off Eddie's mind, too. Suzanne told me so."

"I've hardly done anything yet."

"You've kept Clete Barrow working, and that's no mean feat."

"All I've done is keep Clete company. He's behaved like a gentleman every step of the way."

"He doesn't always, dear. Remember that. Once he gets a skinful, he's a wild man."

"I'll keep that in mind," Rick said.

They changed around, and Rick and Adele played a set against Eddie and Garbo, then another against Cukor and Suzanne, then they broke for lunch, which was served in the cabana next to the pool.

The servants had set up a little buffet, and there was champagne, which Rick avoided, since he didn't know whether he was supposed

133

to play again. He had just begun to relax in Garbo's presence when a servant came down from the house and spoke quietly to Eddie. Eddie motioned with his head for Rick to follow, so he put down his half-eaten lunch and tailed Eddie into the main house.

"Trouble," Eddie said as they went inside. "I didn't want to take this call in the cabana." He picked up a phone in the hall. "Yes?" He listened for a moment. "What is her current condition?" He listened again. "I don't want her moved from the emergency room until her physician arrives. Dr. James Judson. Please see that that happens. Thank you." He hung up and turned to Rick.

"One of our contract players is in the Cedars-Sinai emergency room, an apparent suicide attempt. I want you to change and get down there right away and hold the fort until Jim Judson arrives. You met him at Clete's cottage that first night."

"Right. I'm on my way."

"Rick, a few things: Make sure that she's not admitted and that Dr. Judson takes any record they've made when he leaves. And no member of the press gets to her, and the staff understands that they're not to talk. This is a valuable girl with a real future, and she has to be protected."

"I understand."

"Her name is Glenna Gleason. Now get going. I'll call Judson."

★ ★ ★

Rick sprinted past the pool toward his cottage, spent thirty seconds in a cold shower, threw on some clothes, grabbed some cash and jumped into his car. Ten minutes after the phone call, he was on his way, annoyed that his first and probably only opportunity to get to know Greta Garbo had vanished into this stupid girl's problem. And he was still hungry.

20

As he pushed through the swinging doors of the Cedars emergency room, the scent of disinfectant brought on a wave of déjà vu. He had been in that moment at least a couple of dozen times as a cop.

Since it was Sunday, business was slow, and there were few people to be seen. The reception desk was manned by a single woman in a nurse's uniform.

"Hey, where do you think you're going?" the woman called as he breezed past her.

He ignored her and walked through the doors of the treatment area. A large man was lying on a bed, a slab of gauze on his bloody forehead.

The man lifted his head. "Are you the doctor?"

"No, he'll be along in a moment," Rick said. "Was a girl brought in here a few minutes ago?"

"Down there," the man said, indicating the other end of the long room.

Rick walked toward a curtained-off area at the

end of the room and looked behind the curtain. A woman lay in a bed, her hair wrapped in a white cloth, and another cloth over her eyes, apparently unconscious. A sheet was pulled up to her chin. Rick walked to the end of the bed and looked at the chart on a clipboard attached to the bedframe. No name was written at the top. He walked around the bed and found a silk dressing gown and a handbag lying on a steel chair. He found a wallet in the bag and a California driver's license in the wallet, in the name of Louise Brecht, who lived at 8152 Sunset Boulevard.

"Shit," he said aloud under his breath. Gleason must have already been admitted.

Rick heard the curtain being yanked back and looked up to find a young man in a white coat standing there. A stethoscope peeped from a pocket.

"Who are you?" he asked.

Rick produced a card. "I'm looking for Glenna Gleason," he said. "An apparent suicide attempt."

The young doctor pointed at the bed. "This is the only female patient in the emergency room."

"Did you admit a Miss Gleason earlier?"

"This is the only woman brought in this morning," he said. "The police were here but have already gone."

"The Beverly Hills Police?"

"Yes, I think so."

"Do you recall the officer's name?"

The doctor looked at the ceiling. "Let me see . . ."

"Uniformed officer or detective?"

"Uniformed. Terry, that was his name. Last name."

Rick knew him. "Thank you. Is this woman an attempted suicide?"

"I don't really see how" — he looked at Rick's card again — "some studio's security could be related to this woman."

"If she's the attempted suicide, I'm here to protect her," Rick said.

"Well, I'm in the process of admitting her right now. She's been sedated, and when she wakes up, I'll ask her if she wants to see you. You can wait outside, but it could be several hours."

"Doctor, please tell me if this woman is an attempted suicide."

"That information is available only to her next of kin or her personal physician."

"I am her personal physician," a voice said, and both Rick and the doctor turned to see Dr. James Judson, dressed in casual clothes, standing behind them. "Dr. Judson," he said to the young doctor, extending his hand. Without waiting for further conversation he went to the bed and pulled back the sheet to reveal two bandaged wrists.

"Doctor, I was just admitting her," the young man said.

"That won't be necessary. She's being moved

to a private hospital right now. I have an ambulance waiting." He picked up the chart from the end of the bed. "How long ago did you sedate her? It's not marked here."

"I haven't completed the chart yet. I don't even know her name."

Rick had only been there for two minutes and he knew her name.

"That's all right," Judson said. "How long ago?"

"Perhaps forty minutes," the doctor replied.

"Have her wounds been sutured?"

"I was about to do that when you arrived."

Judson pulled back the curtain and waved at two men in white uniforms standing by a stretcher. "Over here," he said.

The two men came and gently moved the girl to a stretcher on wheels.

"You know where," Judson said. "I'll be right behind you." He turned to Rick. "You're Barron? I remember you."

Rick nodded. "I'll follow you."

Judson ripped the page from the chart and stuck it in his pocket.

"Just a minute," the young doctor said, "that's her only medical record. We need it for our files."

"No, you don't," Judson said. "She hasn't been here." He handed the doctor his card. "Give this to your chief and have him call me if he has any questions." He turned to Rick. "Pay her bill, then come along." He handed him a card with the address of the Judson Clinic on it.

Rick nodded. "Thank you, Doctor," he said, gathering up the girl's dressing gown and handbag and walking back to the front desk. "A bill for the young lady," he said to the nurse.

"She doesn't have one yet. It will take a while to generate it."

Rick put two fifties on the desk. "Don't bother generating it," he said. "She's being moved." He added another fifty to the pair. "And if anyone asks, she wasn't here."

The woman swept the money off the counter. "Sure thing," she said, smiling.

Rick left the building and found his car, parked in a space reserved for doctors. A moment later he was gone, and so was any trace of Centurion's young actress. He checked the address on Judson's card and aimed the Ford in that direction.

21

Rick caught up with the ambulance just as it turned into the circular drive of a large Colonial-style house in the heart of Beverly Hills. There was no sign outside.

Rick had often driven past the address and had never known the house was a clinic. He parked behind the ambulance and watched as the two attendants removed the stretcher and wheeled it into the house. Dr. Judson awaited them in the lobby.

"Upstairs," Judson said. The two men sighed simultaneously, then slowly and carefully humped the stretcher up the stairs. Judson turned back to Rick. "I don't know what else you can do here," he said.

"Just a moment," Rick said. He opened the handbag again and rummaged through it: sixty-odd dollars in cash, a checkbook, showing a balance of more than three thousand dollars — more than he had in the bank — and the driver's license. He didn't have to memorize the address, he knew it. All he needed was the bungalow number. He handed the purse and the silk dressing gown to the doctor. "This is what she was wearing, and her handbag. Her driver's license says she's Louise Brecht, so I don't even know if we've got the right girl."

Judson pointed. "There's a phone over there. Call Eddie."

"What can I tell him about her condition?"

"She's sedated and stable. I'll get a plastic surgeon in to suture her wrists. Apart from that, we'll just have to wait for her to come to, then I'll have a psychiatrist see her."

Rick nodded, went to the phone and called Eddie. He had to wait while he was called from the cabana to the phone.

"Rick? Do you have her?"

"I think so. Is her real name Louise Brecht?"

"Yes. The studio changed it to Glenna Gleason. How did you know her name?"

"She still has a driver's license in her old name." He gave Eddie Judson's report.

"That's fine. She's in good hands."

"I'm going to take a look at where she lives and see if I can find out why this happened."

"Good idea. Call me in the morning and let me know what you've found out."

"Will do." Rick hung up, went to his car and headed for Sunset. 8152 was the Garden of Allah, and he knew it well. The silent star Alla Nazimova had owned a mansion at the corner of Sunset and Crescent Heights, on several acres, and she had turned the place into an apartment house and built a hotel and a dozen or so cottages on the property, going broke in the process. She now lived in a corner room of her old home.

Rick parked on the street and walked through the hotel lobby into the garden, which was surrounded by the cottages. There was a restaurant and bar in the hotel and a nice pool in the garden. The Garden of Allah was home to screenwriters like Dorothy Parker and Robert Benchley and various film-community transients. It was not an inexpensive place to live, and Rick wondered how the girl could afford it. Then again, she had three grand in the bank, and that wasn't hay.

He found bungalow seven and knocked on the door. No answer. He tried the knob, which turned easily, and he was in. A tiny foyer gave way to a sitting room, nicely furnished and neatly kept. At the rear was a small kitchen. Rick looked in the icebox, which held a couple of bottles of champagne and some half-eaten Chinese food. Glenna Gleason must eat out a lot, he imagined.

On one side of the sitting room a door was ajar, and Rick looked inside to find a bedroom with an unmade bed. He stepped over a blood-stain near the door and went into the bathroom, which had spatters of blood on the sink and floor. He went back into the living room and saw another door on the other side. He opened it; another bedroom, occupied. Someone was under the covers, blond hair sticking out.

"Excuse me," he said loudly.

The girl threw back the covers and sat up. She was naked and had quite beautiful breasts. "What?" she said. Then she realized a strange man was in the room and clutched the covers to her chest. "Who are you?"

"My name is Barron," Rick said. "I'm from Centurion Studios."

"Oh."

"Get something on and come into the living room. I need to talk to you about Glenna." He closed the door and went into the kitchen, where he found some coffee and put the pot on. He went back to the front door, found a DO NOT DISTURB card and hung it on the outside doorknob. He had already poured himself a mug of coffee when the girl emerged, wearing a little sunsuit and nothing else.

"What's going on?" she asked.

"That's what I want you to tell me," Rick said. "What happened here this morning?"

"I don't know if I should talk to you," she said, accepting a mug of coffee and finding some sugar in a cabinet.

Rick handed her his card. "I have to know what happened so I can help Glenna."

She peered at the card. "Well, I guess it's all right," she said. She went into the living room and sat down on the sofa.

Rick took a chair beside her. "What's your name?"

"Martha Werner," she said. "Glenna and I are both from Milwaukee, Wisconsin. We went to high school together."

"Do you work at Centurion?"

"No, I'm not that lucky. I do extra work, when Central Casting calls me, which they don't do often enough. Glenna is the one with the studio contract."

"How long have you and Glenna lived here?"

"Glenna's been out here for more than a year. I came a couple of months ago."

"How long has she lived at the Garden of Allah?"

"Since she got her contract, I guess — six, eight months."

"How does Glenna afford the rent? Do you share it?"

Martha shook her head. "I don't make enough to share it. Glenna gets a hundred and fifty a week from her contract, and she's got money from her father. He died last year."

"How about her mother?"

"Died when we were seniors in high school."

"Tell me what happened this morning."

"I had a date last night and got home around midnight. Glenna was in her room, and I could hear her arguing with a man."

"Arguing about what?"

"I couldn't tell, through the door. It didn't seem like anything very serious, so I went to bed. I woke up around ten and went to use her bathroom, because my toilet is clogged up. She

145

was lying on the bathroom floor, bleeding."

"What did you do?"

"I put some towels around her wrists and called the police."

"Did you call them through the desk at the hotel, or directly?"

"Directly. The number is in the front of the phone book. They came, and an ambulance was right behind them. Is Glenna all right?"

"What did you do then?" he asked, ignoring her question.

"They said she'd be okay, that they were taking her to Cedars-Sinai, and that I wouldn't be able to see her until this afternoon, so I went back to bed. I was — am — kind of hungover. Is Glenna all right?"

"She's in a private clinic. She'll be fine, but she'll be there for a few days. Do you know who she was arguing with last night?"

"No, just a man. I try not to pry."

"Who else knows what happened here?" Rick asked.

She shrugged. "Nobody, I guess. Just the police and ambulance men."

"All right, Martha, here's what I want you to do: I want you to clean up Glenna's bathroom and soak the towels in the tub in cold, not hot water, and do it before you let the maid in. Do you understand?"

She nodded.

"And I don't want you to talk to anyone at all about this. Do you understand? It could hurt

Glenna's career, and then you wouldn't have anyplace to live."

Martha nodded dumbly.

"This sort of thing can get around this town in a hurry, and we don't want that to happen, do we?"

Martha shook her head.

"You've got my card," Rick said. "Call me if anything else happens — call me first, do you understand?"

"Yes," she said.

"Remember, clean up before the maids come."

"All right."

"And if you do as I say, I'll see if I can do something for you at the studio."

"Oh, that would be wonderful," she said.

"Now you can go back to bed."

She got up and went back to her bedroom, closing the door behind her.

Rick went back to Glenna's bedroom and went through all the drawers, finding nothing that wouldn't ordinarily be in a girl's room. Then, as he was about to leave, he noticed that the bloodstain by the door had an odd, crescent-shaped imprint at one edge. After a moment's staring, he realized it was part of a man's shoe print. So whoever had been there had left after she cut her wrists. Nice guy.

22

Rick was still hungry, having had his lunch interrupted, so he stopped at a drive-in restaurant and had a cheeseburger. The waitresses were in short skirts and on roller skates, and they were amusing to watch.

He finished his burger and checked his watch. Time to go. He drove to the Beverly Hills PD station and sat in the parking lot, checking his watch again. Cops were arriving for their shift, and he exchanged greetings with a few of them, enduring comments about his new job and his new car. Then the patrol cars began returning to the station, to be turned over to the next shift.

Tom Terry was a big, good-natured Irishman from Boston who had decided he would continue the family tradition of police work in a warmer climate. Rick waved him over as he got out of his patrol car, carrying a clipboard.

"Hey, Rick," Terry said, grinning at him and offering his hand. "I hear you landed in a pot of jam."

"Jam is a nice place to be," Rick said. "I'm available, if you need an assistant."

"I'm afraid I'm not important enough for an assistant, but if anything comes up, I'll let you know." Rick wasn't lying to Tom Terry; he was just the sort of guy he would call. "I hear you made a stop at the Garden of Allah this morning."

Terry laughed. "You get around, don't you?"

"I do. It's the new job."

"Was she one of yours at Centurion?"

"Let's just say I'll give you fifty bucks for your report."

Terry's face lit up. "Those things are numbered, you know."

"Yeah, but nobody's counting, and she's a nice kid who doesn't need her name in police records."

Terry looked through the sheets on his clipboard and tore one out. "There you are," he said, handing it over.

"And there you are," Rick said, looking around the parking lot for trouble, then handing over the fifty.

"It's a pleasure doing business with you, buddy," Terry said.

"Spread the word among the fellows that I'll always be generous where the studio's interests are concerned."

"Will do. I gotta check in. You take care." Terry turned and walked into the station, and Rick pointed the Ford toward home. He thought about tracking down the ambulance drivers, but if they were going to sell the story, they would have already done so. Anyway, the name Louise Brecht wouldn't mean anything to them.

He arrived at home and, as he parked the car, saw Eddie Harris sitting alone by his pool, reading a script, his guests having gone. Rick walked over and sat down next to him.

"You were a long time," Eddie said.

"I had a lot to do."

"What did you find out?"

"Glenna has a roommate named Martha Werner, a high-school chum of Louise Brecht. She found Glenna on the bathroom floor, bleeding, and called the cops and an ambulance."

"So there'll be a police report?"

Rick took the sheet from his pocket and handed it over.

Eddie smiled broadly. "Good boy!"

"Martha Werner has been doing extra work. It would help her to stay quiet if she got a small part in a Centurion movie. She's decorative, and she's on file with Central Casting."

Eddie made a note of the name on the back of his script. "I can do that."

"There was a man in Glenna's room after midnight, and he left a partial shoe print in her blood on the bedroom floor, which means he was there either when or after she cut her wrists.

150

That probably didn't happen until morning, or she might have bled to death before Martha found her. Martha heard arguing after midnight."

"Any idea who?"

"No. I went through her things. There was no address book or any sign of a man. No stains on the sheets."

"Sometimes this is a tawdry business," Eddie said sadly. "Frankly, I wouldn't have figured Glenna as a girl to get into this kind of trouble. She seems to have a level head on her shoulders."

"It's man trouble," Rick said. "That happens to a lot of women. They tend to believe what they're told."

"I hope Judson can get her back on her feet," Eddie said.

"He said he'd have her wrists sutured by a plastic surgeon and have a psychiatrist see her."

"Good. She's not working this week, anyway."

"Might be good to get her back to work as soon as she can. Get her mind off what happened."

Eddie nodded. "And I want you to find out who this man of hers is and see what you can do about keeping this from happening again."

"All right." Well, this was different, he thought. When he had been a cop, he would have dropped her off at the emergency room, and that would have been that. "Let me know what film you assign Martha Werner to, and I'll have

151

another chat with her while she's on the lot."

"I'll take care of it tomorrow and let you know. Did you get lunch?"

"Yeah, I stopped at a drive-in."

"Garbo liked you."

Rick grinned. "I liked Garbo."

"Don't let it go to your head. She doesn't like men all that much. I mean, in that way. She prefers other company, when she can be discreet."

"Oops. I'm glad you told me."

"You want to be careful with women who are at or near the top of the ladder out here. They tend to think of themselves first, and no man likes that. If they somehow thought you might impede their progress, you could end up with high-heel prints up your back."

Rick laughed. "That's good advice, Eddie."

"I'm full of good advice," Eddie said, "but hardly anybody ever takes it."

"I'll take it."

"You having dinner with Clete tonight?"

"I'll call him."

"We're down to the home stretch on this film now, and every frame we shoot of him counts."

"He seems to be holding up well."

"He always seems that way, right up to the moment when he falls off the wagon and does something crazy."

"I'll watch for signs of that." Rick thought of bringing up Clete's concerns about a war between England and Germany, but he held back. He and Clete were becoming friends, just as he and Eddie were, and he would have to pick his way through all this, trying not to betray either of them.

Rick thought of something. "Can I see that police report again?"

Eddie handed it to him.

He read it carefully and handed it back. "I just wanted to get the details firmly in my head."

"Sure."

"See you later." He got up and went to call Clete.

23

Rick went back to the cottage, called Clete, got a busy signal. Feeling sweaty, he showered and changed, then called again; still busy. He tried three more times over the next hour and still got a busy signal. He called the operator.

"Central," she said.

"This is Lieutenant Barron, LAPD," he said. "Please check a constantly engaged number for me."

"Please hold." She went away and came back. "Nobody's on the line," she said. "You want to listen?"

"Yes, please."

There was a click, and Rick listened intently. He thought he could hear the sound of ragged, distressed snoring. "Thank you," he said, and hung up.

When he walked through Clete's unlocked front door, he immediately smelled alcohol. He walked faster. "Clete?" he called. No answer, but he heard the snoring.

He walked into the living room, and the smell of scotch was overwhelming. Clete was sprawled in a living room chair, one foot on an ottoman, slumped so far down in the chair that his head was nearly on the seat. The snoring was ragged because his head was at an odd angle, and his feet were bloody. The smell of scotch came from a broken bottle near the bar.

Rick walked over to him and shook him. "Clete? Wake up."

Clete didn't stir.

Rick pulled him farther down in the chair and put both his feet on the ottoman, so that he was horizontal. The snoring stopped, but the breathing was still ragged. A telephone lay on the sofa, the receiver off. Rick hung it up.

Rick examined Clete's feet and found bloody glass in both of them. The cuts were more than Rick could handle. He tried again to wake up Clete and failed, so he flipped through his notebook and found Dr. Judson's home number.

"Hello?"

"Doc, it's Rick Barron. Twice in the same day. Sorry about that."

"What's up, Rick?"

"Clete Barrow is passed out in his living room. I can't wake him up and I don't like the sound of his breathing. Also, he's cut both feet badly on a broken liquor bottle, and I think he's going to need stitches. I'd rather not take him to the emergency room."

"He's at home?"

"Yes."

"I'll be there shortly. Make sure his airway is clear, that he hasn't vomited. Turn him on his side, if you can."

"Will do." Rick hung up and got Clete turned onto his side, and he seemed to breathe easier. He went to the kitchen, found a mop and a bucket and cleaned up the glass and spilled scotch on the tile floor of the living room. By the time he was finished, Judson was there, and so was an ambulance. The doctor went to Clete, listened to his heart and breathing with a stethoscope, then he turned to the ambulance men. "You can go," he said, and the men left.

"He's all right, then?" Rick asked.

"He's just very, very drunk, but not quite at the point of alcohol poisoning. How long have you been with him?"

"I had dinner with him last night, and he was fine. I arrived here less than half an hour ago and found him like this, so I called you."

Judson began examining Clete's feet. "You were right; he needs suturing." He opened his bag, took out a large pair of tweezers and began plucking glass from Clete's soles. "Get me something to put the glass in, will you?"

Rick found an empty nut bowl on the bar and brought it over.

"How did he do this?"

"There was a broken scotch bottle on the floor when I arrived. He seems to have walked

156

through the glass. I cleaned it up."

Judson began swabbing Clete's feet with alcohol, then he laid out some instruments and started suturing the cuts. "It's just as well he's out," Judson said. "I don't have any Novocain with me." He finished, then applied bandages to both feet.

"How long is he likely to be out?" Rick asked.

"Hard to say. He could sleep straight through the night. Can you stay with him?"

"Sure."

"It's important he doesn't drink any more tonight. I've seen Clete put down a lot of liquor and still walk and talk. It must have taken a hell of a lot to put him in this condition, and he's going to have a hell of a hangover tomorrow."

"Eddie's going to expect him to work tomorrow morning," Rick said. "What about his feet?"

"He's just going to have to tough it out," the doctor said. "I'll go by his bungalow at the studio at eight tomorrow morning and rebandage his feet. If he busts his stitches, call me and I'll resuture them." He took a small bottle of pills from his bag. "You can give him one of these every four hours if he's in pain, but no more than that. For God's sake, don't let him have the bottle."

Rick nodded.

The doctor packed up his equipment. "When he wakes up, he may get . . . obstreperous. Keep him off his feet and don't let him drink any more."

"Okay."

"Call me if you can't handle him, and I'll come over and sedate him."

"Okay."

The doctor left, and Rick called Eddie Harris.

"What now?" Eddie asked, when he had been called to the phone.

"Clete's had an accident and cut both feet pretty badly. Dr. Judson was here and sutured them, but it's going to be painful for him to walk tomorrow."

"Oh, shit, is he drunk?"

"Yes, and passed out. I'll have him at work tomorrow. What time is his call?"

"Not until nine."

"You might think about shooting scenes in which he's sitting down, if there are any like that."

"I'll call the director and see what we can do to keep him off his feet. Thanks." He hung up.

Rick hung up and went to Clete. He pulled him into a sitting position, got down on one knee and rolled him onto his back, in a fireman's carry. He staggered to his feet, barely managing it, then carried Clete into his bedroom, pulled the covers back and lowered him as gently as he could onto the bed. He got the robe off him, then pulled the covers over his naked body.

Rick went back and took the bloody cotton

slipcover off the ottoman, took it into the kitchen, ran some cold water in the sink and left the slipcover to soak. He looked in the icebox and found some cold chicken and potato salad and had some dinner, then he found a magazine and went back to Clete's room, settling into an easy chair.

It was going to be a long night.

24

Rick was jarred out of a sound sleep by a loud groan. He lifted his head off the back of the chair and was greeted by a terrible pain in his neck, the result of sleeping upright. Clete was sitting up on his elbows.

"Christ!" he said. "What happened?"

"You tied one on, pal, that's what happened."

Clete rolled over and started to get up.

"Careful, you cut both feet on a broken scotch bottle."

Clete felt at both feet carefully, then he put them on the floor and stood up slowly. "I can walk on the outsides of my soles," he said, making his way awkwardly toward the bathroom. "Anyway, I've got to pee or die trying." He peed loudly, then returned. "What time is it?"

Rick glanced at his watch. "A little after seven. We've got to get you to work. You want some breakfast?"

"Good God, no," Clete replied, pulling some clothes from a drawer. "I'll have some coffee at the bungalow."

Rick helped him to the car and drove toward Centurion. "How often does this happen?" he asked.

"What?"

"Getting drunk and passing out."

"Oh, not too often, sport. Now and then it all gets to be too much, you know?"

"No, I don't know. What set you off?"

"I don't remember a hell of a lot about last night. The servants were off, and I meant to fix myself some dinner, but I guess I drank it, instead."

"You keep at it and you're going to end up with brain damage, drooling your way through your days in some nursing home. Not to mention what you're doing to your liver."

"Heard it all before, sport," Clete said, waving the words away.

"How are you feeling?"

"Like death, once removed."

"Oh, yeah, I forgot about death," Rick said. "That could happen, too."

"Please, please. Wait until dinnertime, then you can chastise me all you like, but not now."

They arrived at the bungalow, and Rick helped Clete inside and into his makeup chair. "See what you can do with this," he said to the makeup girl.

"I've dealt with worse," she said, then went to work.

"Anybody home?" The voice of Eddie Harris rang out from the front door. He came into the

161

makeup room pushing a wheelchair. "I hear you're non-ambulatory," he said to Clete.

"Don't worry, I can work."

Eddie looked at his bandaged feet. "The doc will be here in a minute. I want him to have a look at them before we leave for the set."

"He's already had a look at them. I'm fine."

"We've got three scenes to shoot today that we can accomplish with you sitting," Eddie said. "Tomorrow, you're going to have to bite the bullet."

"Then bite it I will," Clete said. "I want to finish this bloody picture almost as much as you do."

"If you can hobble through the rest of August, we'll have it in the can."

"Then hobble I will."

Rick made some coffee and had a cup waiting when the makeup girl finished.

"Do I need pants for these scenes?" Clete asked. "I don't relish pulling those jodhpurs on and off."

"Maybe not. We'll take them along, just in case."

Dr. Judson showed up, unbandaged Clete's feet and inspected and rebandaged them. "I've brought some sulfa," he said, drawing some into a syringe. "Let's not wait until you have an infection."

"Oh, all right," Clete said, offering a bare arm.

Rick pushed the wheelchair to an electric

162

cart, helped him in, and stowed the chair in the rear. They drove to the set, and Rick got him inside. The setup was of a broad veranda outside military headquarters, and they got Clete into one of two wicker chairs drawn together with a tray of cold drinks between them.

Clete sampled a drink and wrinkled his nose. "Could somebody put some gin in this, please?"

"Absolutely not," Rick said. "You're going to have to do this sober."

"Who says I'm sober?" Clete read through a couple of pages of his script, another actor sat down beside him, and he did three flawless takes. He didn't even look hungover.

After a break for lunch, Clete changed into a dress uniform tunic, complete with medals, and was wheeled onto a dining room set, where a table had been lavishly decorated with dishes, glasses and food. Other actors came in and took their places, and they ran through a brief rehearsal.

Rick thought one of the girls looked familiar, and it took him a couple of minutes to see past the ball gown and the wig and recognize Martha Werner. She had two lines, and she delivered them with a perfect English accent.

Eddie dropped by and watched a take, including Martha's performance. "She's not bad," he said to Rick.

"You sure got her here in a hurry," Rick replied.

"I think we'll put her under contract. We can

hardly call her Martha Werner, though. Think of a new name for her." He left.

Rick sat down in Clete's set chair and took out his notebook. Yet another new assignment.

When there was a break, Rick went over to Martha. "You were very good," he said.

"Oh, hi," she chirped. "You must have put in a word for me." Her Midwestern accent was incongruous, given her costume.

"Eddie Harris liked your work today," Rick said. "Expect something good to come of that."

"Oh, really? You're not kidding?"

"You'll be hearing from him. In the meantime, you need a name change. Martha Werner won't do."

"Barbara Kane, with a *K*," she said immediately.

"That's not bad," Rick said, putting away his notebook with its list of names.

"It's my mother's maiden name," she said.

"Mention it to Eddie when he speaks to you."

She stood on tiptoe and pecked him on the cheek, leaving a smear of makeup. "Thank you, Rick," she said. "All I wanted was a chance."

"Well, now you've got it."

A makeup man came and patched up her face.

They shot one more scene, then Clete wheeled himself over to where Rick stood.

"Had you nothing better to do all day but watch this boring stuff?"

164

"It was pretty interesting, actually," Rick replied. "I learned something about how movies are made. Tell me, why don't they use more than one camera, instead of shooting a scene over and over with the one, in order to get all the angles?"

"Because actors are cheaper than cameras, old sport. Now get me out of here. I need a drink."

Rick pushed Clete's wheelchair out of the soundstage to the cart, determined not to make a career of keeping him sober.

25

After driving Clete back to his bungalow, Rick called his office to check for messages.

"There's somebody here to see you," Jenny said.

"Who?"

"His name is Ben Siegel."

Rick was taken aback. "He's there now?"

"Reading one of my movie magazines. He's been here for over an hour."

"How did he get past the front gate?"

"I don't know. What do you want me to tell him?"

"Tell him I'm on my way over there." He hung up and went to Clete, who was applying cold cream to his makeup. "You look darling," he said.

Clete laughed. "If my fans could see me now."

"I have to go over to my office for a few minutes. I'll come back and drive you home before long."

"I can get a studio car to take me."

"Stick around. I'll be back."

166

"Whatever you say, old dear."

Rick drove his car back to the administration building and parked. He had thought this business with Stampano was over, but what the hell was Bugsy Siegel doing in his office? He took a few deep breaths so that it wouldn't seem that he had hurried, then walked into his office.

Siegel was stretched out on his leather couch, reading a *Photoplay.* He sat up and offered his hand. "How are you, Rick?"

"Just fine, thank you," Rick replied, shaking the hand. He took the armchair next to the sofa. "What can I do for you, Ben?"

Siegel sat back on the sofa. "I just wanted to see if Chick is leaving you alone."

Rick shrugged. "Haven't seen hide nor hair of him."

"Good."

There was a silence, and Rick wondered again what the guy was doing in his office.

"How'd you get onto the lot?" Rick asked.

"Through the main gate."

"Without a pass?"

"I'm known all over," Siegel said, smiling.

"Oh." He would damn well see that the gangster wouldn't be known next time.

Another silence.

"Come on, Ben, what's this about?" Rick tried to keep his voice genial.

"Well, there is a little business we could discuss."

"Business?"

"How's the new job coming along?"

"Just fine."

"You enjoying it?"

"Yes, I am." Why wouldn't the guy get to the point?

"I'm just wondering if you're the right guy."

"The right guy for what?"

"For the job."

"For my job?"

"No, for the other one."

"I'm sorry, Ben, but I'm not getting you."

"Your predecessor . . ." Siegel drew out the word syllable by syllable, as if trying it out ". . . did a little business with me from time to time. I was thinking that maybe you and I could do a little business."

Now a dilemma: Rick wanted to know about this, but he didn't want to know about it. If he asked, he might hear something he didn't want to hear. He decided to say nothing.

"It wouldn't require a lot of your time," Siegel said.

Rick still said nothing.

"In fact, hardly any time at all. And the money's good."

Rick decided he didn't want to know. "Ben, I'm afraid that this job takes all my time."

"I said it wouldn't take a lot of time."

"I'm on call twenty-four hours a day," Rick said. "There's no time for anything else." Suddenly, he really wanted to know. "What was Kean doing for you?"

Siegel shrugged. "If you don't have any time at all, then maybe you don't need to know that."

"Maybe I don't."

"There's something else."

"What's that?"

"I hear you do some flying."

"I used to. That's something else I don't have the time for anymore."

"Once in a while I take a trip to Mexico. Maybe you could fly me down there — just overnight, sometimes not even that long."

Rick shook his head. "I'm afraid not, Ben, but you can go out to Clover Field and pick up a charter."

"Maybe from your old man?"

Rick felt a little chill. Siegel was letting him know he knew about his father.

"I'm afraid he can't send airplanes to Mexico," Rick lied. "He had some problems with the authorities on the other side of the border once, and it took him nearly a month to get his airplane back. Cost him a lot of money."

"We don't have problems with authorities," Siegel said. "We solve that kind of problem on the spot."

"It's a small business, and he has his hands full."

"We could put some money in his hands."

Siegel had started saying "we," and Rick didn't like that at all.

"Can I be frank with you, Ben? Without meaning any offense?"

169

"Sure you can, Rick."

"You seem like a nice guy, but I don't want to be in business with Jack Dragna and Chick Stampano."

"Jack's a nice guy, too," Siegel said. "As for Chick . . . Well, he doesn't have too much to do with business."

"I don't want anything at all to do with him."

"What you got against Jack?"

"Nothing, personally, but people who do business with him sometimes end up dead."

"If you're straight with Jack, he'll be straight with you."

"I'm sure you're right, but still . . ."

"You know, our money is just as good as Eddie Harris's and Sol Weinman's. Spends real nice, and it's always cash — no taxes, no bother."

"Thanks, Ben, but no thanks."

"If that's how you feel about it."

"I'm sorry, but yes, that's how I feel about it. I'm speaking for my father, too."

"Oh, I'll bet he could use some nice, tax-free cash."

"Ben, I would take it kindly if you didn't speak to him about this, and I'd appreciate it if you'd see that nobody else speaks to him about it, either."

Siegel stood up. "Whatever you say, Rick. Why don't you and I have dinner sometime, maybe with some girls?"

"Right now, all my evenings are taken up with

170

studio personnel." That was certainly no lie, but it probably sounded like one. "Eddie has me bird-dogging his favorite leading man, making sure his picture finishes on time."

"Maybe later, then."

"You never know."

Siegel shook his hand. "Be seeing you, Rick."

Rick certainly hoped not. He walked Siegel to the door and said goodbye.

As soon as Siegel had time to drive out of the parking lot, Rick headed for the fourth floor and Eddie Harris's office.

26

Eddie was standing, clearing his desk, stuffing papers into drawers, when his secretary showed Rick in.

"Hey, boy, what's up?" he asked.

"I just had a visit from Ben Siegel," Rick said.

Eddie stared at him for a moment, then sat down. "What the hell did he want?"

"He wanted to hire me."

"To do what?"

"We never really got around to that, because I turned him down flat before he got started."

"Well, I'd hate to think you'd leave us so quickly."

"He didn't want me to leave. He had some sort of side deal in mind, payment in cash."

"And he wouldn't tell you what?"

"At first, I didn't really want to know, and by the time I decided I did, he wouldn't tell me."

"Oh."

"The only real information I got is that my predecessor, the late John Kean, was working for Siegel."

Eddie's eyebrows went up. "What do you think he was doing?"

"I don't know, Eddie. I wish I'd strung Siegel along for a while, until I found out."

"Me, too."

"He also made noises about hiring my father, but I think that was just to let me know he knew about my father."

"He was trying to intimidate you?"

"It was very subtle, but yes, I think so."

Eddie turned and stared out the window.

"Eddie, you mentioned that you didn't want to be involved with these people. Have they approached you in the past?"

Eddie nodded slowly. "Last year, when we were starting to build the two new soundstages, we had a little difficulty with the banks, and suddenly Ben Siegel was there, offering the money."

"At loan shark rates, I imagine."

"No, at a very good rate. But he wanted equity."

"In the studio?"

"Yes. He was representing Jack Dragna and his friends in New York, like Meyer Lansky, of course, but he made out that it was his own money. I didn't buy that for a minute."

"Why would they want into a movie studio? I wouldn't think they would like the return on investment. They'd make a lot more money on gambling and prostitution and loan-sharking, and it would be tax-free."

"You're right, of course. My thought was that

173

they wanted access to the girls we have signed to contracts, but that doesn't really make sense. If they're looking for whores, they'd do better among the girls who come out here and don't get signed."

"Of course," Rick said. "What else would the studio have that they'd want?"

"Glamour? The chance to rub shoulders with movie stars?"

"Siegel is already rubbing shoulders with movie stars. He and George Raft were childhood buddies, and Raft has introduced him to everybody he knows. I can't see them investing money for that."

"What else have we got?" Eddie asked.

Rick thought about that. "Real estate," he said finally.

Eddie shook his head. "Nah, we're in the low-rent district. If we didn't own the back lot, it would just be scrubland."

"Eddie, do you remember your advice to me to invest in real estate?"

"Sure."

"Why?"

"Because it's going up."

"Then that's why the mob wants it. They want in for the long haul, and when you think about it, the movie studios own land all out of proportion to most businesses. We're talking about hundreds of acres, not a few lots."

"We've got over six hundred acres," Eddie said, "but still . . ."

"Look at this town," Rick said. "Where was it ten years ago? Twenty?"

"God knows it's growing fast."

"And we've been in a depression for years, so land values are artificially low right now. Perfect time to buy in, if you have a lot of cash sitting around — the fruits of criminal enterprise. Who knows what your six hundred acres will be worth in another five or ten?"

Eddie nodded. "You make a lot of sense. I've been shortsighted." He stood up. "Well, we're going to keep them out. I'm not taking a dime from them, and when I talk to Sol about this, he'll feel the same way. I'm going to talk to Eddie Mannix, too. We'll get the word around town; we'll freeze them out."

"What do you want me to do if Siegel comes back to me?"

"Act like you're softening up a little. See if you can find out what he wants."

"Okay. I'll have a word with my dad, too; warn him not to take any business from these people."

"Oh, by the way, I looked into buying a DC-3. There's one available down in San Diego, at Montgomery Field. Will you go down there and take a look at it?"

"Sure, and I'll take Dad, too. He can go through the logbooks and do compression checks on the engines. There's a lot you need to find out about an airplane before you buy it."

"I'd appreciate that, Rick, and thanks for

talking to me about Siegel."

"Sure thing."

"Where's Clete?"

"Waiting for me at his bungalow. I'd better get over there."

"Good job getting him here this morning. I was afraid something like this might happen."

"Oh, by the way, I had a talk with Martha Werner."

"Did you come up with a name?"

"She did: Barbara Kane." Rick spelled it for him. "It's her mother's maiden name."

"Great. I'll get her in here in the morning and make her an offer."

"Good night, then." Rick left Eddie's office and headed over to Clete Barrow's bungalow.

The actor was sitting on the front porch in his wheelchair, waiting, like a good boy.

As they drove away, Rick regretted that he hadn't told Eddie about the gun, the photograph and the money in his safe. He kept meaning to tell him, and he kept forgetting. He kept forgetting to look into that, too.

27

Rick rotated the yoke, and the Lockheed Vega lifted off runway 21 at Clover Field. His father was supposed to be checking him out in the airplane, but Jack Barron said nothing, just kept an eye on the instruments.

Rick made a climbing right turn and leveled off at three thousand feet, heading south. He could cross Los Angeles Municipal Airport at this altitude without interfering with its traffic, and that took only a couple of minutes, since the newer airport was just next to Clover Field. It had been a bean and barley field until eleven years before, when it had been built in time for the 1928 National Air Races.

Rick stayed at three thousand. "Nice airplane," he said.

Jack still said nothing.

"Anything wrong, Dad?"

"Nope," Jack replied.

"Tell me, have you heard anything from somebody named Siegel?"

"Bugsy Siegel?"

"You know who that is?"

"I read the papers."

"He came to see me yesterday, and I thought he might have come to see you."

"He didn't, but another fellow did."

"Did you get a name?"

"No, but he said he worked for Jack Dragna."

"Anything come of it?"

"Nah. I told him I had all the business I could handle."

"Good move. How'd he take it?"

"He just stared at me for a long time, so I stared right back."

"Good. If you hear anything more from him, will you let me know?"

"Why?"

"I just need to know."

"Why?"

"Those people are trying to worm their way into the studio, and it's not working."

"You afraid they'll get rough?"

"No, but I still don't want them around."

"I've still got my Colt side arm from the war; got a shotgun, too."

"Try not to shoot anybody."

"I'll try, but I won't make any promises. Pissed me off, that fellow did. I don't want anything to do with Jack Dragna and his boys."

"Good."

The rest of the short flight passed in silence. Rick ran through the checklists a couple of times, to get it all straight in his head, then he set down at Montgomery Field in San Diego.

The DC-3 turned out to be very nice. While Jack ran his compression checks, Rick climbed aboard. The company that owned the airplane had put in a comfortable interior, with a sofa you could stretch out on and some comfortable chairs. You could seat eight — ten in a pinch, if you put down the folding seats, and there was a toilet in the rear.

The radios were the latest, and the pilots' seats were covered in sheepskin, which made for comfort on long flights. There were oxygen masks throughout the airplane, so hopping over weather wouldn't be too much of a problem. He went back outside, put on some coveralls and began to help his father.

"I wouldn't have thought you'd get involved with gangsters, working at a movie studio," Jack said.

"Neither would I," Rick replied, handing him a wrench.

"You sure you're in the right business?"

"Dad, it's a dream job. I'm my own boss a lot of the time, and there's room to rise in the organization, once I get a grip on the business."

"I read in Hedda Hopper that you're a nursemaid to Clete Barrow."

"You read Hedda Hopper?" Rick asked, astonished.

"I like her better than that other one," he said. "She's bitchier."

Rick hadn't seen the item. "What did she have to say?"

"Oh, just that the two of you were dining at the Brown Derby or someplace."

"Dave Chasen's."

"Yeah, I guess. And that you had to keep him on the wagon."

"She said that, in so many words?"

"Not exactly, but she implied it."

"Well, she's right. Clete is finishing up a big picture that's important to the studio, and they don't want him falling off the wagon."

"I guess it means money to them."

"It means a lot of money to them."

"You enjoying the work?"

"It's not so bad, because I like Clete Barrow. We're getting to be friends."

"You're not a drunk, are you?"

"No, Dad, I'm not. I don't even try to keep up with Clete."

"Good. Liquor will get the best of you, if you're not careful. God knows, I like a snort now and then, but you don't want to let it get ahold of you."

"You're right about that."

Jack returned his tools to the toolbox. "Looks like this is a pretty good airplane," he said. "Let's take a look at the logbooks."

He went through the engine and airframe logbooks carefully, noting each entry. "She's well maintained," he said, "and she's only got a little over four hundred hours on her."

"What's she worth?"

"Oh, I'd be in way over my head there. I'll make some calls and get you a figure." He closed the logbooks. "Let's get out of here," he said.

Less than an hour later, Rick was landing at Clover Field.

"You comfortable with the airplane?" Jack asked.

"Real comfortable. Any advice?"

"Nope. You did it like I taught you. You're a good pilot, boy. I don't have to worry about you."

"When Clete finishes his picture, I'll fly him up to Oregon on that fishing trip."

"I never knew you to fish."

"I thought I'd try it out."

"Can't hurt to have a hobby," Jack said. "Mine's airplanes."

Rick laughed with his father. He put the airplane to bed and got out of his coveralls. "I'd better get back to work," he said.

"You do that. I'll keep my Colt handy."

"Call me if you have any problem at all," Rick said.

"If it's anything I can't handle," Jack replied.

28

Rick got Clete to the set the following morning on time and still in the wheelchair. Clete was complaining, saying he could walk perfectly well, but after another examination and rebandaging by Dr. Judson, he agreed to use the wheelchair except when commanded to rise by his director.

Rick went back to his office and read a magazine for a while, then Jenny buzzed him.

"Eddie Harris wants you to come over to his office right now," she said.

Rick went quickly to the fourth floor and presented himself to Eddie's secretary. Barbara Kane, née Martha Werner, was sitting in the waiting room, and they spoke to each other as he passed through.

Eddie looked up from his desk as Rick entered. "Come in and sit down," he said.

Rick took a chair.

"Miss Kane and Centurion Studios have reached an agreement," he said. "I'm waiting for her new agent to arrive now, so that we can sign the contract that's being typed up."

Rick noted that the negotiations had, apparently, taken place in the absence of an agent. "Good," he said.

"There's something that has to be accomplished before we sign her, though, and now is as good a time as any."

"How can I help?"

"Miss Kane has to have an abortion."

The word made Rick's stomach feel funny. He'd gone through this with Kathleen, Captain O'Connell's niece, only recently, and he hadn't liked the experience. "I see," he said.

Eddie tore a page off a notepad and pushed it across the desk. "This is the name of a doctor who has been recommended."

"Not Dr. Judson?" The good doctor seemed to do everything else for the studio.

"No, Jim Judson doesn't do this sort of work."

Rick picked up the piece of paper. "Dr. Paul Smith," he said aloud, reading from the paper. "In Pasadena."

"I'm told he's a competent man," Eddie said. "It's going to cost two hundred dollars. Draw that from the cashier and take Miss Kane out there."

"When?"

"Right now. The doctor is expecting you."

Rick gulped. He'd hoped to have time to find a way around this. "Is she ready for this?"

"This is at her request. I think it's better for

everybody if we get this taken care of as soon as possible."

"I see."

"I know this is distasteful, Rick, but sometimes business is distasteful. I want you to know that I didn't ask her to do this, that she disclosed it to me and told me this is what she wants. She is under no duress."

Except for the impending contract, Rick thought. "I'll drive her out there now," he said.

"Good. Let me know how it goes."

Rick stood up. "What if there are complications?"

"The man is a doctor; he'll know what to do. If she needs a hospital, call Jim Judson. He doesn't mind getting involved after the fact."

"All right." Rick put the paper in his pocket and left the office. Barbara Kane stood up when she saw him, a question on her face.

Rick nodded. "Come with me," he said.

He stopped at the cashier's window and drew two hundred dollars, then took her out to the parking lot and put her in his car.

"Can we have the top down?" she asked cheerfully.

"Sure." He put the top down and started the car. "Ready?"

"Sure."

He drove out of the studio and headed toward Pasadena.

Barbara laid her head against the seat back and angled her face to catch the sun. "Don't you just love the weather out here?" she asked. "I mean, we have some nice weather in Wisconsin in the summer, but it's nice all year round out here."

"Yes, it is," Rick replied. She seemed awfully calm about this. "How are you feeling?" he asked.

"Oh, I'm fine. I mean, I'm pregnant, not sick."

Rick couldn't think of anything to say, so he just drove, while the girl dozed in her seat.

The doctor's office was a bungalow in a middle-class area of Pasadena, and there was no shingle outside. The address was correct, though.

Barbara opened the car door. "You don't need to come in," she said.

"Are you sure?"

"Look, I've been through this before; nothing to it."

"All right, I'll wait here," Rick said, trying not to sound grateful. "Just shout, if you need me." He gave her the two hundred dollars.

"I shouldn't be more than half an hour," she said. "Forty-five minutes, tops, but I may be a little groggy when I come back."

Rick nodded.

She walked up the steps of the house and rang the bell. Someone — Rick couldn't see who — let her in.

Rick sat and waited, missing smoking again.

He was unaccustomed to killing time without smoking a cigarette. He had nothing to read, nothing to do, and the time went slowly. He put his head back on the seat, tipped his head forward and tried to doze.

He was awakened by the sound of a screen door slamming. He sat up and looked toward the house. Barbara Kane was standing on the front porch, looking unsteady on her feet.

Rick got out of the car and ran up the steps to help her. As he did, he saw a trickle of blood run down her legs and into her shoes. "Are you all right?" he asked. "You're bleeding."

"The doctor said it's to be expected," she said, holding up a paper bag. "He gave me some gauze."

He helped her down the steps and into the car, and she stuffed a wad of gauze up her skirt.

"Just take me home," she said. "I want to sleep."

Rick got the car started and headed back to Los Angeles. He was on Sunset, nearly to the Garden of Allah, when Barbara suddenly bent forward and made a terrible noise. Her face was very white.

"What's wrong?" he asked.

She didn't seem able to form words. She clutched her belly and kept up the noises.

Rick made a U-turn, nearly causing an accident, and shifted down to accelerate. It took only ten minutes to get to Judson's place.

"You stay here," he said. "I'll get some help." He rang the doorbell, and a woman came to the door. "I'm from Centurion Studios," he said. "Tell Dr. Judson I need him and a stretcher down here right now."

He went back to the car to check on Barbara. She was doubled over in the front seat, moaning.

Judson came out the front door in his shirt-sleeves, followed by two men with a stretcher. "What is it?" he asked.

"She's had an abortion," Rick said, "and apparently something went wrong."

Judson and the two men got her on the stretcher and into the house.

"I'll call you when I know something," Judson said, then closed the door.

Rick went back to his car. There was a pool of blood on the front seat. He drove back to the studio and left the car at the motor pool to be cleaned up, then he went back to his office and called Eddie Harris.

"Everything go okay?" Eddie asked.

"No," Rick replied. "She was bleeding when she came out, and we were nearly back to her place when she had some bad pain. I took her to Judson's."

"You did the right thing," Eddie said. "I'll call and see how she's doing. Don't blame yourself, Rick."

"I don't," Rick replied, but he wasn't so sure.

29

The next day, Rick drove into Beverly Hills to the Judson Clinic and presented himself at the reception desk. He had a suspicion, and he wanted it confirmed or denied. After a short wait, Dr. Judson appeared.

"Good morning, Rick," he said. "What can I do for you?"

"How are our two girls doing?" Rick asked.

"I'm afraid Miss Kane had a perforated uterus — the result of an abortion that was little more than butchery. I moved her to Cedars yesterday and she had an emergency hysterectomy."

The thought made Rick angry. A young girl who would now never have children. "Is she all right?"

"She's being treated with sulfa drugs. She's stable and resting comfortably," Judson replied. "It will be at least a couple of weeks, and perhaps as long as a month, before she'll be able to work."

"I'll let Eddie know."

"Our Miss Gleason recovered quickly from

her wounds. Turned out she'd been drugged with morphine."

"Orally?"

"No, there was a needle mark, but she has no memory of receiving the injection."

"Where is she now? Can I see her?"

"She's seeing the psychiatrist right now; she sees him every day. He says we can probably release her tomorrow. I'd rather you didn't see her until then."

"All right. Do you know if she's said who she was with?"

"No, I don't. Her conversations with the psychiatrist are confidential, of course, and anything he tells me with regard to her treatment has to be held in confidence, as well."

"The same with Miss Kane, I suppose."

"Yes, the same. When they're both ready to talk, you can put your questions directly to them." Judson picked up a pad on the reception desk, jotted something on it and handed it to Rick. "In future, if you should encounter another situation like this, you might contact this doctor. He's a good man who does this work as a matter of conscience as much as for the money, and he won't butcher the girls the way this fellow in Pasadena did."

Rick looked at the paper. It was the same doctor who had performed the abortion on his former girlfriend, Kathleen. "Thank you, Jim. Do you know this fellow in Pasadena? Dr. Paul Smith?"

"I've never heard of him, and he's not listed in

the California medical register. It's probably an alias, and he may not even be a doctor."

"Thank you, Jim. May I use your phone?"

"Of course. Use the one by the chair."

Rick called his office and told Jenny that he wouldn't be in for a couple of hours. He got into his car and drove out to Pasadena, to the house where Dr. Paul Smith was plying his trade.

He parked out front, walked up the steps and rang the doorbell. He could hear the chime inside. No one answered. He tried the front door, but it was locked, so he walked around to the rear of the house and began looking in windows. He found an open window in the dining room, and it took only a moment to remove the screen and get inside. There were a couple of straight chairs in the living room and no other furniture in sight. He walked through a kitchen strewn with used paper plates and dirty utensils, down a hallway and into a rear bedroom. A doctor's examining table occupied the middle of the room, complete with stirrups. A single cabinet stood against a wall, holding some bottles and stacks of gauze pads. A number of bloody instruments were scattered on a tabletop.

He opened the steel wastebasket with his foot and found a mass of bloody gauze, covered in flies. There was a phone on the wall, and he got a dial tone. He called the operator and asked to be connected with the police.

"Pasadena Police Department," a woman's voice said.

"Let me speak to the chief of detectives," Rick said.

"Just a moment."

There was a click and a ring. "Lieutenant Henderson," a man said.

"There's an abortionist working in your town," Rick said.

"Who is this?"

"That doesn't matter. The man calls himself Dr. Paul Smith, but that name is not on the medical register, and he may not even be a doctor."

"Who is this?"

"A girl was butchered here yesterday. She had to have emergency surgery at a hospital to save her life."

"We don't take anonymous tips," Henderson said.

"Then you're a lousy police officer and a fool," Rick said. He read out the address. "If you take the trouble to look, you'll find a lot of evidence. If you put a watch on the place, you'll catch him before he kills somebody."

"I told you, I don't listen to this kind of anonymous crap."

"Then Smith must be paying you off," Rick said. "I'm going to watch the papers. If I don't read of the arrest of this man and the closing of his butcher shop, I'm going to go to your city council and expose you as corrupt."

"Do anything you like," Henderson said.

"I'll give you forty-eight hours to roll him up,

191

and then I'll start spreading the word to the newspapers, too." He hung up and left the house the way he had entered it.

Rick drove back to the studio and went up to Eddie Harris's office, but he was told that Eddie was somewhere on the back lot. He drove out there and found Eddie watching the shooting of a gunfight scene on a Western street set.

Eddie came over when the director had cut. "What's up?"

Rick told him about his morning.

"You did the right thing," Eddie said. "You think Henderson will act on this?"

"My guess is that if he does, 'Dr. Smith' will be long gone. You know anybody in the Pasadena city government?"

"No, but I know someone who does."

"Somebody needs to make a call to get a fire built under Henderson."

"I'll see that it gets done."

"In the meantime, Jim Judson gave me the name of another doctor, one I happen to know is good at his work."

"Fine."

"Eddie, where did you get Smith's name?"

"From your predecessor, John Kean," Eddie said. "I'm sorry to have sent that girl to someone like Smith."

Rick nodded. "Judson says it will be two to four weeks before she can work."

"She'll be on the payroll. You see that the bill

192

at Cedar's is paid, and look in on her when she's up to talking to you."

"I intend to."

30

The following morning, Rick stopped at a news-stand and picked up a Pasadena paper. The story was on page twelve, and small:

Pasadena police raided a local house which, police say, was being used as an abortion mill. Evidence of past "operations" was discovered, but the abortionist, who sources say is a Dr. Paul Smith, had fled the scene and is being sought by Pasadena police. They were uncertain as to whether this name is an alias, since there is no Paul Smith on the California medical registry.

Well, Rick thought, somebody got to Lieutenant Henderson, probably Eddie Harris's friend of a friend. He had the feeling that "Dr. Paul Smith" would never be found — at least, not by the Pasadena Police Department.

Rick had been in his office for half an hour when Jenny buzzed him.

"There's a woman on the phone who says she

works at Cedars-Sinai — something about a Martha Werner."

"I'll take it." Rick picked up the phone. "This is Rick Barron."

"Mr. Barron, I'm a nurse at Cedars-Sinai," a woman's voice said. "Martha Werner is a patient here. She says you know her."

"Yes, I do. How is she?"

"She's doing all right, now, and she asked me to call you. She wants you to come and see her."

"Certainly, I will," Rick replied.

"You can visit between two and four this afternoon," the woman said. "Goodbye." She hung up.

After lunch in the studio commissary, Rick drove to Cedars-Sinai and presented himself at the front desk.

"I'd like to see Miss Martha Werner," he said to the woman at the desk.

The woman flipped through a patient list. "Are you a relative?" she asked.

"I represent her employer," Rick replied. "I'm here at her request."

"And who is her employer?" the woman asked, looking suspicious.

Rick handed her his card.

"Oh," she said. "You'll have to have her doctor's permission to see her."

"I already have it. You may telephone Dr. James Judson, and he will confirm it. Would you like his number?"

195

The woman shrugged. "I guess it's all right. Room 211, second floor. The elevators are to your left."

Rick went upstairs and found the room. He knocked softly, and a nurse came to the door. "Yes?"

"My name is Barron. Miss Werner asked me to come and see her."

"Just a minute." She closed the door. A moment passed, then she opened the door again. "She's very tired; don't be long."

"I won't." The nurse left, and Rick stepped into the room and closed the door behind him. Martha Werner/Barbara Kane looked smaller than he remembered, and paler. He pulled up a chair to the bed and sat down. "How are you feeling?" he asked.

She regarded him with sleepy eyes. "I could be worse," she said. "They told me the sulfa saved my life."

"I'm sorry you had to go through this," Rick said, aware that he and the studio were responsible for taking her to the abortionist. "I should have found a way to check out this guy."

"It's not your fault," she said. "I got myself into this."

"You had help," Rick pointed out. "Do you want me to contact the father?"

She managed a little smile. "I'm afraid there's more than one candidate," she said. "I haven't been as careful as I should have been."

"Is there anything I can do for you?"

"I just want to tell you about Louise — Glenna, I mean."

"She's doing very well, I hear. She'll be back at work soon."

"She came to see me at Dr. Judson's place, and we had a talk. She doesn't know what happened to her."

"Do you?"

"I know more than I told you. At least, I suspect more. She'd been seeing a man named Chick Stampano."

"Do you think he's the one who hurt her?"

"I don't know, but he's the kind of guy who would do it."

"Did you see him in the cottage?"

"Not that night, but he'd been there before." She blinked rapidly and turned her face toward the window. "He would be one of my candidates for fatherhood, though. I mean . . ."

"I understand. How did you get involved with him?"

"Oh, you know, you meet people. He was nice, at first, until after he screwed me. Then he didn't want to know me."

Rick nodded. "He's that kind, I hear." Rick had a thought: "Did you ever know a man named John Kean?"

She screwed up her forehead, looking comical. "That's a familiar name, but I can't place it."

"He had my job before I did," Rick explained.

She shook her head. "Doesn't mean anything to me. Chick Stampano does, though. Is there

197

anything you can do to keep him away from Louise and me?"

"I'll see what can be done."

"I would appreciate that, and I'm sure Louise would, too."

Rick wrote his home number on the back of his card and pressed it into her hand. "If either of you hears from him or sees him again, please call me, day or night."

"All right."

"Eddie Harris sends his best wishes. He told me to tell you you're on the Centurion payroll, and the hospital bill will be taken care of. He's looking forward to having you back at work."

She brightened a little. "That's nice of him."

"Is there anything you need me to do for you?"

She shook her head, and her eyelids were drooping.

He patted her hand. "You get some rest. I'll come and see you again."

"No, don't," she said. "I don't want the studio involved any more than this."

"Let me worry about that."

"Thank you for coming to see me."

He left her and went downstairs, where he found a florist's shop. He ordered a large bouquet to be sent to her room, then he left the hospital and got into his car.

Stampano's bloody paw prints were everywhere, all over everything and everybody, he thought. Maybe it was time to use that phone number Eddie Harris had given him.

31

Rick went back to his office and dug the slip of paper out of a little business card file in his desk drawer. Al was only a phone call away, and he was angry enough to make the call.

Still, he had never killed anybody, not even as a cop, and he wasn't sure he wanted to start now. He thought about it, then he dug out another business card and made the call.

"Ben Siegel," the voice said.

"This is Rick Barron."

"Well, hello, pal," Siegel said smoothly, as if they were old friends.

"Can I buy you a drink later today?"

"I'll buy you one."

"Okay, someplace quiet, where we can talk."

"And we've got a lot to talk about, huh?"

"Where and what time, Ben?"

"Come to the Trocadero at six. We'll have the place to ourselves."

"See you then." Rick hung up. Well, he thought, it was worth a try. He called Eddie Harris's secretary and made an appointment.

Eddie was looking at a model for a set design — a sort of Art Deco battleship with guns pointing upstage and tiers for dozens of girls to tap-dance on. "Look at this," Eddie said proudly. "I think I like the models more than the sets themselves."

"It's beautiful, Eddie," Rick said admiringly.

"Take a seat," Eddie said, waving him to a sofa. "What's up?"

"I've got a date for a drink with Ben Siegel at six," Rick said.

Eddie looked surprised. "What for?"

"Chick Stampano may be the father of Martha Werner's child."

"You mean Barbara Kane."

"Yes, I have to get used to that."

"Did she tell you this?"

"Yes."

"And she said he may be the father?"

"She isn't sure."

"Oh, it's like that."

"Yes. And there's more: Jim Judson tells me that somebody injected, ah, Glenna Gleason with morphine before her wrists were slashed."

"She didn't do it herself?"

"No, there were no drugs in her cottage."

"Any idea who?"

"Can't you guess?"

"Stampano again? Jesus!"

"I can't prove it, because Glenna doesn't remember anything, but he's the leading candidate."

"Is this why you're seeing Ben Siegel?"

"Yes. I thought it might be worth one more try to get Siegel and Jack Dragna to do something about Stampano."

"Do what, kill him?"

"Quarantine him from anything to do with Centurion girls."

"You might as well include Metro and the others, too; they'd appreciate the favor."

"All right, I will. I have your permission to do this, then?"

"If you think it's the right thing to do."

"It's all I can think of, short of calling Al, and that might have repercussions."

Eddie leaned back and put his feet on the coffee table. "It occurs to me that warning Siegel first might increase the possibility of repercussions, should we later have to bring Al into it."

"I'm doing my best not to bring Al into it."

"But you understand, if you meet with Siegel and ask him to 'quarantine' Stampano, as you put it, and later, you have to call Al, then Siegel's going to know where the bullet came from."

"I understand."

"I mean, all you can tell Siegel is that if Stampano isn't reined in, there will be serious consequences, then when the consequences occur, he'll know their origin."

"I suppose he will."

"I don't think you're getting it, Rick."

"Sure I am."

"I mean, he might fixate on you as the source

201

of the problem, and you might end up offshore somewhere, wearing cement shoes."

Rick blinked. "You're right, I wasn't getting you. I was thinking more along the lines of Siegel taking out some sort of retribution against Centurion or the other studios."

"Like what?"

"Like an extras strike."

"Could happen. I would be equally unhappy if there were retribution against the studios or against you, personally."

"Thank you. Either of those outcomes would make me unhappy, too, though not equally."

"Let's think this through: Is there some other way to deal with Stampano less drastically, but equally effectively?"

"The nice thing would be to get him convicted of the attempted murder of Glenna Gleason and send him up to San Quentin for twenty years or so, but we don't have the evidence for that."

"I like the idea of a conviction," Eddie said, "and I don't care what it's for. Surely Stampano, given his line of work, is guilty of all sorts of things."

"Very probably. I have a friend in the LAPD who works on organized crime cases. He's overworked and understaffed, but . . ."

"I would be happy to offer him some sort of, ah, motivation, if you think it would help."

"It might. Probably half the force is taking a bribe for something."

"Is it a bribe when you pay a cop to do his job?"

Rick laughed. "I don't think you would get convicted of that. Anyway, it's possible that my friend already has enough on Stampano for a conviction, but that he's holding out in the hope of catching bigger fish."

"That sounds good."

"What's more likely is that he knows Stampano has dirt all over him but that he can't make a case."

"Then maybe what your friend needs to do is to create a case that can be made."

"It wouldn't be the first time," Rick admitted.

"I'll bet it would be the first time he got paid for it."

"Probably."

"Go ahead and keep your appointment with Siegel, but assume it's not going to work. Then see your friend and see what can be worked out."

Rick looked at his watch and stood up. "I'm on my way."

Driving out the main gate, Rick felt relieved that he had an alternative to out-and-out murder.

32

The front door to the Trocadero was locked, and Rick knocked loudly on it. Then he saw a doorbell to one side and rang that.

Ben Siegel opened the door. "Hello, Rick," he said, shaking hands. "Come on in."

The place was strangely empty. The tables were set for dinner, and there was a slight scent of disinfectant.

Siegel walked him to the bar, offered him a stool, then let himself behind the bar. "What'll it be?"

"Bourbon. Old Crow is good, over ice, no water."

Siegel filled a glass with ice, then with bourbon, then poured himself a scotch. He set Rick's drink on the bar and raised his own. "What'll we drink to?"

"Happy days," Rick said. He took a breath and started to speak, but Siegel interrupted him.

"Where you from?"

"Originally? A small town in Georgia, but I've

been out here since I was ten."

"I thought I heard some accent. I'm from New York, you know."

"Are you?"

"I'm a Jew. Did you know that?"

Rick shrugged. "Half the people I know are Jews."

"Some of your best friends?" Siegel smiled a little smile.

Rick took him seriously. "Not really."

"You got any problems with Jews?"

"Not in the least."

"Then you got no problem with me?"

"Not personally."

"With my business?"

"I don't know what your business is, except you seem to be in business with Jack Dragna, and I guess I pretty much know what he does."

"Yeah? And how do you know that? You ever done any business with Jack?"

"I used to be a cop. You hear things — not to mention what you read in the papers, and Dragna's been in the papers from time to time."

Siegel laughed. "Yeah, I guess he has been. I was hoping you were going to tell me we could do some business together."

"I'm not in business, Ben. I'm just a studio cop, and part of my job is to keep the studio out of some kinds of business."

"You said something like that before."

"Yes, I did, and nothing's changed."

"So why did you want to see me?"

"Things have taken a bad turn with your friend Stampano."

"Oh, shit, not that again."

"I'm afraid so."

"What's Chick done now?"

"He got one of Centurion's actresses pregnant, and he may have tried to kill another one."

"Oh, come on. Girls in this town get pregnant all the time."

"Sure they do, and when they're Centurion's girls, the studio has to take care of them and clean up after them, which means I have to take care of things." He noticed that Seigel had not addressed the charge of attempted murder.

"And that's what you're doing now."

"That's right."

"What do you want *me* to do? I haven't gotten any of your girls pregnant."

"What I want, what Centurion wants and what all the studios want is for Stampano to stay away from girls who are under contract to them."

"You mean you expect Chick Stampano, who thinks of himself as God's gift to women, to stay away from half the girls in LA? Come on, Rick. I can't put a lock on the guy's cock."

"You can if you want to."

"How'm I gonna do that?"

"Maybe he would be happier back in New York. Surely there's work for him to do there."

"That's not my call."

"Maybe you could speak to your friends in New York about it."

"I can mention it, sure, but that doesn't mean they're going to do anything about it."

"Ben, maybe you can explain to them that Stampano's romantic adventures are making things tough for everybody. The guy's a loose cannon."

"You know, I never really knew what that meant — a loose cannon."

"It goes back to the days of sailing warships. If a cannon wasn't tied down, what with the ship rolling in the seas, it might roll around the decks, killing people and otherwise doing great damage. You get the picture?"

"Yeah, yeah, I get it."

"You never know the kind of damage a loose cannon can do until it's too late. So you have to tie it down or, maybe, kick it overboard before it gets people hurt."

"Is that some kind of threat?"

"No, Ben. I think you know it's not. The studios have a legitimate beef against Stampano, and your people are in charge of him."

"So you want us to tie him down or kick him overboard?"

"They want you to do whatever it takes to end the problem."

"And what are they going to do for us?"

"You deal with Stampano, and everybody benefits."

"And how do we benefit?"

"He's aboard your ship. You deal with him, and he doesn't bump into your people and your businesses." Rick had an idea. "You know, Ben, I don't know Stampano well, but I know the type."

"What type is that?"

"I've seen tough guys like Stampano brought into a police station and charged with something, and first thing you know, they're singing like a bird to keep themselves out of jail."

Siegel shrugged. "Our people don't do that," he said, as if stating a simple fact.

"One of these days, one of them will, and Stampano strikes me as the type." It wouldn't hurt to plant a few seeds of doubt in Siegel's mind.

"If you're running a legitimate business like I am, you don't have to worry about that stuff."

"Come on, Ben, how long do you think Stampano would last with a legitimate business? He goes around beating up girls, getting them pregnant, then taking a powder. Any legit business would fire him out of hand. What does it say about your business that you keep somebody like that on the payroll?"

Siegel looked into his glass and rattled the ice. "Chick works for a liquor distributor that I have an interest in, that's all."

Rick tried another tack. "I think I get it," he said.

"Get what?"

"He's somebody's cousin or nephew, right?

Somebody important enough not to insult by dealing with him."

"Chick has friends."

"People like Chick don't have friends, they just have relatives."

Siegel finished off his drink and set down his glass. "Okay, I'll talk to New York, but I'm not making any promises."

Rick finished his drink, too. "Do what you can, Ben. It'll make life easier for everybody."

They shook hands and Rick let himself out of the club. He saw a pay phone across the street and headed for it.

33

Rick called the LAPD and asked to speak to Ben Morrison, his acquaintance who handled organized crime.

"Detective Morrison."

"Ben, it's Rick Barron."

"Hi, Rick. What's up?"

"I'd like to buy you a drink."

"Why?"

"Some business to discuss. Could be profitable."

"When?"

"How about right now? It's after work."

"Jimmy's in half an hour?"

"Good. See you then." Rick hung up and called Clete Barrow. "Evening. How about some dinner?"

"I'm not drinking, so I don't need my hand held."

"Shucks, I just wanted to have dinner with a movie star, and you're the only one available."

"Well, since you put it that way. Brown Derby?"

"How'd you like to experience a little local color?"

"Why not?"

"Remember the gun shop Al's, on Melrose?"

"Sure."

"Right across the street, place called Jimmy's. It's a cop bar, and they have simple but decent food."

"When?"

"An hour?"

"See you there."

Rick hung up and went back to his car. He sat there for a few minutes, thinking, then he started the car and drove to Jimmy's.

The place was noisy, filled with police officers — some of them off-duty — and cigarette smoke. He spoke with half a dozen cops he knew at the bar, fending off jibes about his new line of work and buying some drinks, then he found an empty booth at the back where he could still see the door. A waiter made a half-hearted pass at the booth, but Rick put him off. "When my friend gets here," he said, "and I'm paying." As if Ben Morrison would reach for a check.

Ben showed up ten minutes later, worked his way down the bar, and finally settled into the booth with Rick. A waiter appeared.

"A double Johnnie Walker Black, neat," Ben said. He pointed at Rick. "Hollywood Joe here is buying."

"Old Crow, ice, no water," Rick said.

Ben tossed his hat onto the seat beside him and slicked back his hair. He was fortyish, thicker around the middle than he used to be and with a little less hair to slick back. "So, what? You're gonna make me rich and famous?"

"Just a little more comfortable," Rick said. "You might be able to figure a way to get a promotion out of it."

"Yeah, sure," Ben snorted. "I made sergeant eight years ago, and that's it for me, pal. I got eight more years till pension, and I'm going to sit it out keeping tabs on the organizational activities of spics, niggers and goombahs."

"I knew there was crime to be found among our Spanish and darker friends, but I didn't know it was organized."

"Oh, there's a thriving marijuana trade among the wetbacks, and the darkies have learned to steal cars. We got an actual ring going out there."

"How's it going with our Italian community?"

"Jack Dragna has learned from experience. He's trying to make it look legit where he can, which makes it harder for me, but he's not fooling anybody. Bugsy Siegel is shoving him aside, anyway, and he apparently has Luciano's backing."

The drinks arrived and they raised their glasses.

"How many guys working for you, Ben?"

"I've got two detectives, and I can borrow bodies as needed."

"That's not much."

"You're telling me! The department is going to go on ignoring organized crime, and one day that attitude is going to rise up and bite them on the ass."

"Last time I talked to you, you were interested in one of Jack's minions, Chick Stampano."

"I'm still interested. How about you?"

"More than ever," Rick said.

"Why?"

"He's causing serious problems for the studios."

"That's gotta mean women. I heard about the thing with the girl over at Metro."

"It's that sort of thing, but it's multiplying and spreading. Have you got anything on this guy?"

"Nothing I could nail him for. I mean, he's got a no-show job at Siegel's and Dragna's wholesale liquor business, but that's not a crime."

"Is he important to you as a means of getting at Jack or Ben Siegel?"

"He could know a lot. I hear he's got a connection to somebody big in New York who's watching over him. He got sent out here because he was doing the same stuff there that he's doing here. He's got a weakness for women, and he likes them bruised."

"Aye, there's the rub."

"Don't start talking like Long John Silver. I'll

think you've gone queer on me."

"Fuck you, it's Shakespeare. I think."

Ben laughed. "So what do you want to do about Chickey baby?"

Rick shrugged. "I tend to think it would be a public service if somebody found him a cell at Quentin."

"Who could argue with that?" Ben took a slug of his scotch. "What did you have in mind?"

"I don't know, maybe he could somehow become attached to some unsolved case that's still open?"

"Or we could just wait awhile and he'll kill some girl."

"I think he's already tried," Rick said.

Ben looked interested. "Anybody I know?"

"A contract player."

"Details?"

"I think he shot her up with morphine, then slashed her wrists for her. She'd have bled to death on her bathroom floor if her roommate hadn't called it in."

"You keep saying, 'I think.'"

"If I could prove it, I wouldn't be offering you a bonus for doing your job."

"How much of a bonus?"

"A grand, plus expenses."

"My price for railroading innocent goombahs is five grand."

"Two and a half, Ben. Don't push it."

"You got any ideas on how to accomplish this?"

"Well, if I were doing it myself, I'd round up four or five of the LAPD's biggest and best, give 'em a hundred apiece to beat the guy to within an inch of his life, then charge him with aggravated assault on a police officer. That ought to get him a dime upstate, don't you think?"

Ben shook his head. "Nah, Jack Dragna's got enough of our upper ranks on his payroll to get that tossed."

"I was hoping you might come up with something more subtle, something that would stick — something so disgusting that even the LAPD and the DA's office couldn't look the other way."

"What, plant a Boy Scout in his bedroom?"

"More like a troop of Boy Scouts, all oiled up and ready."

"Something that would humiliate him before his peers?"

"Something so bad that Siegel and Dragna couldn't kick back. He's been talked to once about this, and I talked to Ben Siegel a second time this afternoon."

"So, something bad happens to Chickey, they look at you."

"Probably, unless you're ingenious enough to do this so well that they'll never suspect me."

"Ingenuity comes high."

"All right, three grand, and when you have a plan, talk to me about it and I'll give you a down payment and expense money."

"Let me sleep on it," the cop said.

"Something else, Ben: You know anything about the deaths of John Kean and his wife? He had my job before I did."

Ben shrugged. "Sure, I heard about it. I know the sergeant who ran the investigation."

"What was his off-the-record opinion? Could it have been a double murder?"

Ben shook his head. "From what I heard, it was a straight older-man, younger-wife murder/suicide. This guy reckoned Mrs. Kean was doing the horizontal jitterbug with some young stud; Kean confronted her, she spat it in his face and he reacted badly. When he realized what he'd done, he put a bullet in his own head rather than face the consequences."

"That's an old story."

"It is."

"Did he have any ideas on who the young stud was?" Rick had an idea.

"He didn't turn up anybody."

"I think it was Stampano," Rick said.

"You got Stampano on the brain," Ben replied. "You got anything to back that up?"

"Not that I'm ready to talk about."

They both became aware that the whole of Jimmy's had suddenly gone silent. They looked toward the door, where Clete Barrow was standing, resplendent in a double-breasted blue blazer with brass buttons, vanilla ice cream–colored trousers and brown and white wingtips.

"Jesus, a movie star," Ben said. "Whatshisface."

"He's with me," Rick said. "Beat it."

Ben tossed off the remainder of his scotch. "You're amazing, boy. I'll get back to you."

"Bye-bye." Rick waved to get Clete's attention, and the actor made his way to the booth.

"I haven't made an entrance like that since my last time treading the boards in the West End," he said.

34

The drinks were set on the table. Clete seemed deep in thought, which was unlike him.

"Something on your mind?" Rick asked.

Clete lifted his head, took a swig of his drink and looked at Rick. "You haven't heard the news, have you?"

"What news?"

"I heard it on the car radio, on the way over. The Germans and the Russians have signed a non-aggression treaty."

"That doesn't make any sense," Rick said. "Hitler hates the Communists, and they hate him, especially after the German bombings in the Spanish Civil War."

"It makes all the sense in the world, from their point of view," Clete said. "To Stalin, it means that he's got Hitler off his back, at least long enough for him to build up his forces. To Hitler, it means that he's free to do whatever he wants in Europe without Soviet interference — that England and France can't count on the Soviet Union in the event of war with Germany."

There was a roar of laughter from the bar.

"Listen to them," Clete said, nodding at the group. "They don't know what's happening to them, do they?"

"Neither do I," Rick said. "What's happening to them?"

"We're all going to be at war soon," Clete said. "Half the men under thirty in this room are going to die in it."

Rick took a gulp of his drink. "That's sort of a pessimistic point of view, isn't it?" He was, after all, under thirty.

"Nobody in this country seems even to remember the last war. England lost a million men — the cream of a generation."

"This country is not going to war," Rick said. "Even Roosevelt says that."

"Well, my country is, and soon. I don't see how it can be stopped, not with Chamberlain giving Hitler whatever he wants. God, if Churchill were only in charge."

Rick was at a loss. "Do you think England can win a war against Germany?"

"I think we can. We've only got ten divisions, but the French have ninety. Together, that makes us equal to the Germans' hundred divisions. They're way ahead in aircraft and artillery and training, though. Have you read Churchill's speeches?"

"No."

"I get the *Times* by post. Churchill's been warning the government for years to increase aircraft production, but they've ignored him, for the most part." Clete waved at the bartender for another drink. "The Russians have a huge army, but now they're out of play."

"What's going to happen next?"

"I'm going to get roaring drunk, that's what's going to happen next."

Rick sighed. "Well, one of us better stay sober." He handed Clete a menu. "I recommend the meat loaf," he said.

Clete looked astonished. "What the fuck is meat loaf?"

Rick dumped the unconscious movie star on his bed, pulled off his shoes and got his jacket off. He threw a blanket over him, walked back into Clete's living room and called Eddie Harris.

"Hello?" Eddie didn't sound sleepy.

"It's Rick. I hope I didn't wake you."

"Nah, I'm reading a script."

"What time is Clete due on the set tomorrow?"

"Why, is he drunk?"

"Drunker than I've ever seen him; unconscious drunk."

"The German-Soviet thing?"

"Yeah."

"Clete takes the European news too seriously. This has been going on for a year or more."

"He may have a point. He's very convincing on the subject."

"I'll juggle some scenes and buy him until noon."

"That would be a big help."

"If you can't wake him by ten, call Judson and get him over there. He can give him something to keep him on his feet."

"Right. Oh, I had a chat with my detective friend at the LAPD this evening."

"About our Guinea friend?"

"Yeah."

"He have any suggestions?"

"He's thinking about it. This is going to cost you four or five grand before it's done."

"I'll spring for that," Eddie said. "It's cheaper than hiring Al."

"Safer, too. The idea is to hang something on him, get him sent upstate."

"I like that idea."

"When is Clete's film going to wrap?"

"Next week, if you can keep him working."

"I'll see what I can do," Rick said.

"You sound tired, yourself. Get some sleep."

"Okay, I'll bunk in here tonight, and I'll call Judson in the morning if I can't get Clete moving."

"Take it easy." Eddie hung up.

Rick headed for the guest room.

Rick woke a little before eight. He showered and got dressed, then looked in on Clete. To his astonishment, the actor was dressed, showered and shaved. To his further astonishment, Clete was dressed in a British military uniform, looking at himself in a mirror.

"What the hell are you doing?" Rick asked.

"Just wanted to see if it still fits. It does." Clete tossed his cap on the bed and started unbuttoning his tunic. "I think I'll get wardrobe to run me up a couple more," he said.

"You're not due in until noon," Rick said, wanting to change the subject. "You want some breakfast?"

"If you're having some."

Rick went into the kitchen and found the Filipino houseman, Manuel, who went to work on the food.

They breakfasted on the terrace.

"Aren't you hungover?" Rick asked.

"Not really," Clete replied.

"I don't know how you do it."

"Did you get the schedule pushed back?"

"Yes, until noon. I called Eddie last night."

"There was no need, but it's nice to have a morning off." He looked out over the city. "It's so beautiful here. I won't see many more mornings like this."

"There is an unlimited supply of mornings like this," Rick said. "Don't worry about it."

"A month," Clete said.

"What?"

"I give it a month, six weeks at most. We'll be at war by then."

"Come on, Clete, there's a lot that can be done in a month. I'm sure the diplomats are working on this full-time."

"We wrap the film next week. We're still on for that fishing trip, aren't we?"

"Sure we are. I've got the Lockheed booked. What's the nearest airport to the camp?"

"No airport. There's a pasture along the river; you can set down there. I can show you on a Sinclair road map."

"I hope we have good weather."

"It's going to be wonderful," Clete said. "I can feel it."

"I'll get the charts and a road map and have a look. We're going to need someplace to refuel for the trip back."

"You do that, chappie. I want this trip to go well. I want to remember it." Clete took a notebook from his pocket and began making a list. He tore off the page and handed it to Rick. "Here's a list of gear you're going to need for the trip," he said. "I don't have enough to loan you these things, but don't buy any actual fishing equipment. I have plenty of that, and anything I'm short of, the other two fellows will have."

"Where do I get all this?" Rick asked, looking at the list.

"Abercrombie & Fitch," Clete replied. "They have a branch on Wilshire."

"I'll be ready," Rick said.

"By the way, Artie Shaw and his band are opening at Ciro's tonight. Want to go?"

"Sure, I love Shaw's stuff."

Then Clete seemed to withdraw into himself.

35

Rick went back to his own house to change. Clete would get himself to work, and he had little to do in his office, so he went down to Abercrombie & Fitch and spent nearly two hundred dollars on waders and clothing and a duffel to put it all in.

Rick was beginning to see a conflict ahead for himself. Clete still had another four years on his contract with Centurion, but he knew that if England went to war, Clete would bolt for home. He wasn't sure if Eddie Harris knew, or if he should tell him. His loyalty was supposed to be to his employer, but he and Clete had become good friends, and he didn't know what to do.

On the way back to the studio, he stopped for a fill-up at a Sinclair station and picked up their road maps for California and Oregon, then he drove out to Clover Field to see his father.

"Morning," the old man said as Rick walked into the hangar. "You still going to use the Lockheed next week?"

"Yes, that's why I'm here. You got the current chart for Oregon?"

"In the office. You know where."

Rick went into the office and dug out the charts. He found the Rogue River in Oregon, but he didn't yet know where on the river he'd be landing. There was an airport at Grants Pass, though, and another at the mouth of the Rogue River, where he could refuel. It all looked straightforward.

He went back into the hangar. "Got what I needed," he said.

"Good."

"You heard anything more from those Italian gentlemen?"

"Not a peep. Haven't seen any strangers around, either. Been pretty quiet."

"That's good news. Well, I'd better get back to work."

"What kind of work they got you doing these days?"

"No two days are the same," he replied. He didn't want to tell his father how he was occupying his time. "See you later."

"Bye."

That evening, Rick and Clete arrived at Ciro's in their dinner jackets to a wave of popping flashbulbs outside. There was a line of people making its way slowly into the nightclub. Photographers were yelling at Clete to look this way and that, and Clete obliged, laying on the smiles and charm. He was good at it, too, Rick thought.

Soon they were inside and being shown to a ringside table. No sooner had they sat down than Hedda Hopper sat down with them.

"No girls this evening, Clete?" she said, after a perfunctory handshake with Rick.

"Not tonight, my dear. I've got an early call tomorrow, so Rick and I are just going to catch the first show, then head to our respective homes."

Rick wondered why it was necessary to say that. Was Clete worried that Hedda might think them queer for each other?

Hedda asked a few more questions, then turned to Rick. "I'm seeing you everywhere around town," she said. "You must be enjoying the new job."

"I just go where the work takes me, Miss Hopper," he said.

"Please," she said, putting a hand on his arm, "you must call me Hedda. All my friends do, and a great many people who aren't my friends."

"Hedda it is," Rick said, giving her a smile.

"You're good-looking enough to be a leading man," she said. "Have you ever considered acting?"

"Not for a moment," Rick laughed. "I see what Clete has to put up with, and I don't think I could handle it."

"You seem to be keeping him out of trouble."

226

"Oh, I'm just along for the ride."

"Well, I have my rounds to make," Hedda said. "Nighty-night." She got up, allowed Clete a peck on her cheek and moved on.

A trio had been playing, but now they stopped, and members of the Artie Shaw band began filtering onstage, making tuning noises with their instruments.

Rick had expected an announcement, but suddenly the entire club went completely dark for a few seconds, then a spotlight came on, finding the drummer. The great Buddy Rich launched into a head-pounding drum solo that introduced "Traffic Jam," then another spot came on and found Artie Shaw himself, who had come onto the bandstand in the darkness. He slid up to that high note, and the band was off and running on the up-tempo arrangement, with Shaw leading the charge.

They finished to a roar of cheers and applause that sounded like something from a football stadium, and when it finally died, a disembodied voice said, "Ladies and gentlemen, Artie Shaw and his orchestra, featuring Buddy Rich on drums!"

The band swung into "Begin the Beguine," and people began to dance. A waiter brought drinks and took Clete's and Rick's dinner order. The set continued on through "Frenesi," "Japanese Sandman" and "Yesterdays."

Rick looked around the room and saw Chick Stampano seated on the other side of the dance floor. They were in exactly the same seats as the last time they had been at Ciro's.

Clete followed Rick's stare. "Oh, I see our old friend Mr. Greaseball is back. Is he behaving himself these days?"

"No," Rick said, "he's not. I had a little meeting with Ben Siegel about him yesterday."

"Don't stare at the man," Clete said, "or we'll just have another confrontation."

"You're right," Rick replied. "I'll just forget he's there." He turned back toward the band and began to enjoy the music again.

Shaw played a novelty version of "Donkey Serenade," then segued into "Dancing in the Dark," while the dancers swayed with the music.

"Good," Clete replied.

Artie Shaw had stepped up to the microphone again and held his hands up for quiet. "Ladies and gentlemen," he said, "one of Hollywood's most beautiful and promising actresses is with us this evening as our special guest singer. She's starting a new musical at Centurion Studios next week, and we're very lucky to have her. Here's Miss Glenna Gleason to sing 'Stardust'!"

The band swung into the introduction, and a lovely girl in a sequined dress came across the stage to the microphone and began to sing.

Rick was frozen in his chair. It was not the first time he'd seen Glenna Gleason, though her eyes had been covered at the hospital, but he was not prepared for the shock. The last time he'd seen that face had been in a bedroom photograph with the late Mr. and Mrs. John Kean — and, of course, with Chick Stampano.

36

Rick now realized why Eddie Harris was so high on Glenna Gleason: The girl was simply gorgeous. She couldn't be more than twenty-two, he thought, but there was a calm maturity about her. Luxuriant auburn hair fell to her shoulders, and her tall, slim body and full breasts were something to behold in the low-cut, sequined dress. The girl had a beautiful voice, and she sang with a simplicity and sweetness that was overwhelming.

Rick looked around the ringside tables and saw that everyone else was having the same reaction, men and women alike. This girl had something very rare. Clete Barrow sat and stared, like Rick, transfixed.

She finished the song, then sang another Hoagy Carmichael tune, "Skylark," then finished with "I Get Along Without You Very Well," accompanied only by the pianist. When she was done, the crowd was on its feet.

"Don't worry," Shaw shouted over the din, "she'll be back for the second show."

As the girl began to leave the stage, Clete rose and strode across the dance floor. He took her hand and whispered something to her, then led her back to the table.

Rick was on his feet, holding her chair.

"Miss Gleason," Clete said, "may I present my friend Rick Barron?"

A flash of recognition passed across her face. She held onto his hand and bent close to whisper, "I owe you a great deal. Thank you so much."

"I was very happy to do what I could," Rick managed to reply, though he seemed to have some difficulty speaking.

Clete ordered champagne, and they all raised their glasses. "To the beginning of a big career," he said.

Then Rick looked up and saw Chick Stampano striding toward their table, apparently to congratulate her. Rick stood and walked around the table, placing himself squarely between Stampano and the girl.

There was a moment when Rick thought Stampano would keep coming, but instead he stopped, looked hard at Rick for a moment, then changed direction and went to another table, where he spoke with some people. Rick waited for him to finish talking with them and return to his table before he sat down again.

"Thank you again," Glenna said.

"Not at all," he said. "If he should ever try to contact you again, please let me know immediately."

She smiled her gratitude.

The three of them sat, talking and drinking champagne through the rest of the show, then through the intermission. The second show began, and after a few numbers Artie Shaw called Glenna to the stage again, and she gave another affecting performance, earning another standing ovation from the audience.

When she had finished, Glenna came back to the table for a moment. She put her hand on Rick's wrist and looked at his watch. "I really must go," she said. "I have a dance rehearsal first thing in the morning."

"Let us take you home, then," Clete said.

"Thank you, that's very kind."

They worked their way through the crowd, with Glenna accepting congratulations from many people, among them Eddie and Suzanne Harris.

Eddie whispered in Rick's ear, "I saw that. Thanks for watching out for her."

"It was my pleasure," Rick replied. He left Clete and Glenna talking with the Harrises and went to get the car. When they came out of Ciro's, he had the motor running.

The three of them sat in the front seat on the short drive to the Garden of Allah, and Rick was conscious of Glenna's scent and of her thigh pressed against his in the close quarters. He waited in the car while Clete walked her to the door.

"My God!" Clete said when he was back in

the car. "Isn't she something?"

"She certainly is," Rick replied. "I can tell I'm going to have to fight you for her." He put the car in gear and pulled away from the curb.

"You're that attracted to her?" Clete asked.

Rick was about to answer when he glanced in the rearview mirror and saw a car he recognized pulling into the place where he had parked. It took him a minute to make the U-turn in traffic, and by that time Stampano was out of the car, striding quickly toward Glenna's cottage.

Clete spotted him, too. "And he's got two gorillas with him," he said, nodding in the direction of the car, where the hulking figures sat.

Rick reached into the glove compartment, retrieved his little .45 and handed it to Clete. "Stop them, but try not to shoot anybody. There's one in the chamber." He hopped out of the car and went after Stampano, who had disappeared around the corner of the cottage. He looked back to see Clete standing between the cottage and the two men, who were getting out of their car.

Rick turned the corner of the cottage and ran straight into a sucker punch that staggered him but didn't take him off his feet. He saw the second one coming and blocked it, getting in a couple of quick jabs before Stampano could step back.

Stampano reached into a hip pocket and came out with a blackjack. Rick knew that if he took the thing in the head, he'd be unconscious and helpless. As Stampano started his swing, Rick, instead of stepping back or ducking, stepped into Stampano's body, blocking the blackjack and getting in a hard right under the man's heart that made his knees buckle.

Rick got ahold of the blackjack and twisted it from Stampano's hand, then tossed it into some bushes. "Now," he said, "it's just you and me."

Stampano circled him warily, looking around for the blackjack. "Hey, boys!" he shouted. "Get over here!"

"They're busy," Rick said, then staggered him with a left hook. As Stampano was regaining his balance, Rick aimed a right at his nose and felt the crunch as it sailed home. Stampano sat down on the flagstone path, blood gushing all over his white dinner jacket.

Rick grabbed him by the collar and hoisted him to his feet, then grabbed the seat of his pants with his other hand and marched him down the pathway on his toes. When he came around the corner, Clete had the two goons at bay, the .45 in his hand. "Get the back door," Rick yelled.

Clete stepped to the car and opened the back door in time for Stampano to sail past it into the rear of the car. "Get him out of here," he said to the two men. They got into the car and drove Stampano away.

"Well," Clete said, inspecting a bruise on Rick's chin, "I'm glad to see he was the one bleeding. Did you enjoy that?"

"More than I should have," Rick replied. "I don't think we'll see him out in public for a few days. He's going to have a pair of beautiful shiners, and he'll have to have his nose set."

Rick looked up to see Glenna standing at the corner of the house. He ran up to her, took her arm and steered her back toward her front door. "Nothing to worry about," he said.

"I saw some of it from my door," Glenna said. "And I have to say, I enjoyed it."

Rick laughed.

"Once again, I'm in your debt," she said, when they came to her door. She kissed him on the corner of the mouth, then went inside and closed the door.

Rick felt weak in the knees, but he made it back to his car.

Clete laughed. "You look sort of stunned."

"She kissed me," Rick replied.

"Now you're in for it," Clete sighed.

Rick got into bed but had trouble falling asleep. A montage of Glenna Gleason ran through his head, not excluding the photograph of her with the Keans and Stampano. He found himself wanting to do to her what Stampano was doing in the photo, but more tenderly. Or maybe not.

37

Rick woke in the following morning and, in the bathroom mirror, inspected his bruised and swollen face where Stampano had sucker punched him. After he had dressed and shaved, he put an ice pack on it for a few minutes, taking comfort in the certainty that Stampano was going to see worse in his own mirror.

As Rick walked into his office, Jenny was answering the phone. "It's Eddie Harris," she said.

He went into his office, closed the door and picked up the phone. "Good morning, Eddie," he said.

"That remains to be seen," Eddie replied.

"What's up?"

"I had a call from Ben Siegel late last night, and he was furious."

"Oh?"

"He says you and Clete beat the shit out of Chick Stampano last night."

"That's only partly true, Eddie."

"Which part?"

"*I* beat the shit out of Stampano while Clete held off his two goons."

"How the hell did he do that? Is he hurt? Has he got any marks on him?"

"Not a scratch. Clete showed them my gun and kept them out of it, while I dealt with Stampano."

"What did you do to him?"

"Well, I'm pretty sure I broke his nose, and he's going to need a new white dinner jacket."

Eddie emitted a long chuckle.

"And did I mention that this happened outside Glenna Gleason's house?"

"*What?*"

"Clete and I drove her home after her second show, and as we were leaving, Stampano and his two goons showed up. I followed him around the corner of the house, and he was laying for me, sucker punched me, then he pulled a blackjack. I took it away from him, tossed it away and hit him a few times, then I threw him in his car and we left."

"Well, at least no gunfire was exchanged."

"I was pleased about that, too."

"And Clete had a gun in his hand?"

"Eddie, the guy's a Royal Marine, for Christ's sake. He knows how to handle a weapon."

"Oh, yeah."

"What exactly did Siegel say?"

"He was ranting about how you had lured Stampano into a fight. He said *you* had the blackjack."

"Nuts! Did he mention that I had warned him

a second time to keep Stampano away from our people?"

"No, but I did, and that seemed to stymie him a little. What I'm worried about is, he hinted that you could expect Stampano to get even."

"I hadn't thought about that, but it doesn't surprise me. He may just be blowing hot air."

"Maybe, but maybe not, so here's what I want you to do: Wherever you go, until further notice, I want two studio cops with you — one in your car and one in another car, and I want them armed."

"That's a little overcautious, isn't it, Eddie? I can handle Stampano."

"Yeah, but how many of his goons can you handle all at once? And another thing, I don't want you and Clete out on the town together for a while. If you want to have dinner, go out to Santa Monica or Pacific Palisades, and stay out of Ciro's and, above all, the Trocadero. The Brown Derby and Chasen's, too."

"All right, Eddie," Rick sighed. Then he had a thought. "Eddie, it occurs to me that Stampano might try to retaliate against my old man."

"Then put a couple of studio cops on his place of business, too, and around the clock. I'm not going to have him hurt because of studio problems."

"That's going to stretch our people pretty thin," Rick said. "How about if I hire a few off-duty cops to help out?"

"Good idea. It wouldn't hurt to have a real cop around if something happens."

"I'll make a call."

"Good. And thanks again for taking such good care of Glenna."

"I enjoyed that part."

"See you later."

Rick called the Beverly Hills department, asked for Tom Terry and was told that it was his day off. He dug out his address book and called Terry's home.

The phone rang half a dozen times before a gruff voice answered. "Yeah?"

"Wake up, Tom, it's Rick Barron."

"Hey, Rick," Tom replied, a little more brightly.

"You want to go Hollywood a little?"

"You going to fix me up with Lana Turner?"

"Nah, I'm going to fix you up with me."

"You're not my type."

"I need three or four off-duty cops for some bodyguard work."

"Who's the body?"

"Me and my old man. He's got a flying business out at Clover Field."

"Somebody dogging you?"

"You know Chick Stampano?"

"I've heard the name, saw him once at the track with some starlet."

"You get on the phone, round up three other guys who aren't working today and get them over to Centurion. I'll leave a pass at the gate in your name."

"Okay. Gimme a couple of hours?"

"Sure; say, noon?"

"That's good. What can I promise them?"

"Long hours and good pay, but no movie stars."

Tom laughed. "They'll do it twenty-four a day and for nothing if you can promise them movie stars."

"See you at noon, Tom." He hung up and called his father.

"Hello?"

"Morning, Dad. You okay?"

"Shouldn't I be?"

"I've had another run-in with the Italian people. I'm going to send a couple of guys over to your place around midday, and there'll be somebody there twenty-four hours a day until things calm down."

"What do I have to pay 'em?"

"Not a dime. It's all on Centurion Studios."

"Then it's jake with me."

"Talk to you later."

Rick hung up and looked at his watch. He had a couple of free hours. He buzzed Jenny. "Call the production office and find out where the new musical is rehearsing."

38

Rick drove over to the soundstage where rehearsals for the musical were going on. He'd
seen the big battleship set under construction,
but now it was about finished, and there were at
least fifty dancers, boys and girls in rehearsal
clothes, lining up along its tiers for their
number. Rick spotted Glenna and her partner at
center stage, she dressed in a tight bodysuit and
black net stockings that accentuated the length
of her legs. A colorful silk scarf was tied around
her waist.

"All right!" an assistant director yelled
through a megaphone, "Places, everyone!"

Rick found a spot where he could stand behind the camera without interfering.

"We'll go on the first beat of the playback,"
the director said.

"On the first beat of playback!" the assistant
yelled. "Playback!"

There were four loud, rhythmic clicks from
speakers, and the music started. The dancers
began their routine, making a racket with their

taps over the music and mouthing the lyrics to the prerecorded soundtrack.

"Cut!" the director yelled.

"Stop playback!" the assistant shouted.

The director stood up with his megaphone. "You're all half a beat behind the playback!" he yelled. "Pick it up. I want it right on the money! And let me see those smiles!"

"Places!" the assistant shouted, and the dancers resumed their first postures.

"Playback," the director said.

"Playback!" the assistant shouted.

The four loud clicks came again, and the dancers began on the first beat of the music. This time it seemed crisper, and the dancers more enthusiastic.

When the number was done, the director stood up and clapped his hands together. "Great! Now we're going to break for two hours while the painters finish and you kids get into costume and makeup, then we're going to shoot it. Back here at one!"

The cast broke up and went to their dressing rooms, and Rick made a point of being at the set stairs when Glenna came down them.

She spotted him and waved. "Good morning, Rick," she said, dabbing at her face with a towel. "Did you see our rehearsal?"

"I did, and I thought it looked wonderful, especially you."

"We had such a good rehearsal, we're going to shoot today, instead of tomorrow. That'll put us half a day ahead of schedule."

"Eddie Harris will like that," Rick said.

"Thanks again for taking me home last night," she said. "And for dealing with Stampano. I'm sorry about your face."

"It's nothing to worry about. Stampano looks worse. But he may try to retaliate, and I think you should move out of your bungalow for a little while. Is there someplace else you can stay? With a friend, maybe?"

"I can move into my dressing room," she said. "They've given me half a bungalow for this film, and there's a bed."

"That sounds good. You'll have plenty of security on the lot."

"It'll save me the commute, too. I've got very early calls every day this week."

"What time will you be done today?"

"It depends on how it goes this afternoon, I guess, but probably it will be at least six o'clock before we're let go. Maybe later."

"I'll go home with you to get your things and see that you get back here all right."

"Thank you. That's very sweet."

"I'll be back late this afternoon, then."

"See you later." She ran for her dressing room.

Rick went to see Cal Herman, his assistant director of security, and told him what he would need, then he went back to his office, where he found Tom Terry and three young officers, in plainclothes, waiting for him. He shook hands all around and told them to sit down.

"Here's what's happened," he said. "I had a little set-to with a guy named Chick Stampano last night, not for the first time. He's been roughing up girls from both here and Metro, and we've had it with him."

"Doesn't he work for Jack Dragna?" Tom asked.

"Yeah, but we're not going to let that bother us. We've heard that he might try to retaliate, and Eddie Harris, our general manager, has instructed me to take some precautions. Our studio cops are going to handle the gates and watch over one of our actresses. Tom, you're going to ride with me, and one of our studio cops will follow in another car. Then, I want two men, twenty-four hours a day, at my father's place of business at Clover Field, in Santa Monica."

"I'm going to need some more guys, then," Tom said.

"Right. Get as many as you need. My father's place is a big hangar, and I want one man inside and one outside, patrolling the perimeter. There are some expensive airplanes in the hangar, and I'm partial to my old man, too, so take care of them all."

"Do we follow him home at night?"

"If I know him, he'll sleep in his office. So who's going to Santa Monica?"

Tom Terry pointed at two men.

"Fine. You fellows armed?"

"We all are," Tom said.

Rick gave them directions to his dad's place. "Introduce yourselves," he said. "Dad knows you're coming. It would be better if you don't shoot anybody, but I expect you to protect yourselves and what you're guarding, whatever it takes."

The two young men left.

"I'm going to need one more man to follow Clete Barrow around," Rick said. "Put your other man, here, on him. My secretary will tell you how to get to his bungalow."

Tom motioned for his man to get going.

"Tom, use my phone and scare up some more guys for the other shifts, then I want you to ride with me back to my place. I'm going to pick up some clothes, then bunk in here for a few days."

"I'm with you," Tom said, then he picked up the phone and went to work.

By late afternoon, Rick had all his bases covered, and he had explained to Clete what was going on.

"I'm going to have a bodyguard?" Clete asked. "I don't need one."

"I wouldn't want anybody to mess up that pretty face," Rick said, "at least not until you've wrapped on your picture. Don't worry, he won't cramp your style."

"Your friend Al has finished building my new

245

gun," Clete said. "I think I'll pick it up on the way home."

"Couldn't hurt," Rick said. "Stay safe."

He drove back to his cottage on Eddie Harris's estate, with Tom Terry in the passenger seat and a studio cop following. He packed a bag and went back to the studio.

"Going somewhere?" Jenny asked, seeing the suitcase.

"No, I'm moving in here for a few days."

"What's up?"

He gave her an abbreviated account of what had happened.

"Your sofa turns into a bed, you know."

"I didn't know, but I'm glad to hear it."

"I'll get housekeeping to send over some fresh sheets and towels."

"Housekeeping?"

"They take care of all the bungalows and dressing rooms."

"Great." He got back into his car and drove over to Glenna Gleason's bungalow. She shared it with another female principal in her film. A studio cop was stationed outside.

"Evening," Rick said to him. "Everything all right?"

"Yes, sir," the man said. "She just got back from work."

"We're going to drive over to the Garden of Allah and pick up some things of hers. I'll ride with her, and you follow."

"Yes, sir."

Rick knocked on the door.

"Come in," she called.

He took a deep breath and went in.

39

They drove in silence for a few minutes, then Glenna turned toward Rick and pulled her knees up on the seat. "Tell me about you," she said. "You don't seem the Hollywood type, somehow."

Rick smiled. "No?"

"I'll bet you came from somewhere else, like everybody else out here."

"Georgia," he said. "A small town. But I came out here when I was ten, so by local standards I'm practically a native. Where are you from?" He knew, but he wanted to listen to her voice.

"Milwaukee," she said. "Home of beer."

"That's right; lots of Germans."

"I'm one of them, I guess, or at least half. But we were talking about you."

He gave her the mini-biography.

"Your dad's a flyer, then?"

"That's right. So am I."

"I've never flown."

"We'll have to remedy that. You'd enjoy it, I think."

"Will you take me flying?"

He took his eyes off the road for a moment and looked into hers. "Maybe I can get Clete Barrow to join us."

"I'd rather you didn't. I mean, he's very nice, but he's a movie star and far above me."

"Not so far, and from what I've seen, when your picture is released the distance will be even less." He was relieved that she didn't want Clete along.

"I think I would have a lot of trouble thinking of myself as a movie star."

"Isn't that what you want?"

"It's what I wanted when I came out here, but now I just want to do the best work I can. The money isn't even all that important."

"Are you independently wealthy?"

"I was, for a while, but not anymore. I mean, it seemed wealthy to me, but . . ."

"You suffered reverses?"

"Well, I had to support myself while I looked for work, and then . . . yes, you could say I suffered reverses."

"You'll make it back in no time."

"Like I said, the money isn't all that important to me."

"Don't ever let Eddie Harris hear you say that. You'll find your attitude reflected in your paycheck — not that Eddie isn't a generous guy."

She laughed.

They pulled up behind her bungalow and

went in. Rick thought the place surprisingly neat for two girls sharing, but after all, the Garden of Allah had maid service.

"There are some Coca-Colas in the icebox," she said. "Make yourself comfortable. I'll only be a few minutes."

Rick found himself a Coke and had a look around the living room. There were some photographs, apparently of her family, in silver frames on a sideboard. Glenna would have been the little dark-haired girl of about twelve in one of them, looking very beautiful even then. There was also a photograph of her in a beauty pageant, with a silk sash over her shoulder reading "Miss Wisconsin," watching another girl be crowned. She was more beautiful than the winner, he thought.

He finished his Coke and stretched out on the sofa for a minute. Then a cool hand was on his cheek.

"I'm sorry I took so long," she said. "You fell asleep."

"I didn't sleep very well last night," he said, looking up at her. The hand was still on his cheek and he took it in his. "I had something on my mind."

"No bad dreams, I hope." She didn't take her hand back.

"Only good ones," he said truthfully. He wanted to tell her that his dreams were of her, but he stopped himself.

"Shall we get back to the studio, then?"

He sat up and rubbed his eyes. "Yes, let's." He was surprised at the number of bags she had, but he stuffed them wherever there was room in her little Chevy.

They drove back in a comfortable silence. "Oh, pull over to that market," she said, pointing. "I want to get some things for my kitchenette."

He followed her into the market, pushing a cart for her.

"If you don't have dinner plans, I'll fix you something at the bungalow," she said.

"That would be nice."

She chose some lamb chops and some vegetables, and he paid the bill.

"You're the guest of the studio while this lasts," he said.

"You're too kind, sir."

They drove back to the studio and to the bungalow. It was about the same size as Clete's, but had been built as a duplex, to accommodate two lesser stars. He carried in the groceries, and she put them away, then unpacked her bags.

"How long will I have to stay here?" she asked.

"I don't know; maybe a few days, maybe longer."

She nodded. "I brought everything. I'm going to check out of the Garden of Allah. The rent is just too much."

"I'll help you find a new place when everything's all right," Rick said, fighting off visions of her moving in with him.

"You're a sweet man," she said. "There's a little bar in that cabinet over there, courtesy of the studio. Why don't you fix us a drink?"

"What would you like?"

"A martini," she said. "I like a martini when I'm cooking."

Rick made the drinks and sipped a bourbon while he watched her move around the kitchen from his perch on a bar stool just outside. There was a big window with a counter and the two stools. The scene was, well, domestic, he thought.

Dinner was good. She knew what she was doing in the kitchen. He had grown up, after his mother had died, cooking badly for his father, and he was unaccustomed to people cooking for him. After dinner, he made her a second martini.

"When will you take me flying?" she asked.

"When will you have a day off?"

"Sunday."

"I'm afraid I'll be away on a fishing trip with Clete and some friends of his," Rick said, with real regret. "I'm flying them up to the Rogue River in Oregon as soon as his picture wraps."

"Oh, then I'll have to wait," she said, pouting.

He loved her pout. "How about the Sunday after? We'll fly out to Catalina for lunch."

She brightened. "You've got yourself a deal, mister."

He liked the deal. When he left, she gave him a little kiss on the lips, and her breasts brushed against him.

He knew she knew he wanted more.

40

Clete's movie finished shooting the middle of the following week, and Clete called Rick at his office.

"We're done, old sport, so we're off for the Rogue River tomorrow?"

"We are," Rick replied.

"Good. I'll let the other chaps know."

"Tell them to meet us at my dad's hangar at eight o'clock."

"I say, that's a little stiff, isn't it, what with the wrap party tonight. How about noon?"

"Make it ten o'clock. We have to get there in good daylight so I can see to land. I'm allowing time so that if we have to stop to refuel because of headwinds we can still make it."

"Oh, all right, I guess I can manage ten o'clock. You coming to our wrap party?"

"If I'm invited."

"Of course you are. Six o'clock on soundstage two."

"See you then." Rick hung up and thought of inviting Glenna, but she was shooting today, and he didn't want to call her on the set.

Rick left his office at six and stopped by Glenna's bungalow, but she wasn't back yet. He left a note on the screen door, inviting her, and drove on.

The crew had still not struck the Indian Army officers' club set on soundstage two, and the party was held there, with the cast still in costume for the final scene, which had been a ball. The women were in full-length gowns, and the men were in dress uniform. Clete sported lots of braid and medals.

"I see you had a good war," Rick said, nodding at the medals.

"Damn good," Clete replied, handing him a glass of champagne from a passing tray. "I killed hundreds of the beggars."

"Which beggars?"

"Oh, you know, whoever were the beggars at the time."

Some studio musicians, also in British Colonial uniform, began a waltz, and a pretty girl in a ball gown asked Clete to dance. They whirled away in what Rick imagined amounted to a restaging of the ball scene.

A moment later, somebody tugged at Rick's elbow, and he turned to find Ben Siegel standing there.

"We gotta talk," Siegel said, taking his arm and steering him off the set and into the shadows of the big soundstage.

When they were out of earshot of the party-goers, Rick stopped. "All right," he said, "let's talk." He was ready to take on Siegel, too, if he had to.

"I want you to know I did what I could," Siegel said. "I talked to Dragna about this, and he agreed that Chick was out of line, but he wouldn't do anything about him. I was hot about what you did to Chick the other night, but I don't think I got the straight story from him."

"He was the one with the blackjack," Rick said.

"I figured," Siegel said. "Here's the problem. It's Luciano," Siegel said. "Jack's scared stiff of him."

"Luciano's in prison, isn't he?"

"That doesn't matter a bit. He still runs things. Jack thinks Charlie Lucky is going to send somebody out here to take over and get rid of him."

"I heard he sent you out here to do that."

"Don't believe everything you hear."

"What does all that have to do with Stampano?"

"Chick is Charlie Lucky's boy," Siegel said.

"So Dragna's not going to do anything about Stampano."

"Not a thing. Jack looks at it like, even if Chick kills somebody, it's okay, as long as there are no witnesses."

"Have you seen Stampano?"

"This afternoon. His face is a mess, so he can't see his girls. He doesn't want them to know what happened to him. So he's mad as hell, and something is going to happen."

"What?"

"I don't know exactly, but if I were you, I'd get out of LA for a few days, until his face gets better and he cools off. Right now, every time he looks in a mirror, he gets crazy."

"As it happens, I'm leaving town tomorrow morning for a few days, but it's nothing to do with Stampano."

"I'll tell him he scared you out of town," Siegel said. "He'll like that. He can brag about it to his pals."

"I don't give a shit what you tell him," Rick said. "I wouldn't cross the street to get away from him. I *want* him to try something."

"Well, I'm not going to tell him that. You just take your trip, and when you come back, be careful. And if you can avoid Chick, do it, because if you hurt him again, Luciano might get into this. You understand?"

Rick took a deep breath. "Look, I've done everything I can to avoid the guy, but he keeps popping up, and you and Luciano and Dragna — all of you — are going to have to understand that my people are not going to put up with Stampano anymore. Either he behaves himself, or there will be more trouble, and it will get worse."

"I hope you're not thinking of capping him, Rick."

"What?"

"Capping . . . killing the guy."

"I'm not a murderer, Ben, but if he comes after me, I'll defend myself."

Siegel sighed. "Well, I tried," he said. "Whatever happens now is on your head."

"No, it's on Stampano's head. Maybe you can communicate that to him."

"I'm out of this from right now," Siegel said, raising his hands in a defensive gesture. "I gave you the message, now I'm gone." He turned around and walked away.

Rick went back and stood by the dance floor, watching the whirling couples. Glenna hadn't shown up.

And something bothered him about his conversation with Ben Siegel. It just didn't sit right.

41

LA was an early town, but none of the cast of Clete's film had an early call the next day, having just wrapped a film, so they stayed late. It was after midnight before the party broke up.

Rick found Clete and edged him away from the parting guests. "You want to change out of that uniform before we take you home?"

"I'm not going home tonight," Clete said, nodding at a pretty bit player. "I brought my gear to the studio this morning, so I'll sleep at the bungalow."

"Good. There'll be a studio cop following you and watching the place tonight. They'll bring you to Clover Field tomorrow morning, too. Don't be late."

"Wouldn't dream of it, old chap," Clete said, then headed for the girl.

Rick looked around for Tom Terry and his studio cop, saw them standing near the exit and walked over. "Listen, fellows, I'm going to go back to my place and pick up some fishing gear, then come back here for the night. I'm leaving town tomorrow morning on a fishing trip. Tom, you're riding with me, and I don't think we'll need to be followed by another car." He turned to the studio cop. "You follow Clete Barrow back to his bungalow and stand guard there." The man left.

They got into Rick's car, and he put up the top, thinking he might be less conspicuous that way. They left the studio and drove toward Beverly Hills, and Rick was satisfied that they weren't being followed.

They had just crossed Sunset Boulevard when suddenly there were two black cars ahead, blocking the street. Instantly, Rick yanked the emergency brake and turned the wheel hard to the left. The car's rear end, with its locked brakes, skidded around, putting him into a hundred-and-eighty-degree turn. Halfway through the turn, Rick heard multiple gunshots.

"Jesus, get us out of here!" Tom yelled, drawing his gun and rolling down his window. He got on his knees facing to the rear and transferred his gun to his left hand.

Rick gave the V-8 all it had, and he winced as Tom fired two rounds at whatever was behind them.

Tom turned and sat down again. "You think they'll follow?"

"I guess we're going to find out," Rick said, turning hard onto Sunset and heading north.

"I'm sure I put one through a windshield," Tom said. "I don't know if I hit anybody."

Rick drove down a block and turned right, putting him on residential streets again. Ahead was a house with huge rhododendrons out front, and he whipped into the driveway and got out, drawing his gun from the shoulder holster. He and Tom stood behind the car, waiting. They saw nothing, and all they heard was the sound of engines roaring down Sunset.

"I guess they didn't like being fired at," Rick said. "I think we can go to my place now." They got back into the car, and Rick drove home without further incident.

As Rick and Tom got out of the car, Tom said, "Hey, look at this." He was pointing to a bullet hole in the passenger door.

Rick checked his own door and found another hole. "Jesus," he said, "it went through your door, then through mine; passed right over our laps."

"That's close enough for me," Tom said.

Rick went into the house and phoned Ben Morrison, waking him up.

"What's happened?" Ben asked.

"An attempt on my life," Rick said.

"Anybody hurt?"

"Not on my team, but my car has bullet holes in it."

"Could you see who it was?"

"Two black cars, big sedans. I couldn't tell who was inside, but we both know who it was. Ben Siegel delivered a warning earlier this evening, told me Stampano was out to get me. I gave him a beating last night, when he bothered one of our girls."

"Where's your car?"

"I'm taking it back to the studio, if you want to take pictures. Do it tomorrow, though. I'm going to get it repaired."

"Nah, why bother? I'll take your word for the bullet holes. Were there any other witnesses?"

"Tom Terry, from the Beverly Hills force, was with me."

"Good. Can I go back to sleep now?"

"Yeah, but I want you to send some people to pick up Stampano right now, then sweat him in the morning."

"Why? He's not going to give us anything."

"I want him to know the police are thinking about him. Maybe it'll help calm him down. By the way, Siegel told me that Stampano is Charlie Luciano's man out here, keeping an eye on Jack Dragna. Dragna's scared of him for that reason."

"That's interesting to know," Ben said.

"I'm going out of town tomorrow for a few days; be back the first of the week."

"Sounds like a good idea, considering."

"Good night, Ben." He hung up.

Rick packed his fishing gear and clothes and tossed them into the backseat of his car.

Back at the studio, Rick told the cop to pick him up at eight-thirty the following morning for the drive to the airport. "Then you fellows will have a few days off from this detail," he said. He turned to Tom. "I'll be okay here on my own. Go home and get some sleep. Our boys will get me to the airport tomorrow morning, and I'll call you when I'm back."

"You want me to make a report of the incident?"

"Yeah, go ahead and do that. It might be good to have it on the record."

Tom left, and Rick hauled his gear into his office. Jenny had made up the sofa as a bed, and he climbed into it with gratitude. It was nearly two a.m., and he had a long flight the next day.

Before he fell asleep, he spent a little time wondering why Glenna hadn't shown up at the party, then he dozed off.

42

The following morning, Rick left a note for
Jenny to have his car repaired, then he left for
Clover Field with a studio cop for company.
The cop drove into the hangar and helped him
unload his luggage, then Rick sent him on his
way, since he knew Stampano would still be in
jail at that hour.

His father came out of his office. "Morning,"
he said. "I gassed her up last night, and I did
your preflight inspection this morning. You
going to have a lot of luggage?"

"Thanks, Dad, I expect so," Rick replied. Jack
got a little tractor and towed the aircraft out of
the hangar and onto the ramp.

Rick was completing his own pre-flight inspection when Clete drove onto the ramp, followed by two men in a pickup truck. Clete
seemed his usual, unhungover self.

Clark Gable got out of the driver's seat of the
pickup, followed by a tall, slender young man
with a mustache.

"You've met Clark, I think," Clete said.

"Sure I have," Rick replied, offering Gable his hand.

"How are you, Rick? Looking forward to some trout fishing?"

"I'm looking forward to learning about it, Clark. It's my first time."

"This is David Niven," Gable said, introducing the young man. "Another Limey."

Rick shook Niven's hand. "Let's get your gear loaded, then we're ready for departure." The four of them loaded their luggage and a lot of groceries into the airplane, including a case of liquor and two cases of Schlitz beer and some soft drinks. Rick threw a cargo net over it all and tied it down. He put Gable and Niven in the rear seat, Clete in the front, then climbed into the pilot's seat.

He ran through his checklist, then primed and started the engine and watched as the gauges came to life. He continued through the checklist, then gave his dad a thumbs-up signal. Jack Barron pulled the chocks from under the wheels, and Rick taxied to the end of runway 21. He went through the runup procedure, listening for any sign of trouble from the big radial engine, then he handed out some earplugs to the others and put on his headset.

"We're going to follow the coast to the mouth of the Rogue River, then follow the river up to the camp," Rick said. "Clete, will you recognize it from the air?"

"I will," Gable said. "There's a big red barn

and a farmhouse, and the strip runs parallel to the river along the north bank. There's a windsock near the barn."

Rick looked to the northeast, to be sure there was no landing traffic, then eased the throttle forward and taxied onto the runway. He didn't slow down, but shoved the throttle to the firewall, and the big single began its takeoff run. A moment later, he eased the yoke forward, and the tail came off the ground, then he rotated and the craft lifted into the air, climbing strongly.

As soon as they crossed the beach, Rick turned north and climbed to three thousand feet. The day was bright and clear, and the California coast was gorgeous. They flew northwest, past Oxnard and Santa Barbara, then more northerly past Morro Bay, Big Sur and Monterey. Rick noted that they had a nice tailwind, so they made good time, and it wasn't going to be necessary to stop and refuel.

They flew past Half Moon Bay, then across the Golden Gate, admiring the new bridge. By noon, San Francisco was behind them.

Gable produced some thick ham sandwiches. "Ma made 'em for us," he shouted. He gave everybody but Rick a beer, and gave him a Coca-Cola.

Another hour and a half brought them to Gold Beach, Oregon, near the mouth of the Rogue River. Rick found the local airfield and started down. "I'm going to refuel here for the flight back," he shouted to the others. "We don't know what the weather will be like for our return."

He set the Vega down on the grass strip and taxied to what passed for the terminal. Half an hour later, they were refueled and climbing out of Gold Beach toward the river, shining in the afternoon sun.

Rick stayed about a thousand feet above the ground, keeping the river off his left wing. For as far as he could see there was nothing but dense forest, broken only by the river and an occasional farmhouse. After half an hour, Gable tapped him on the shoulder. "It's up ahead there. See the barn?"

Rick put the nose down slightly and retarded the throttle. "Got it."

"The windsock is to the left of the barn," Gable yelled. "Usually, you land to the west."

Rick found the windsock. He flew past the barn for a mile, descending to five hundred feet, then turned back toward the runway. It was clearly visible, and a tractor parked near the strip with a big mower attached told him the grass had been cut. He flew past the barn and set the airplane down in a perfect three-pointer, then let the speed bleed off before taxiing back.

"Pull up right there," Gable said, pointing to a spot beside the barn.

Rick taxied into position and shut down the engine. They were met by a tall fat man who was introduced as Jake, and a big Irish setter, introduced as Rocky.

They loaded everything into Jake's pickup, and he handed the key to Gable. "Everything's ready down at the cabin," he said. "I'll see you when I see you."

"Three or four days," Gable said. "We'll see how it goes." Gable got into the truck, and Clete got in beside him, while Rick and Niven got into the back with the luggage and groceries. They bounced along a dirt track along the river for a couple of miles to a big log cabin. Twenty minutes later, they were unloaded and had opened two bottles of whiskey, scotch for Clete and David, bourbon for Rick and Clark.

"Man," Gable said, "I can't tell you how good it feels to get out of the city and up here." He fell into one of the big overstuffed chairs and put his feet up, taking a long pull from his drink. "Rick, tomorrow you're going to see some of the world's best fly-fishing."

"Well," Niven said, "it's pretty, but it isn't Scotland, and trout aren't salmon."

Gable grinned at him. "I can tell we're going to have to shoot you before the weekend's over."

Everybody laughed and settled down to their drinking. Clete turned on a big Zenith radio next to the fireplace. "We'll get the BBC on this thing," he said, selecting the shortwave band. After a few minutes of static and whistling, the radio produced surprisingly good reception of the British station, from which a newscaster was speaking. "We take you now to the House of Commons, where the prime minister is about to speak."

Moments later, the mournful voice of Neville Chamberlain came from the radio. He rambled on for a quarter of an hour, giving the House an account of his government's negotiations with the Germans and outlining steps he had taken to prepare for the possibility of war. Finally he concluded:

"We have no quarrel with the German people, except that they allow themselves to be governed by a Nazi government. As long as that government exists and pursues the methods it has so persistently followed during the last two years, there will be no peace in Europe. We shall merely pass from one crisis to another, and see one country after another attacked by methods which have now become familiar to us in their sickening technique. We are resolved that these methods must come to an end. If out of the struggle we again reestablish in the world the rules of good faith and the renunciation of force, why, then even the sacrifices that will be entailed upon us will find their fullest justification." He finished to a chorus of "Hear, hears."

Clete snapped off the radio. "Well, it seems that even Chamberlain has finally faced facts."

"We'll be at war within a week," Niven said.

"Ah, don't worry about it, David," Gable said. "You Limeys will kick Hitler's ass back to the Rhine in no time."

"I hope you're right, Clark," Clete said.

Later, Gable grilled some steaks, and they had a subdued dinner, washed down with quantities of whiskey. There were two bedrooms in the cabin: Clete and Niven took one, Rick and Gable the other. There were two single beds with lots of blankets, and Rick settled in. He was astonished to see Gable take out his teeth, brush them thoroughly in the sink, then put them in a glass of water beside his bed.

43

The following morning at dawn, Rick was awakened by the smell of frying bacon. He splashed some water on his face, brushed his teeth and got dressed. He found Gable in the kitchen making pancakes.

"Morning, Rick."

"Morning, Clark. Are Clete and David up yet?"

"Those crazy Limeys are having a dip in the river," Gable said.

"Brrrrrr."

"My sentiments exactly. I think it has something to do with their having to take cold baths in English boarding schools."

Clete and Niven suddenly burst through the front door, naked, rubbing themselves with towels. "God, that was wonderful," Clete said.

"Tip top," Niven agreed.

"You're both insane," Gable said. "Get some clothes on. Breakfast is ready and I don't want to look at your dicks while I'm eating."

The two vanished and came back dressed.

Rick had set the table, and they sat down to a huge breakfast. When they were finished, they washed the dishes, then got their gear and set out along a footpath, heading east along the river. After half a mile or so, Gable stopped.

"Rick, you stay here with me, and I'll give you some pointers. Clete, David, go another quarter of a mile, and you'll find a spot nearly as good as ours."

For the rest of the day, Rick was given an intense course of instruction in fly-fishing by Gable, who was clearly a master of the sport.

They returned to the cabin in the late afternoon, laden with enough fat trout for dinner and beyond. They cleaned the fish in the river, then Clete set about making dinner, while the others entertained themselves with music on the radio and generous quantities of whiskey.

After dinner, Clete attempted to get the BBC again and failed. "Well, anyway," he said, "it's the middle of the night over there. Maybe we can get something in the morning."

In the morning, Rick cooked ham and eggs while the two Englishmen threw themselves in the river again. When they were dressed, Clete tuned in the BBC as they sat down to breakfast. Chamberlain was in the middle of speaking in the Commons.

". . . We were in consultation all day yesterday with the French government, and we felt that the intensified action which the Germans were taking against Poland allowed no delay in making our own position clear. Accordingly, we decided to send our Ambassador in Berlin instructions, which he was to hand at nine o'clock this morning to the German Foreign Secretary, and which read as follows: 'Sir; in the communication which I had the honour to make to you on the first September, I informed you, on the instructions of His Majesty's Principal Secretary of State for Foreign Affairs, that unless the German government were prepared to give His Majesty's Government in the United Kingdom satisfactory assurances that the German government had suspended all aggressive action against Polish territory, His Majesty's Government would, without hesitation, fulfill their obligation to Poland. Although this communication was made more than twenty-four hours ago, no reply has been received, but German attacks upon Poland have been continued and intensified. I have accordingly the honour to inform you that, unless not later than eleven a.m., British Summer Time, today, third September, satisfactory assurances to the above effect have been given by the German government and have reached His Majesty's Government in London, a state of war will exist between the two countries as from that hour.' That was the final note. No such undertaking was received by the time stipulated, and, consequently, this country is at war with Germany."

He went on for another minute, but Rick

stopped listening and simply watched the faces of Clete and Niven. Both looked stricken.

"That's it," Clete said, when Chamberlain had finished. "We're in it."

"I feel for you and your country, pal," Gable said, "but thank God we're not in it."

"Not yet," Niven said.

"Roosevelt will do everything he can to keep us out of it," Rick said.

"Yes," Clete said, "and it won't be enough."

"I'm afraid you might be right," Gable said. "If things go badly for England, Roosevelt will try to get us into it." He turned to Rick. "And you know what that means."

For the first time, Rick gave thought to the idea that he, personally, might have to go to war. "I guess I'll have to go," he said. "How about you, Clark?"

"Not me. I'm past draft age, and Ma and I are trying like hell to get pregnant. The combination of those two things will keep me out, I guess. If I were younger and single, I'd go, though. I wouldn't like it much, but I'd go. I talked to Jimmy Stewart last week, and he's been taking flying lessons for a long time, to get a leg up."

"You won't have to take flying lessons, Rick," Clete said. "The army's going to want you."

"I guess you're right," Rick said.

They continued eating breakfast in silence, then Clete put his fork down. "I've got to get back to LA," he said. "I've got things to do."

"So have I," Niven said.

Gable spoke up. "Well, why don't we wrap it up here and go home. Weather okay to fly, Rick?"

"Looks like it."

It took them an hour to get packed and load the pickup. They drove back to Jake's farmhouse, paid him and gave him the rest of the trout and groceries, then loaded the airplane.

Rick did his preflight, then loaded everybody up and got the engine started. They were off by ten o'clock, and the winds were cooperative again, so they set down in Santa Monica shortly before two p.m.

As Rick taxied back to his father's hangar, he saw something that nearly stopped his heart: a corner of the hangar had burned, and temporary timbers had been set in place to support it.

He got the airplane shut down, then ran into the hangar. Jack Barron was sitting at his desk, and he looked up, surprised to see Rick. "I thought you'd be another couple of days," he said.

"What happened?" Rick asked, pointing to the burned corner of the hangar.

"Looks like somebody splashed some gasoline on it and set it alight," Jack said. "Middle of the night, after you left. The night watchman across the field saw the blaze and called the fire department."

"Where were my studio cops?"

"I sent 'em home," Jack said.

"Jesus, Dad."

"Now, don't blame them. It was my decision, though not the best one I ever made. Don't worry about it. I've got insurance, and I've got a builder coming to take a look at the damage today."

"Were any of the airplanes damaged?"

"No, we were lucky."

Rick called the studio and ordered three men out immediately. "In case they come back to finish the job," he said to his father.

Rick went back and helped unload the airplane. When they were done, he said his good-byes to Gable and Niven, then turned to Clete. "What are you going to do?"

"I'm not sure yet," Clete replied, sounding evasive.

"You can tell me, Clete. I won't rat you out to Eddie Harris."

"I'm going to go home and see if I can get a phone call or two through to England. Then I'll decide."

"Wait until my men get here, and one will follow you home."

"Nobody's going to bother me," Clete said. "They think we're still away."

"All right, but I'll have a man at your house inside an hour."

"If you feel you have to," Clete said. He shook Rick's hand and held on to it for a moment. "Thanks for flying us up to Oregon," he said. "I think Niven and I will remember the trip for a long time."

"So will I," Rick replied, and he meant it.

44

Rick went back to his office and found Jenny reading a movie magazine. "Why do you read that stuff?" he asked. "Don't you get enough of the real thing around here?"

"Nope," she said. "And I wouldn't be reading it if I had anything to do around here. By the way, Hedda Hopper is calling you 'the Prince of Beverly Hills.'"

"*What?*"

"No kidding. She says she sees you in all the best places with Clete Barrow, and that you're a prince in shining armor for protecting the studio's actresses from wolves."

"Where the hell did she get that?"

"Who knows? I expect she has lots of sources. She says you dress like a prince, too."

"God, I hope Eddie Harris doesn't see that."

"Why? I should think he'd like it."

"It's embarrassing."

"Getting your name in the papers is not embarrassing in this town, unless you're in jail."

The phone rang, and Jenny picked it up. "Mr.

Barron's office." She held her hand over the phone. "It's Mr. Harris."

"Oh, God," Rick moaned. He went into his office, closed the door and picked up the phone.

"Hello, Eddie."

"Well, if it isn't the Prince of Beverly Hills!"

"Aw, come on."

"That's wonderful! I love it!"

"You do?"

"It reflects well on the studio to have Hedda saying nice things about our people."

"How'd you know I was back?"

"The gate called me. I asked them to when you got in. Why are you back early?"

"We heard the news from London on the radio this morning. It sort of put a damper on things. Anyway, we'd already caught half the trout in Oregon." Rick didn't want him to ask what Clete thought of the news. "Listen, Eddie, my dad's hangar got set fire to a couple of nights ago."

"Oh, Christ, was it bad?"

"A night watchman called the fire department, and they caught it in time. The damage isn't much."

"I'll send a crew of studio carpenters out there tomorrow morning to repair the damage. Your father shouldn't suffer because of the work you're doing for us. By the way, I saw the damage to your car. That must have been scary."

"Happened too fast to be scary."

"Hiram will have it fixed in no time."

"Thanks."

"Do you expect any more trouble from Stampano?"

"It wouldn't surprise me. I haven't had time since I got back to call my man at the LAPD, but I'll call him this afternoon."

"Okay. I heard you've got Glenna living in her bungalow."

"Yes, I thought she'd be safer there. She's given up her place at the Garden of Allah."

"The studio will help her find something new when this blows over."

"Let me call Ben Morrison now, and I'll get back to you."

"Okay."

Rick hung up and called Morrison.

"Lieutenant Morrison."

"Ben, it's Rick."

"You're back?"

"Yeah, we came back early. Stampano set fire to my father's hangar out at Clover Field while I was gone."

"Shit, I hadn't heard about that."

"It wasn't too bad, but I want you to give him as hard a time as possible."

"I can't."

"Why not?"

"He got on the train for New York yesterday. A source of mine says Luciano wants him back there."

"For good?"

"We can only hope. I wouldn't count on it, though, and I wouldn't let my guard down if I were you. He may have left instructions."

"I won't. What did he have to say when you arrested him?"

"Denied all knowledge of everything; barely admitted to knowing you. With two shiners he looked like a raccoon. You must have really busted him one."

"I did my best."

"Anyway, we kept him until around noon, when Dragna heard about it and sent a lawyer over to get him out. At least he knows we're not going to sit by and watch while he tries to kill you. I've taken steps to let Luciano know that, too."

"How can Luciano run the organization from jail?"

"Are you kidding? I hear he's living like the Prince of Wales in there. He probably has a phone in his cell. By the way, congratulations on your ascent to princehood."

Rick could hear the smirk. "Get off my back, will you? Call me if you hear anything else."

"And you call me if you hear from any of Stampano's friends."

"Will do." Rick hung up and thought about calling Glenna, but she would be on the set at this time of day. Instead, he called Hiram in transportation.

"Welcome back, Rick. Your car is ready. Are you in the office?"

"Yes, Hiram, and thanks for doing it so quickly."

"My pleasure. I'll send the car over to you. By the way, I thought it might be a good idea to put a couple of quarter-inch steel plates in the doors. It adds weight, but you won't have bullets going all the way through the car."

"I appreciate that, Hiram." He hung up and called Eddie Harris. "Good news, Eddie. Charlie Luciano has called Stampano back to New York."

"Funny you should mention that — I just got a call to that effect from Jack Dragna. He wanted me to know that there wouldn't be any more problems."

"Well, that's a relief, to hear it from the horse's mouth."

"I guess you can move back home again, and I'll get my girl on finding Glenna a new place. Her roommate is supposed to be out of the hospital next week, and I'm putting her back to work."

"Great news."

"You want to tell Glenna for me?"

"Yeah, sure."

"I thought you might. Welcome home, pal." Eddie hung up.

Rick suddenly felt twenty pounds lighter. It was over. At least, he hoped it was.

He was waiting at Glenna's bungalow when she got home from work, and he gave her the good news. She changed, and they went out for dinner.

That night, he slept in his own bed, for a change, though he wished he were in Glenna's.

45

Rick went out to Clover Field the following morning to see that the crew of Centurion carpenters had their work in hand, and they did, with Jack Barron overseeing them.

"Thanks for sending these people," his dad said. "Now I don't have to explain to an insurance adjustor how this happened."

"The repairs are Eddie Harris's doing," Rick said.

"I've found him a couple of pilots for his new DC-3," Jack said. "They start to work next week, and Harris wants to go to New York right off. The airplane is being delivered tomorrow from San Diego."

"Great news, Dad. That'll bring in some good money for you."

"I can't complain about that."

"My Italian friend has headed off to New York, but I'm still going to keep a couple of men here at night, just in case."

"Whatever you say. I promise not to send them home."

Rick went back to his office and called Clete Barrow. He'd heard nothing from him since their return from Oregon. No one answered the phone. It must be the servants' day off.

Shortly, a script was delivered from Eddie Harris with a note: "Read this. I'm going to produce it myself, and I thought you might like to look over my shoulder while I'm doing it. We go into pre-production tomorrow, so be in my office at nine for the first meeting."

Rick spent the remainder of his day reading the script and making notes to himself about questions to ask. This was going to solve the problem of what to do with his days.

Late in the afternoon, he tried phoning Clete again; still no answer. He left the studio at six and drove over to Clete's house. The Filipino houseman answered the door.

"Please come in, Mr. Barron," he said.

"Is Clete in?"

"No, sir."

"I've been trying to reach him, but nobody answered the phone."

"Mr. Barrow instructed us not to."

"Why?"

The man pointed to an envelope on the living room coffee table. "He asked me to give you that."

Rick picked up the sealed envelope and ripped it open. There was a letter in Clete's public schoolboy hand, a neat copperplate:

My Dear Rick,

I'm sorry I couldn't talk with you about this before I left, but I would have been putting you in a difficult position. By the time you read this, I'll be on an airplane to Montreal, whence I will hitch a ride to England on the first available ship.

My regiment has called up its reserve officers, of which I am one, and my contract with Centurion not withstanding, it's a call I must heed. I've sent Eddie Harris another letter explaining all this, so you won't be on the hook for it.

When this is all over, if it ever is, and if I live through it, I expect to be back, so I've not put my house up for sale. I know you're comfortably fixed in Eddie's guest cottage, but I'd be very grateful if you would move into the house while I'm gone and keep an eye on it for me. Empty houses have a way of deteriorating, and I love the place too much to let that happen. Manuel and Maria have packed up my duds and stored them in the attic, so the master bedroom is all yours. Use it well.

I've paid Manuel and Maria through the end of next year, and at that time you can decide whether to keep them on. You can take care of the phone and utility bills. My car is still being worked on in the studio shop, and I'd appreciate it if you'd see to the return of the loaner to Hiram. The keys to the house and car are in the second envelope.

During the time you and I have known each other, I've come to think of you as a close friend, perhaps the closest I have, and I'll miss your company. Still, I'll have the company of a lot of other good chaps for the duration.

I don't know what else to say. If America comes into the war, and I expect she will, eventually, perhaps we'll meet on the other side of the great pond and raise a glass once again. Until then, take care of yourself, and Glenna, too. I think she's for you. I'll write when I can.

> With my affectionate regards,
> Clete

Rick read the letter again, then folded it carefully and put it into his coat pocket.

Manuel came out of the kitchen. "Shall I tell Maria you'll be here for dinner this evening, Mr. Barron?"

"Not this evening, Manuel," Rick replied. "There's something I have to do. I'll bring my things over tomorrow."

"Very good, Mr. Barron. Maria and I are glad to know you'll be staying here. It would have been very empty without Mr. Clete."

"Thank you, Manuel."

Rick left and drove back to the studio, then to Glenna's bungalow. She was in the kitchen.

"Hi, there. Will you stay for dinner?"

"I certainly will," he said. "Can I fix you a martini?"

"Oh, please do."

He made the drinks and set them on the kitchen counter, then he took her face in his hands and kissed her lightly, then again, more thoroughly.

"That was very nice," she said, putting her arms around him.

"I plan to do a lot more of it," he said. "Has the studio made any progress finding you a place to live?"

"I haven't heard from Eddie's secretary; she's handling it."

"Tell her to stop handling it."

"Oh? What did you have in mind?"

Rick sat down at the counter and took a sip of his bourbon. "Clete Barrow has left for England, to rejoin his regiment."

"Oh," she said, surprised. "I suppose I can understand that."

"So can I, though I'll miss him."

"You're quite good friends, aren't you?"

"Yes, more than I had realized. He's better company than anyone I know, except you."

She brought her drink over to the counter and rested her elbows, bringing her face close to his. "I feel the same way," she said, then she laughed. "I thought I was too shy to say that."

"I'm glad you did, because it makes my question to you easier."

"What question?"

"Clete has asked me to move into his house. It's a lot bigger than mine, and there are servants. Why don't you move into it with me?"

She gulped and took a sip of her martini. "Wow. I hadn't expected that."

"I know."

"I mean, we haven't even . . ."

"We can remedy that anytime you say."

She smiled. "It's an attractive thought."

"I can protect you so much better if I'm around all the time," he said.

"I do need protecting, don't I?"

"And you wouldn't have to find a place to live."

"There is that. What would I do about Barbara? She's out of the hospital next week."

"There's a little guest house on the property. It's hers for as long as she wants it."

"I'm trying hard, but I can't think of an objection to your plan."

He kissed her again, and they forgot about dinner.

46

Rick arrived early for his meeting in Eddie Harris's office the following morning.

Eddie looked up from his desk. "Good morning. I got Clete's note. Did you know he was going to do this?"

There it was, the direct question. "I can't say I was surprised."

"Why didn't you mention it to me?" Eddie's voice was uncharacteristically cold.

"As I recall, you mentioned it to me, on one occasion. It can't have surprised you, either."

Eddie looked out the window. "Goddamnit, I wanted him to star in this script I sent you."

Rick said nothing.

"It was only one more film. He could have waited until the end of the year."

"His letter to me said that his regiment called up its reserve officers, and he was one of them. What else could he do?"

"I had a call from Sam Goldwyn last night. David Niven has gone, too, and Sam is livid."

"It's war, Eddie, and if we get into it a lot of

Centurion people are going to have to go."

"Meaning you?"

"I'm the right age for it. I could get the call."

"I don't mean to sound unpatriotic, but thank God I'm past forty." He tapped the script on his desk. "I've been going over our contract players in my mind, and I haven't been able to cast the male lead. We're going to have to go outside, and it's going to cost us to borrow a star."

Rick was glad for the change of subject. "When I read it, I didn't see Clete in the part," he said. "The character is younger and American, and I've never heard Clete speak with anything other than his own accent."

"You've never heard Errol Flynn speak with anything but his own accent, either, but he sells tickets, even to Westerns."

"This character is American, urban and a little rough around the edges."

"So, who do you think?"

"The week before I came to work here I saw a movie called *Dynamo*, and there was a young actor in a featured part who impressed me. Name was Barry something, or something Barry."

"Never heard of him."

"Maybe it was his first film."

"Which studio?"

"I'm not sure. Maybe RKO."

Eddie pressed a button. "An actor named Barry, first or last name, did a picture called *Dynamo*, maybe at RKO. Get me a print of the picture and find out the rest of his name and who his agent is." He turned back to Rick. "We'll have a print by noon, and we'll take a look at it together. Meanwhile, think of some more names."

"Okay."

"Now, how about the girl?"

"Glenna."

"She's got three more weeks' work on the musical."

"When do we start shooting?"

"Two weeks, and we can't wait. We're shooting in sequence."

"The girl only has one scene in the early part of the film. Maybe we could borrow her for a day from the musical."

"Possibly. Give me some more names for the girl, too."

The box on Eddie's desk buzzed. "Yes?"

"I called RKO, and they didn't want to give us a print of *Dynamo* or even tell us the actor's name, so I found a print we can borrow at a theater in Santa Monica, and I've sent a messenger out there for it. I haven't been able to find out anything about the actor, but we can get his name from the titles, and then I'll track him down."

"Good. Put it up in my screening room the minute it gets here, and call whatshisname, the director of the musical, and tell him I want Glenna Gleason for a day, two weeks from Monday, so he should shoot around her."

"Yes, sir."

Eddie turned back to Rick. "So, who else for the guy?"

"Alan Ladd."

"Not bad, though he's pretty smooth. I see how you're thinking, but he just started shooting a picture at Paramount."

"John Garfield."

"Not available, either. He's in the middle of a film at Warners'. But he would be damn good casting."

The box squawked again. "Mr. Harris, the others are here for your production meeting."

"Send 'em in," Eddie said, and four people walked into the office and were waved to the conference table. Eddie introduced Rick to the director, set designer, costume designer and production manager. "Rick is going to sit in on this production all the way through," he said, and no one objected or even seemed surprised.

Eddie and Rick took seats at the table. "All right," he said, looking at the set designer, "what are we going to need? Let's start saving money right now."

"We've got just about everything we need in storage," the man said. "It's nothing unusual — offices, a hotel room, a bar. I can make it all look fresh. There is a country club scene, though. We might have to do it on location."

Rick had a thought. "The colonial officers' club set is still on stage two, isn't it?"

"Good idea!" the man said. "I can dress it with more modern things and move some windows. It'll work fine."

Eddie gave Rick an approving glance. "Costumes?"

"Pretty much off the wardrobe department's rack," the designer said. "I'll need to do a couple of dresses for the girl, though."

They worked on through the morning, and Rick began to see how a film was put together.

They were about to break for lunch when Eddie's secretary came into the room. "The print of *Dynamo* is ready in your screening room," she said.

"Great," Eddie replied, standing up. "Get the commissary to send over some sandwiches, and we'll eat while we're watching it."

"What's *Dynamo*?" the director asked.

"Something from RKO with an actor Rick likes for the lead."

"What actor?"

"Barry something or something Barry."

Everybody moved into the screening room next door, and the film began to roll.

"Lawrence Barry," Eddie and Rick said simultaneously, as the name came up in the credits.

"Oh, shit," Eddie said, "the guy must get called Larry Barry." Everybody laughed.

They settled in to watch. They were half an hour into it when the sandwiches arrived. Eddie picked up a phone attached to his chair. "Stop for a minute." The film stopped and the lights came up. "Everybody grab a sandwich, and we'll resume."

"I've heard about this picture," the director said.

"We got the print from a theater in Santa Monica," Eddie said. "RKO didn't want us to see it." He picked up a phone. "The actor's name is Lawrence Barry. Find out who his agent is, and get them both in here this afternoon." He turned to the director. "What do you think of Barry?"

"I like him. I've heard a little about him from New York. He did something on the stage last year. I wasn't aware that anybody had signed him."

"Maybe nobody has," Eddie said. "Maybe *Dynamo* is a one-shot deal for Barry, and that's why RKO is being uncooperative." He got a sandwich and sat down next to Rick. "I like the guy," he said quietly. "He and Glenna will look great together, too."

"I thought so," Rick said. Actually, it hadn't occurred to him until Eddie mentioned it, but he was willing to take credit for the idea. "By the way, Clete has asked me to live in his house while he's gone."

"So you're moving out of my place?"

"I guess so. I'm sure you can find somebody else. If Suzanne wants a man in the place for protection, I know a cop who might be good for you."

"What's his name?"

"Tom Terry. He's one of the Beverly Hills officers who helped me with the Stampano thing."

"I'd like to meet him."

"I'll arrange it."

"Or I could offer it to Glenna."

"Well, ah, Glenna is moving into Clete's place with me."

Eddie laughed. "You don't waste much time, do you?"

"I, ah . . ."

"She'll be safer with you than alone, and I guess that's good for the studio."

"I'm glad you think so," Rick said. He was relieved, too.

47

Rick sat in Eddie's office and watched Lawrence Barry. He was dressed in a decent suit and tie, and Rick was impressed with his calm demeanor.

"So," Eddie said, "what do your friends call you? Larry?"

Barry smiled a little. "My middle name is McArthur. I've always been called Mac."

"Good. Did you have a chance to look at the script?"

"Yes, I did, but not thoroughly."

"What did you think of it?"

"I think it could be a good film."

"You think you could handle the lead?"

His agent came to life. "He certainly could. He's had a lot of stage experience."

"Shut up, Jerry," Eddie said. "I'm talking to your client."

"I certainly could," Barry replied. "I've had a lot of stage experience."

Rick liked that, the guy standing up for his agent, and not afraid to be a smart-ass with Eddie Harris.

"Which won't do you a hell of a lot of good in the movies."

"Sure it will," Barry replied. "You saw *Dynamo*. Whatever I brought to that I learned on the stage."

"How do you know I saw *Dynamo*? It hasn't even been released yet."

"Because I wouldn't be here if you hadn't seen it."

It occurred to Rick that Barry was very much like the character in their script. "I think you read the script pretty thoroughly, Mac," Rick said, "because you're doing a very good job of playing the character right now."

Eddie looked at Rick, then back at Barry, then he burst out laughing. "I've been had," he said. "I thought this was an interview, but you're doing an audition."

"It seemed like a good idea," Barry said, smiling.

"All right, you get the part." Eddie turned to the agent. "Standard seven-year contract, five hundred a week."

Barry spoke up. "I got more than that in *Dynamo*."

"Yeah, for four weeks' work. This is seven years, and you get paid every week, with raises as you get better."

"I'm already very good," Barry said.

The agent spoke up. "Mac isn't really interested in the usual long-term contract. He's already turned that down at RKO."

"Then he isn't interested in working?"

"I said the *usual* long-term contract. We'll want script approval and time off for him to do theater in New York, plus salary increases on each film."

"What kind of salary increases?"

"He'll do your first picture for a thousand a week. After that, he gets a five-hundred-dollar raise for each picture."

"Okay, here's my final offer," Eddie said. "He does two pictures a year for Centurion, and he can turn down one script a year. I'll give him three months a year off, so he can dabble with the stage, if he wants to — the dates to be negotiated. I'll pay him a grand a week for the first picture and two-fifty more for each picture after that, but I'll only pay him for the weeks he works. The term of the contract is seven years."

"What about fringe benefits?"

"He'll get star treatment when he shows me he's got what it takes to be a star, and the minute he shows me he can't become a star, then I'll fire him. He starts two weeks from Monday."

Barry spoke up. "I want two weeks' rehearsal with the cast and director on each picture, and I want to be paid for rehearsals."

"I'll guarantee you a week's rehearsal, and I'll give you two weeks when I can, but you'll get half-salary for rehearsing."

Barry looked at his agent but said nothing.

"I think we can proceed on that basis," the agent said. "You want to send me a contract?"

"You'll have it before the close of business tomorrow," Eddie said. "One thing, your leading lady won't be available for rehearsals on this one; she's making a musical. You won't meet her until the first day of shooting."

"Who is she?" Barry asked.

"Her name is Glenna Gleason. She's new, and she's going to be very big. You'll like her."

"I don't know," Barry said.

His agent spoke up. "You're going to have to trust Mr. Harris on this one, Mac."

Barry thought about it, then nodded.

Eddie stood up and offered his hand. "Good to have you aboard, Mac. Come to this office Monday morning, and we'll get you squared away with a dressing room."

"A bungalow would be nice," the agent said.

"Don't push your luck, Jerry. I told you he'll get star treatment when he's a star."

The meeting broke up, and Eddie motioned for Rick to stay. "What you just saw was a good negotiation," he said. "The agent is good. He prepared his client well, though I don't think he told him to audition. The agent knew what he could get for the kid, and he didn't try for more. A negotiation works best when everybody has an idea of what's possible. You get into trouble when you get an agent or an actor who wants more than the situation warrants, or when you get a Joan Crawford — an actress who thinks she's a goddess and wants to be paid for thinking it."

"I enjoyed watching," Rick said. "I think I learned a few things from it."

"I liked it that you picked up that the kid was playing the part. That went right past me, and you caught it."

"It was a smart thing for the guy to do."

"If we can keep that kid sober and out of jail, and if he works hard and doesn't let his ego get the best of him, he'll become a real star. I think he has what it takes."

At the end of the day, Rick drove by the transportation department and borrowed a truck and a driver from Hiram, then he went first to Glenna's bungalow for her things, then to Eddie's guest house for his own stuff. By dinnertime, the two of them had moved into Clete Barrow's house.

They sat on the terrace by the pool, Glenna with her martini and Rick with his bourbon, while Manuel and Maria prepared dinner.

"Eddie asked me to give you some news," Rick said.

"What news?"

"You've got a new film to start as soon as you've finished the musical."

"What is it?"

"The script is in the bedroom. You can read it later. It's called *Caper*, and it's very good."

"What's my part?"

"The lead."

She squeezed his hand. "Oh, Rick, that's wonderful."

"You'll be co-starring with a young actor from New York named Lawrence Barry; his friends call him Mac. Eddie signed him today, and he thinks he'll be a big star. He also thinks that the two of you will look very good together on screen."

"How do you know all this?"

"Eddie asked me to sit in on the production from start to finish. I think he believes I can be a producer."

"Wonderful! Is there a part in it for Barbara?"

"I'll see what I can do."

"Everything is going so beautifully now, after that business with . . ."

"Don't worry about that anymore," Rick said. "He's out of the picture now."

She sighed. "I'm afraid there's a pattern in my life: Just when everything is going well, I seem to find a way to mess it up."

"We'll work on keeping everything going well," Rick said.

48

Glenna took her day off from the musical and worked on the first day of the shooting of *Caper*. She and Lawrence Barry seemed to hit it off and completed two scenes.

Rick returned to his office to find a thick envelope plastered with Canadian stamps waiting for him. Clete must have written from Montreal, he thought, but when he opened it he got a surprise.

LONDON, SEPTEMBER 12, 1939

My Dear Rick,

Hello from London. This has all happened very quickly. After my flight from Los Angeles to Montreal, stopping in Detroit, I was about to head for the port to look for a ship, but I never got off the airfield. I struck up a conversation with an RCAF pilot, who told me he was ferrying a bomber to the south of England, and he offered me a ride.

We took off the following morning and landed in Reykjavik, in Iceland, and stayed the night. Next morning we flew to Glasgow, refueled, then went on to Bekin Hill airport, in Kent. I got a train up to London, checked into the Reform Club and phoned my regiment. I was told not to turn up for another three days, so I've had a nice stay here, seeing a couple of friends and some theater.

Things seem very odd here. There are sandbags piled up around doorways and signs saying "Air Raid Shelter" being put up at the entrances to underground stations, but nothing is happening. No bombs falling, no paratroopers landing, nothing at all. The great difference from life before the war is the blackout, which is stringently observed. No streetlamps or electric signs, and every window is either dark or curtained over. Cars must have their headlamps mostly masked and turned off altogether when the sirens go off.

You drive down a darkened street in a taxi, find a street number using a torch (flashlight, to you), and a curtain is pulled back and you step into a brightly lit restaurant or nightclub, full of jolly people. Later, you walk outside into the darkness again. There's an air raid warden at nearly every street corner, enforcing the blackout and herding people into the tubes when there's a raid warning.

The newspapers have published plans for backyard bomb shelters that you can build yourself, and I'm told people are actually building them. People are planting vegetable gardens, in anticipation of rationing, and Hyde Park is being divided into allotments, where people can grow their own food.

Conscription is in full force, and young chaps are lining up to sign up with the RAF. Everyone, it seems, wants to fly a Hurricane or a Spitfire. They're calling this the "Phony War," because nothing is happening yet. I've used my time here to be measured for some additional kit, and the two uniforms that Centurion Wardrobe ran up for me have come in very useful.

The best news I've had since I returned is that Chamberlain has offered Churchill the post of First Lord of the Admiralty, something like your Secretary of the Navy, which is a very powerful position, given our reliance on the Royal Navy. It's the next best thing to being Prime Minister. My own opinion is that Chamberlain won't last long, and that the Conservative Party will turn to Churchill to lead the country.

On the appointed day, I entrained for Southampton, then took a ferry to Cowes, on the Isle of Wight, off the south coast, where my regiment is undergoing commando training. We've taken over the Royal Yacht Squadron, England's most prestigious yacht club, which occupies a castle built by Henry VIII to ward off the French, who never turned up. The

Castle, as the building is called, is a stone pile with a dozen or so bedrooms, one of which I've grabbed, though it's a single room and I have to share it with another officer. We bathe in the club's locker room, dine in its dining room (quite elegantly) and read in its library.

Our training, at this stage, is heavily slanted toward physical conditioning, and I confess, I'm having a hard time of keeping up after my dissolute existence in your West Coast Babylon. We're doing weapons training, too, of course, and there's talk that we'll be sent to France before too long.

I've already been promoted from lieutenant to captain, such is our need for officers, and been given command of a company, comprising about a hundred and twenty men. They're a good lot, with some veterans of the last war, and a lot of raw recruits, who are undergoing what amounts to basic training. My acting skills have been useful in playing the forceful and crotchety CO, but eventually they'll find me out, I'm sure, but at the moment they don't know that I'm a teddy bear inside.

Some other news: I discovered that while my RCAF bomber was between Iceland and Scotland, my uncle, my father's elder brother, died of a heart attack. Since his son and heir had been killed in the first war, my father, who went into the Church, like many second sons, has now succeeded to the dukedom. Oh, God,

I never told you, did I? My uncle was Duke of Kensington. What does this mean? Well, I'm afraid I've succeeded to my father's title, Marquess of Chelsea, and shall ever be known as such on this side of the water.

I haven't told my colleagues in the Royal Marines yet. I want them to get used to Captain Barrow, so that they'll continue calling me that when word gets around.

The whole thing will mean little to me as long as there's a war on, but when Pater shuffles off this mortal coil, if I don't precede him, then I'll be a fucking duke. Can you believe it? The good news is that there's a fine house in London (in Kensington, of course) and a great pile in Sussex, where one can ride to the hounds, if one is so inclined. My parents are in the process of packing up the Manse in Wiltshire that they've occupied for the past ten years, and moving up in the world, while I've got my face in the mud of a Wight field on a daily basis.

Good <u>news</u>: There's a Canadian journalist with us who's getting a flying boat to Montreal tomorrow morning (they take off in the Solent, which is the body of water that separates the Isle of Wight from mainland England) and he's going to mail this letter for me, so it will reach you a lot sooner than it would otherwise.

My mailing address, for the moment, is simply, The Castle, Cowes, IOW, England, if you'd care to write and tell me about the glamorous Hollywood life that has, no doubt, continued in my absence. Send it via air mail.

I hope you're in the house by now and enjoying it. Why don't you ask the lovely Glenna to share it with you? I'll wager she would accept such an invitation.

I'll get a missive off when I can, though I can't promise such accelerated delivery as this one will no doubt have. I'm not missing the high life, but, of course, I miss you.

With warm regards,
Clete

Rick found some paper and began writing him back immediately.

49

Everything went well on *Caper*, at first. Glenna finished her musical and started the new film as scheduled. She seemed to thrive on the work, arriving home in the evenings tired but excited.

Her enthusiasm for Rick in bed seemed as great as that for her work, and they explored each other as new lovers do, experimenting with giving each other pleasure.

Rick loved working on *Caper*, and soon he was doing a lot more than observing. Eddie Harris took him aside a couple of weeks into shooting. "I'm going to back off this picture now," he said. "There's another project I want to get ready for the new soundstage, and I'm going to pretty much leave this one to you. The director, the cast and the crew are already looking to you, and you've made that happen remarkably quickly. You can always come to me if you have a problem you can't solve, but I want you to try your best to solve it before you do. I would con-sider it a bad sign if key people on the film started coming to me because they couldn't agree with you on some point, but you're going to have to use your best judgment to figure out how much authority you can exert. Don't overstep, but don't be a pushover, either.

"I'm going to give you an associate producer's credit on *Caper*, and I want you to start looking for a project that you can produce on your own. You can go through the scripts we've on file, or option a book, if you find something you like. Keep it small and controllable. You'll have plenty of time to get involved with big-budget, Technicolor extravaganzas later, when you've got your feet firmly on the ground."

Eddie said nothing to the crew about his absence from the set, and neither did Rick. A couple of times, when the director had questions for Eddie, Rick made the decision, and it stood, and soon on the set it was as if he had always been the producer.

They were a week away from wrapping, with four of the most important scenes yet to be shot, when Rick worked late one evening and came home to find Manuel taking an empty martini glass from the table beside Glenna's poolside chair and bringing her a second. Rick had never known her to have a second drink before dinner. He asked Manuel for a drink and sat down.

Glenna seemed tense and drawn and, for the first time, exhausted. "Hi," she said softly.

Rick waited for his drink to be delivered and for Manuel to go back inside before he spoke. "What's wrong?" he asked.

She shook her head. "Nothing, I'm just tired."

He took her hand. "It's more than that," he said. "Tell me, and I'll try and make it better."

She pulled her hand away and used it to grasp the new martini. "I'm perfectly all right," she said. "I asked Barbara to join us for dinner." Barbara Kane had been living in the guest house since leaving the hospital, and Rick had found her a juicy part in *Caper*.

"Fine," Rick said, but he had the feeling that Glenna had asked Barbara to join them so that she wouldn't have to talk.

Barbara arrived and ordered a drink, then they went in to dinner. Rick and Barbara kept the conversation going during the meal without much help from Glenna, and when dessert was served, she stood up.

"Please excuse me," she said, "I'm going to turn in. Try not to wake me when you come to bed, Rick."

"All right," he said, kissing her on the cheek.

He and Barbara finished dessert, then sat on the living room sofa with an after-dinner drink.

"I know you know what's going on," Rick said, "and I need to know, too."

Barbara looked away. "I don't know what you mean."

"It's obvious that something happened between the time Glenna left work and I got home," he said. "I can't help her if I don't know what it was."

"I'm sure she's just tired," Barbara said, knocking back the remainder of her drink. "So am I. Please excuse me." She got up and went back to the guest house.

Rick finished his drink and read a script he'd brought home from work, then he went into the bedroom. Glenna was lying on her side, facing away from his side of the bed. He was sure she wasn't asleep, but she had asked not to be disturbed, so he undressed, got into bed and, eventually, drifted off.

When he woke the following morning, Glenna was gone. Usually, he was the one to wake first, and they always had breakfast together before leaving for work.

The breakfast table was set for two, so she hadn't told Manuel that she wouldn't be there. Rick ate quickly, then showered and shaved and drove in to work.

He had been using a makeshift office on the soundstage, and when shooting broke for a scenery change, he went to his desk and called Ben Morrison.

"Ben, it's Rick."

"Hey, buddy."

"Is Stampano back in town?"

"Funny you should mention that," Ben said. "I got a call five minutes ago from a source. Stampano got in yesterday, all healed up and looking his usual self."

"Can you think of an excuse to roust him?"

311

"Not after last time. I got heat from above about that. I'd need an actual crime and some witnesses. Has Stampano done something?"

"I'm not sure," Rick said. "How about the fire at my father's hangar? Can you haul him in for questioning about that?"

"I can't tie him to it. I can't tie anybody to it. I got the Santa Monica cops to send an arson investigator over to look at the scene, and all he could say was that gasoline was used. He got nothing else."

"Keep an eye on Stampano, will you, Ben?"

"Sure, I will. I'll call you if I hear anything."

Rick hung up. The director was standing in the door.

"What's the matter with Glenna?" he asked. He knew they lived together; everybody did.

"What do you mean?"

"She can't remember her lines, and she looks like hell. Did you two have a fight?"

"No. I'll talk with her."

"I can give her another hour before the next setup."

"Thanks." Rick left his office and walked over to Glenna's dressing room on the stage, a small trailer. He rapped on the door.

"Not now," Glenna called.

"It's Rick."

"Not now, please, Rick."

"I have to talk to you."

"Please, Rick, not now. I have lines to learn."

Rick went back to his office and read scripts

until an assistant director called him to the set.

Mac Barry and Glenna were in their places, and the director had a quick word with each of them, then went back to his chair beside the camera.

"Quiet on the set!" an assistant director yelled.

"Roll camera," the director said.

"Speed," the camera operator replied.

"Action!"

Barry spoke his first line and waited. Glenna stood, staring into the middle distance, saying nothing.

"Cut!" the director called.

Barry spoke his line and waited. Glenna stood very still for a moment, then fainted.

50

Rick sat next to Glenna, who was stretched out on a sofa in her trailer dressing room, and held her hand. The makeup lady had put a cold compress on her forehead.

"Give us a minute," he said to the makeup lady, and when she had gone, he tapped his fingers lightly on Glenna's cheek. "Come on, baby, wake up," he said. "It's just me. There's nobody else here." He knew Dr. Judson would be there soon, and he wanted to talk to her before the doctor gave her anything.

Glenna's eyelids fluttered, and she finally was able to focus on Rick's face. "I'm sorry," she said.

"Nothing to be sorry about," Rick replied. "The doctor's going to take a look at you in a few minutes, and then we'll see if you feel like working any more today."

"I'll be fine in a few minutes," she murmured.

"We have to talk before the doctor gets here."

"What about?"

"About Stampano. I know he's back in town."

Tears spilled from her eyes. "I don't want to talk about it."

"Listen to me, Glenna. We're going to have to face this and deal with it, or it will never end."

"I don't know what you're talking about."

"I've seen the photograph," he said.

She turned toward him and sat up on one elbow. "That's not possible."

"I assure you, I've seen it."

She fell back onto the sofa. "I'll move out today," she said. "I know how you must feel."

"Sweetheart, the only thing I feel is love for you. If you'll trust me, I'll handle this."

"How can you handle it?"

"First, you have to tell me everything that's happened, then I'll know what to do." He handed her a box of tissues.

She wiped her eyes and blew her nose. "Do you have to know the details?"

"Yes, that's important."

It took her a moment to screw up her courage. "It started with your predecessor and his wife."

"The Keans."

"Yes. I met them in the commissary shortly after I was signed by Centurion. They were very kind to me, and they invited me out for dinner at a restaurant in Malibu."

"Go on."

"When we got to the restaurant, Stampano was waiting at our table, and the Keans introduced us. He was very charming, and I was enjoying our evening. After dinner, he insisted that

315

we have a cognac. I declined, but he persisted, so I had, maybe, half the drink. A couple of minutes later, I began to feel oddly, and the Keans said I should go home and lie down. They helped me to their car, and I guess I passed out. The next thing I remember, I woke up in a motel room, on the bed. I was naked, and so was Stampano. The Keans were getting dressed.

"I asked what was going on, but they ignored me, then the Keans left me alone with Stampano. He told me to get some sleep and he'd come back for me, then he got dressed and left. I tried to get out of bed, but I couldn't, and I passed out again. When I woke up I felt terrible, and it was mid-morning. Nobody was there. I got dressed and walked to the motel office, and they called a taxi to take me home. I missed a photo session that morning at the studio.

"I didn't hear from them for a couple of days, then when I came home from the studio, an envelope had been shoved under the door. There were half a dozen photographs of me in bed with Stampano and the Keans, most of them close-ups of me that didn't reveal any other faces. I burned them and flushed the ashes down the toilet. Then, later that evening, Stampano phoned.

"He sounded shocked when I told him about the pictures, and he said we must have been photographed from the room next door through some kind of mirror. He said he would get to the bottom of it.

"The next day, as I was leaving for work, he turned up at the bungalow. He said he had been to the motel and had found out how the pictures were taken, and he implied that he had beaten up the motel owner. Then he said he had gotten a blackmail note. Whoever had taken the pictures wanted money from all of us. He asked me how much I could raise.

"I drove to the studio and went to John Kean's office and told him about the conversation with Stampano. He said he'd gotten the same letter."

"Did you see either letter?"

"No, but Stampano and Kean both told the same story. Kean said he was scrambling to get together as much money as he could and that I should do the same. I asked how much, and he said whoever was blackmailing us wanted fifty thousand dollars. I was stunned. I had inherited some money from my father when he died, but I had spent some of it to support myself after I came out here and started looking for movie work. Kean said he thought he could raise ten thousand by borrowing on his house and asked how much I could come up with.

"I was a fool, I know, but I told him I might be able to get twenty-five thousand. He said he would talk to Stampano and see if he could come up with the rest."

"Did you ask him or Stampano how you came to be in the motel in the first place?"

"Of course, and they both said I was enthusiastic about the idea after we had left the restaurant."

"So did you give him the money?"

"I gave him twenty-two thousand dollars. It was all I had left."

"What happened then?"

"Stampano called me a couple of days later and asked where the money was, that the blackmailer was threatening to send the photographs to Eddie Harris. I told him that I had given it to Kean, and he hung up. A few days after that, both the Keans were dead. The police said John had shot his wife, then himself."

"Did you call the police?"

"No, I was afraid to."

"When did you hear from Stampano again?"

"About a week after the Keans died. He said Kean had stolen the money I gave him and nobody could find it, and that the blackmailer was still after us, that he was going to send the photographs to the studios and the gossip columnists and the movie magazines."

"And he wanted more money."

"Yes. He said he had already given the blackmailer twenty-five thousand dollars, and I had to come up with as much before he would give us the negatives. I told him that I was broke, that all I had was my salary from my contract.

"He finally said that he would pay the other twenty-five thousand, but that I would have to pay him back. I agreed to that. Then he took me out to dinner and told me that he now had the negatives, and had burned the ones with him or the Keans in them, and that unless I started giving him money every week, he would go to Eddie Harris. When I didn't give him enough, he came to the bungalow, held me down and injected me with something, and that was the last thing I remembered until I woke up in Dr. Judson's clinic with my wrists bandaged."

"Thank you for being frank with me about all this. First of all, you're going to get back your twenty-two thousand dollars. I found it locked in Kean's safe in the office when I came to work, along with a photograph of the four of you. I haven't told anyone about it. It seems obvious that Kean was in on the blackmailing scheme from the start and that he tried to hold out on Stampano."

"You think Stampano killed the Keans?"

"Yes, or he had it done. And when he thought he had gotten all he could from you, he tried to kill you, too, so that you could never prosecute him for blackmail. Now we can have him arrested, on your testimony."

"Oh, Rick, I can't testify against him. If any of this becomes public, I'm finished, don't you see?"

She was right. "All right, we'll see that it doesn't become public."

"How are you going to do that?"

"Leave it to me. Did you hear from him yesterday?"

"Yes, he said he wanted all the money in three

319

days, or he would send the photographs to everybody in town."

"How did he tell you to get in touch with him?"

"He gave me a phone number. It's on a pad on my dressing table."

Dr. Judson rapped on the door, then came in.

Rick took him aside for a moment. "She's very upset about something, but don't ask her about it."

"Do you want me to give her a sedative?"

"Yes. I think she needs the rest. I'll call off the rest of the day's shooting, but tomorrow she will want to work. I'll want you on the set early in the morning."

Judson nodded and went to work.

Rick took her hand and kissed it. "You get some rest. I'll come back later today."

"All right," she said.

Rick took Stampano's phone number from Glenna's dressing table, told the director to wrap for the day and to be ready to shoot the following morning, then he left the soundstage and went to look for Eddie Harris.

51

Rick got into an electric cart and headed for the administration building. Halfway there he nearly ran into Eddie Harris in another cart at an intersection. Rick waved him down.

"Jesus, you're driving fast," Eddie said. "You could have killed me."

"Sorry about that, but we have to talk."

"Problems on *Caper*? I thought everything was going smoothly." He got into Rick's cart.

Rick drove a block over to the New York street set, which was not being used that day, then stopped. "Stampano's back, and this time it's bad."

"Oh, shit. We've got to do something about that bastard."

"You're right about that." Rick told him the whole story from the beginning.

"You mean you've had that photograph since you came to work here?"

"Yes, but for a long time I had no idea who the girl was. I'd never seen Glenna's face until that night at Ciro's, when she sang with Artie Shaw."

"I think it's time to call Al," Eddie said.

"I'm not sure that's the way to go," Rick replied. "Not yet, anyway. He may be in this with Jack Dragna or Ben Siegel, and they may have access to the photographs."

"You mean, you want to pay the son of a bitch? That won't work. He'll just keep coming back for more. That's what blackmailers always do."

"We may have to pay him, as a last resort."

"I take it you have a plan."

"Sort of. Stampano has the negatives, but I think he would have destroyed the shots that had the Keans in them. I have one that shows the Keans and Stampano with Glenna, and, with Glenna's testimony about the twenty-two thousand that Kean was holding back from Stampano, that would give him a motive for murdering the Keans, something the police could act on."

"But if Stampano is prosecuted, Glenna would have to testify, and her public testimony would have the same effect as the worst Stampano could do."

"If what I want to do works, he won't be prosecuted, and we'll get back the negatives."

"But we'll never know how many prints he's made."

"Maybe not. All we can do is to make it extremely unprofitable for him to do anything with them."

"I don't know, Rick."

"Eddie, if you have a better idea, tell me what it is and I'll do it."

Eddie sighed. "I don't have a better idea. What do you need from me?"

"I need the studio still photographer to make some copies of the photograph of Stampano, Glenna and the Keans — I'll cut Glenna's face out of it before I give it to him — and I'll need five five-thousand-dollar bills that can't be traced back to us. And I'll need Al."

"Five James Madisons," Eddie muttered. "I think I know where I can get them."

"If you go to Centurion's bank and ask for them, there'll be a record that the police can check, if something goes wrong."

"No, I know another way."

"Good. You'll need to get them today, tomorrow morning at the latest."

"I can do that. I'll call you when I've got them, but I want to know what to do with them."

Rick gave him a rough outline of his plan, and Eddie agreed.

Rick looked at his watch. "I've got a lot to do. I'd better get going. Send the money over to my office when you get it, and let the photographer know I'm coming."

Eddie got back into his cart and drove back toward the administration building. Rick found a phone and called Ben Morrison at the LAPD.

"Ben, can I buy you a drink at Jimmy's this

323

afternoon? It's something I don't want to talk about on the phone."

"Sure."

"Five o'clock?"

"Sure."

"See you then." Then he called Tom Terry and invited him, too. Rick hung up and went back to his office. He opened his safe, took out the envelope with the photograph in it, found some scissors and cut Glenna's head out of it. He burned that part of the photograph in an ashtray, then put the eight-by-ten glossy in an envelope and drove to the studio still photographer's office. He took the man into his photo lab and handed him the photograph.

"I want you to make ten copies of this," he said. "Wipe it down before you shoot it, then I want to watch you develop the film and make the prints."

"Okay. I can make an eight-by-ten contact negative and print from that. It'll take about an hour."

Rick looked at his watch. "Go to it," he said. "An hour is all I've got."

He watched the work being done, then put the new prints and the original, along with the contact negative, into an envelope and left. He went back to his office and put the photographs in his safe and locked it, then he got his handcuffs from a desk drawer. He checked the ammo in the little .45 and stuck it in his shoulder holster, cocked and locked. He walked out to Jenny's desk.

"I'm going to be out for the rest of the day," he said to her. "If Eddie Harris sends over an envelope, put it in my safe. The envelope is very important."

"Gee, can I look inside?"

"If you open it, it'll explode."

He got into his car and headed for Malibu.

52

It was a pleasant day, and with the top down, he soaked up the Southern California sun as he drove down to Santa Monica and peeled off on the Pacific Coast Highway.

Malibu was a small community of beach houses scattered along miles of beach, some of them widely separated, so the Pacific was easily seen and enjoyed in the gaps. He saw half a dozen FOR SALE signs along the way, and it occurred to him that, if he ever got far enough ahead to start investing in real estate, buying a lot out here might be a good place to begin.

He drove past the little business district, which consisted of a filling station, a grocery store, a hardware store and not much else, and finally came to the Moon Rise Motel. He knew the place. It had a reputation for renting rooms by the hour, as well as by the night, no questions asked. At this hour of the day the place was pretty much deserted, so he figured he wouldn't be disturbed. He parked out front and walked into the little office at the end of the row of rooms. A man in shirtsleeves and a necktie sat behind the counter at a desk.

"What can I do you for?" the man asked.

Rick looked at the business license hanging on the wall nearby. "Are you Melvin Carson?" he asked.

"That's me. If you're selling something . . ."

"I'm not selling, I'm buying."

Carson looked at him narrowly. "Buying what?"

"Information."

"Information about what?"

"Let me lay it out for you, Melvin," Rick said, retrieving a fifty-dollar bill from his pocket and laying it on the counter. "That's two weeks' rent for any room in the place."

Carson looked interested. "So?"

Rick produced his lieutenant's badge, showed him the handcuffs and gave the man a hard look. "Here's the alternative," he said. "Arrest, trial and conviction in a blackmailing scheme."

"What are you talking about?" Carson asked indignantly.

"Let's you and I take a walk. Come on."

Carson got up and lifted the flap of the counter. "Where we going?"

"We're going to look at the two rooms my suspect rents when he wants to take pictures."

"Now wait a minute, mister . . ."

"Lieutenant."

"Lieutenant, then. You're a little out of your jurisdiction, aren't you?"

"I'm a deputy sheriff, too."

"Well, you ain't got nothing on me."

Rick slapped the man across the face with his open hand. "I don't want to hear one more word of denial out of you, Melvin, because I've got a stack of photographs in my desk drawer that shows a lot of detail about the furnishings of one of your rooms, and I've got a witness, a victim, who is ready to testify in court that she was brought to this place against her will. Now, do you want a piece of a kidnapping and black-mailing charge? Because you're going to do the same time as the other guy."

"Which other guy is that?" Carson asked.

"That's Chick Stampano," Rick said. "Why? You got any other 'business partners'?"

"Look, that guy is connected, you know what I mean?"

"His connections are nothing compared to mine. I'm connected to the district attorney and to the warden at San Quentin. How does twenty years sound?"

"You're putting me in a spot, Lieutenant."

"That's exactly what I'm doing, Melvin. Now, which room did Stampano use?"

"Down at the end," Carson muttered, taking his passkey from his pocket. He led the way to the last room in the row and opened the door.

Rick followed him into the room and had a look around. It was seedy but clean, and the fur-niture could have been worse. He walked over to the mirror over the dresser, facing the bed, and peered into it, then he lifted it off the wall and had a look behind it. There was a hole in the wall, about four inches in diameter. Rick held the mirror up and looked at the reverse side. He could see clearly right through it. "Very cute," he said.

"Look, I didn't do that, and I don't know who did."

"Let's take a look next door." He followed Carson into the next room and found an identical setup. "Very nice. You can shoot from either room into the other."

"I swear I didn't know nothing about that."

"Let's go back to your office, Melvin." He situated Carson at his desk. "I'll bet you've got some stationery with the motel's name on it, haven't you?"

"Yessir."

"Get out a couple of sheets."

Carson opened a desk drawer and removed some stationery.

"Now, I want you to write me an account of how Chick Stampano came out here and made his deal with you. I want to know how many times he came, and who came with him, and don't leave anything out."

"Look," Carson said, "I'd like to help, but that guy wouldn't think twice about killing me."

"He can't kill you from San Quentin, so don't worry about it. Anyway, I'm sure Stampano threatened you in some way to get you to do this awful thing. Maybe he even beat you up."

"Well, yeah, that's how it happened."

Rick stood over him and supervised a first draft of his statement, then made him make a clean copy.

"Your fifty is on the counter, Melvin," Rick said, "and it would be a very big mistake for you to get in touch with Stampano, you understand?"

"Yessir, Lieutenant," Carson said.

"Enjoy your time as a free man, Melvin, and remember, it could come to an end at any time if you screw around with me."

"I won't say a word, Lieutenant."

"And don't leave town." That always sounded good.

"No, sir."

Rick got back into his car and drove back toward Santa Monica. At the place where the Pacific Coast Highway met Sunset Boulevard, he pulled into a parking lot next to a public beach, parked and got out. The beach was doing a little business today, with a lifeguard on duty and a few dozen people sleeping in the sun or bathing. There was a small brick building with a flat roof, situated maybe eight feet above the beach, that housed a men's room at one end and a ladies' at the other, and next to it stood two public telephone booths. He made a note of the numbers.

He turned around and looked at the hillside behind him. The houses were close together here. There was no really good spot. He turned and looked at the little building again, then he dragged over an empty garbage can, turned it upside down, climbed on top of it and had a look at the low roof. There was a parapet about eighteen inches high. That would do, he thought.

He had one more look at the view from the building down to the beach, then he got into his car and headed for Melrose Avenue, where he had two appointments to keep.

53

Rick got to Jimmy's before the others. He went to the pay phone and called Al, across the street in his gun shop.

"Hi, Al, it's Rick Barron."

"How are you, Rick?"

"Just fine."

"You enjoying my little .45?"

"Well, I haven't killed anybody with it yet, but you never know. You going to be around the shop for a while?"

"I close at six."

"Wait for me until I show up, will you? There's something I want to talk to you about."

"Yeah, sure."

Rick thanked him and hung up, in time to see Ben Morrison and Tom Terry walk in together.

"You two know each other?" he asked them, shaking hands.

"We've met a couple of times," Morrison said.

Rick took them to a booth in back. "What are you drinking?"

"Some of that twelve-year-old scotch, if

you're buying," Morrison said.

"Same here," Tom said.

Rick got the drinks and brought them back to the booth. They raised their glasses.

"Now, what's up?" Morrison asked.

"Stampano." He gave them a brief rundown on Glenna's experience with the man, then he showed them the motel owner's statement and the photograph of Stampano with the Keans and Glenna, with her face cut out. "He wants twenty-five grand for the negatives."

"You going to pay?" Tom asked.

"I haven't decided yet. Ben, do you think you could get a conviction of Stampano on the murder of the Keans and the kidnapping of Glenna with this evidence?"

"No, I don't," Morrison said. "All right, sure, he's got a motive for the Keans, what with their holding out on him and all, but I can't put him at the scene, and the guy in charge of that investigation says there's no physical evidence. As for the kidnapping, the motel owner's statement was written under duress, right?"

"Sort of."

"So we're nowhere."

"I thought so," Rick said.

"So why are we here?"

"If I can't get the guy sent up, then I want to make him harmless."

"And how are you going to do that?"

"I think Glenna hasn't been his only victim," Rick said. "My guess is that he's got photos and negatives of other actresses from other studios and that he's making very nice money from it. But none of them is ever going to testify against him. What I want is for you two guys, with whatever help you need, to steal the material from him while I keep him busy."

"You know where he's keeping them?" Tom asked.

"I think in one of four places," Rick said. "His home, his office at the liquor distributor's or the office at the Trocadero."

"That's only three."

"The fourth is a darkroom somewhere on the premises of the Trocadero."

"Why do you think that?"

"Where is Stampano going to get the film developed? He can't take it to a drugstore or to a photo lab — they'd call the cops as soon as they saw what was on the film. But Ben Siegel runs the Trocadero, and there's a woman there who goes around taking pictures of the guests, then developing them on-site."

"Sounds good," Morrison admitted.

"You know where Stampano lives?"

"Yeah. He's got a house up in the Hollywood Hills, not all that far from your place."

"Good."

"I don't think the liquor distributor is a good spot to search, though," Ben said. "Stampano doesn't have an office there, and I've never known him even to visit the place."

"Okay, then we're down to three spots."

334

"When do you want this done?"

"Probably at dawn tomorrow morning."

"Well, there won't be anybody at the Trocadero at that hour, but how are you going to get Stampano out of his house?"

"You leave that to me. I want you to stake out his place from about five o'clock tomorrow morning, and as soon as you see him leave the house, get in there."

"Do you know where he keeps the prints and negatives?"

"My guess is he has a safe, so I want you to take a safecracker with you. You know Hans?"

"The little German guy? Sure. Will he do it?"

"Show him a badge, and he'll do it." Rick peeled off five hundred dollars and gave it to Morrison. "Give Hans a hundred, and you guys split the rest."

"Okay."

"I'll call you tonight and confirm that I have Stampano set up."

"Okay."

"And, Ben, Tom: Don't get any ideas about hanging onto some of what you find for entertainment purposes, you understand me?"

"Rick, you wound me," Ben said.

"I want all of it, so that I'll know it's been destroyed."

"Of course."

"How you going to get Stampano out of the house?"

"I'm going to offer him money."

"That ought to do it."

"Okay, fellas, go home and wait for my call." He got out his notebook and wrote down two phone numbers. "And when you've finished the job at all three places, call me at one of these numbers. Let it ring once, then hang up. Then call again and let it ring twice and hang up. Then I'll know you were successful. If you don't find the stuff, just let the phone ring until I pick it up, and that may take a lot of rings."

"Whatever you say, Rick."

Rick tossed off the rest of his drink. "I've already paid for another round, so take your time." He shook hands with them, then left Jimmy's and walked across the street to Al's gun shop. The lights were still on.

Rick let himself into the shop and looked around. Al waved from his desk at the rear of the shop. He was the only one in the place. Rick locked the door and turned around the CLOSED sign, then walked to the rear.

"Have a seat," Al said. "You want a drink?"

"I just had one, thanks."

"What's up?"

"Let me get right to the point: Eddie Harris has told me I can call on you for, ah, extracurricular work."

"He did?"

"He did, and I need some done."

Al regarded him evenly, then he sat back in his chair. "Who do you want killed?"

"Nobody yet, I hope. But I need you just the same. What kind of shot are you with a rifle?"

"I can shoot the eye out of an owl at three hundred yards," Al said. "If it ain't too windy and I can choose my weapon."

Rick explained what he wanted done. "What kind of weapon would you use?"

"For a long-range kill?"

"No, for short range — say, twenty-five yards, and to frighten, not kill, unless it becomes necessary."

Al beckoned for him to follow, then led him downstairs to the basement, where he had a firing range. He took a big rifle from a rack and handed it to Rick. "I'd use that," he said.

"Pretty heavy," Rick said, hefting it. "What is it?"

"A BAR — Browning Automatic Rifle. The army used it in the last war. It'll fire semiautomatic, or full automatic, five hundred and fifty rounds a minute. Takes a magazine of twenty, fires a 30–06 round. Highly accurate with a scope, highly frightening without one, on auto."

"Sounds perfect," Rick said. He told Al what he wanted done. "Here are the signals I'm going to use." He showed Al the signs.

"Got it."

"And if anybody so much as points a gun at me, kill him."

"I'll want a grand to be there. If I have to kill anybody, it's five grand apiece."

"I'll bring cash," Rick said. He gave Al a full briefing, then left the shop and returned to the studio.

Glenna was still sleeping peacefully, and he did not disturb her. He went to his own office on the stage and dialed Stampano's number.

"Hello?"

"This is a friend of Glenna," Rick said. "She's asked me to deliver your money."

"It's Barron, isn't it?"

"That's right. If you want the money, there are rules to follow. Deviate from the rules and you don't get paid. Is that clear?"

"Tell me your proposition."

"There's a public beach where Sunset ends at the Pacific Coast Highway. Know it?"

"Yeah."

"You show up there tomorrow morning at six o'clock sharp, and I mean sharp. Come alone. You park at the extreme south end of the parking lot, walk down to the beach and walk north on the sand. I'll be walking south on the beach. Got that?"

"Why the beach?"

"So that I can see you're alone. You bring all the negatives and prints of any photographs showing Glenna. I'll bring twenty-five grand. You hand me the prints and negatives, I hand you the money. We both walk away. Glenna never hears from you again and no photograph of her taken at the motel is ever published any-where. That's it. Take it or leave it."

There was a silence.

"Well?"

"I'm coming armed."

"That's okay, so am I, but you'd better not have anything in your hand at any time."

"I don't like the sound of all this."

"Then go fuck yourself."

"All right, all right," Stampano said quickly. "I'll be there."

"At six a.m., before there's anybody on the beach. Don't be late." Rick hung up. He checked on Glenna again, then ordered dinner sent over from the commissary.

He slept on the floor next to Glenna that night.

54

Rick woke at four a.m. without an alarm clock. Glenna was still asleep, and he didn't disturb her. He went to his office, showered and got Eddie Harris's money from the safe.

He examined the five five-thousand-dollar bills closely, since he had never seen one before. James Madison's picture was, indeed, on the notes. He stacked them together squarely, then took some scissors from his desk and cut them in two, lopping off the right-hand one-third of each. Then he took cellophane tape and joined them together again and returned them to the envelope.

He checked his .45 again, put on his coat, put the money in a pocket, then went to his car and left the studio. He was parked at the north end of the beach lot at five-thirty. It was still dark and very foggy.

He got out of the car, walked over to the little building housing the toilets and checked both pay phones to see that they had a dial tone. "Al?" he called. "You there?" He couldn't do this without Al.

Al's voice came from the roof of the building. "I'm here."

"Can you see the beach in front of you?"

"Just barely. The fog should begin to lift a little when it gets light."

Rick hoped so. He hadn't counted on fog when he'd made his plan. "Okay, I'm going down to the beach." He walked down a flight of concrete steps to the beach, found a rock and sat down on it. The light was slowly coming up, and he could just make out the line where the water met the sand. The tide was low, leaving a wide stretch of wet, packed beach. He waited as patiently as he could, checking his watch frequently. It was at times like this that he missed smoking.

At five minutes to six, he heard a car, then the engine stopped and a car door slammed, then another. Stampano hadn't come alone.

Rick got up and walked down to where the sand was wet and waited. The light was coming up fast, now. He unbuttoned his jacket, reached inside it and unsnapped the thumb break on the shoulder holster, made sure the gun was cocked and locked.

Then, as he gazed into the fog, a single figure materialized. Stampano kept walking, then stopped about ten feet from Rick.

"Okay, let's do it," Stampano said.

"Tell the other guy to come up here and stand next to you, where I can see him, and tell him his hands better be empty."

341

Stampano thought about it, then turned and called out something to somebody. A moment later a large man appeared, his hands empty but his jacket unbuttoned. He came and stood next to Stampano.

"All right," Stampano said, "I'm here."

"I told you to come alone," Rick said. "You broke the rules."

"I'm here. Let's get this done."

Rick opened the right side of his jacket so that Stampano could see there was no gun there, then he reached into the inside pocket and took out the envelope. He removed the five bills, spread them out and held them up. "Five five-thousand-dollar bills," he said. "Let me see the prints and negatives."

Stampano reached under his jacket for the small of his back.

"Careful," Rick said. "Do it slowly, and don't show me any hardware."

Stampano slowly produced a large brown envelope and held it up. "Here they are."

"Show me."

Stampano reached into the envelope and pulled out some eight-by-tens. "Six prints," he said. He replaced the prints and pulled out half a dozen negative strips. "Here are the negatives; twenty-four exposures."

"Stand very still," Rick said. "Either of you moves a muscle, you're dead."

The big man's hand began to move inside his jacket.

Rick raised his left hand and pointed one finger at the sky. Half a second later, a burst of automatic fire erupted, making a row of explosions in the sand between Rick and the other two men. They froze.

"You bastard," Stampano said.

"You brought backup, I brought backup," Rick said. "Now I want you to walk over to me and hand me the envelope. I want to inspect the goods. If they pass inspection, you'll get your money." He pointed at the other man. "And if you move a muscle, your head will explode." He beckoned to Stampano.

Stampano walked slowly forward and stood three feet from Rick, who held out his left hand. Stampano gave him the envelope.

Rick opened it, looked at the prints, which were all of Glenna and Stampano, but with his face cropped out. He held the negatives up to the increasingly bright sky. They were all duplicates of the print of Glenna. None showed the Keans or Stampano's face.

"Take five giant steps backward," Rick said.

"Gimme the money."

"In a few minutes. We're going to wait for a phone call."

"A phone call? What are you talking about?"

"Shut up and walk backward if you want the money."

Stampano backed up. "What's going on?"

"Be patient, Chick. We'll be done in a few minutes."

The three men stood on the beach, staring at each other. Ten minutes passed, then another five. Twenty minutes were gone before Rick heard a phone ring once, then stop. He held up his hand. "Stand still." A moment later, the phone rang twice, then stopped. Rick smiled. "All right, Chick, come and get the money."

Stampano walked up and held out his hand. "Gimme," he said.

Rick opened his envelope and removed the print of the four people, with Glenna's face cut out, and handed it to Stampano. "You cheap little chisler," Rick said, "you held out on me."

"Where'd you get this?" Stampano demanded.

"It shows you with the Keans, doesn't it? And only a few days before you killed them. This photograph, along with Glenna's testimony, can put you in the death chamber up at Quentin."

"Sez you."

Rick took the five bills from the envelope, ripped them apart where they had been taped, and handed the short ends to Stampano. "Here's all the money you're going to get for now. A year from today, you'll get the rest — on the following conditions: One, Glenna doesn't hear from you again, and neither does *any other actress* in town. Two, none of the photographs of Glenna or any of the other girls is circulated or published. I'd better not ever even hear of a rumor to that effect. I'm not going to ask you for the rest of the prints and negatives because I already have them. That's what the phone call was about."

"What do you mean?"

"You're all cleaned out, Chick, but there's more. If Glenna or the other girls hears from you again, *ever*, you're dead. You get a bullet in the brain. If any of them, or me, for that matter, stubs a toe, or gets so much as a flat tire, you're dead. If I or any of them ever walks into a restaurant or a club and you don't leave immediately, you're dead. Do you understand everything I've said?"

Stampano stood, his jaw working, but speechless.

"Or I can just lift one finger, and you die right here on this beach, right now, you and your man. You hear me, Chick?"

Stampano still didn't speak.

"Say it."

"I hear you," he finally managed to say.

"Now go get in your car and drive away from here. And remember this: You ever mess with anybody in this town again, Ben Siegel won't be able to help you; Charley Luciano won't be able to help you. You'll be done."

Stampano turned around and walked down the beach, followed by his man. The fog had lifted, so Rick could see them all the way to their car, see them drive away.

"Okay, Al!" he shouted. "Come get your money, and let's go home!"

55

Rick drove back to the studio, to his office, and waited. Ten minutes later, Ben Morrison and Tom Terry showed up with a handful of envelopes.

"You got it all?" Rick asked.

"We cleaned out two safes, one in Stampano's house, one in Ben Siegel's office at the Trocadero and a locked filing cabinet in the photographer's darkroom. You were right, Glenna wasn't the only girl he was blackmailing. There's pictures of Lara Taylor and some others."

"Did you pay Hans?"

"We did."

"Here's another five hundred apiece for a job well done." Rick doled out hundreds. "Ben, thanks for your help. I still want you to keep an eye on Stampano, especially for the next month or so."

"Will do."

"I need to talk to Tom for a minute, so I'll say goodbye." They shook hands and Morrison left.

"Sit down, Tom."

Terry sat down.

"Tom, it looks as though I might be moving up at the studio pretty soon. How would you like my job?"

Terry grinned. "I'd like that just fine."

"Don't say anything to anybody yet. I still need to get Eddie Harris's approval, and that may take some time, but I think we can get this done by the end of the year. You'll like the money, I promise."

Terry left, grinning broadly, and Rick began opening envelopes. Stampano had been a busy boy. He had photographs of half a dozen actresses at different studios. Rick locked all of them in his safe, except those of Glenna and the Keans, then he left his office and went to the soundstage and Glenna's trailer. She was just waking up as he came in.

"You slept well," he said.

"I must have been out for nearly twenty-four hours," she replied, kissing him. "What's happened?"

"We're done with Stampano," he said, holding up the envelope. "I have all the prints and negatives. Do you want to see them?"

She shook her head.

Rick retrieved a steel wastebasket and set fire to the envelope, and they both watched it reduced to ash. "Now all you have to worry about is doing good work on these last scenes," he said.

She stood up and came into his arms. "I will, I promise."

"This is going to be a good film," he said, "and with this success on top of the musical, you're going to be the newest star in this town."

He watched her work that morning, then, satisfied that she was doing well, he went back to his office, retrieved the photographs of the other actresses and went to see Eddie Harris.

Eddie was at his desk, going through a budget. "How's *Caper* going?" he asked.

"On schedule and a little under budget," Rick said. "We lost a day's shooting, but Glenna is back on the job, and she's looking great."

"How did it go with Stampano?"

Rick handed him the envelope with the five five-thousand-dollar bills. "I gave him a third of the notes and told him he'd get the rest in a year if he behaved himself. Frankly, I don't care whether you give it to him or not. You've got two-thirds of each bill there, and that's enough to take them to the bank. He can't do anything with what he's got, except frame them."

"You think he'll behave himself?"

"I've explained to him that if he doesn't, bad things will happen to him. Do you have any way to get to Luciano?"

"I know somebody who knows somebody who knows him."

"I think he's the key. If you can persuade him to bring Stampano back to New York permanently, then he'll be out of our hair for good."

"He's going to want something from us to do that."

"Tell him we've got the goods to send Stampano to prison for twenty years."

"Do we?"

Rick handed him the envelope with the photographs of the actresses. "My guy took these out of two safes and a filing cabinet in Stampano's house and at the Trocadero while I was talking to Stampano out at the beach."

Eddie went through the envelope quickly. "This is the most appalling stuff I've ever seen," he said. "There are two girls from Metro here, one from RKO, one under contract to David Selznick and one with Sam Goldwyn."

"And they've probably all paid Stampano money."

"I'd love to prosecute the guy, I really would, but I can't see these girls or the studios ever testifying against him."

"He's counting on that, I think, but maybe the threat will keep him in line."

"I hope so."

"You should know that some of those came out of the safe in Ben Siegel's office at the Trocadero, so he's got to be in on this."

"Then I'm going to have to get to Luciano, one way or another."

"That would be a good idea. There's something else I'd like to talk to you about."

Eddie grinned. "You found a property."

Rick nodded.

"I was impressed with how quickly you learned on *Caper*, and I've seen the rough cut to date, so I think you're ready. What do you want to do next?"

"I found a script in your slush pile that I like. It needs some work, though."

"What is it?"

"It's a kind of screwball comedy called *Ready to Go*."

"I remember liking that when I read it, but you're right, it needs work. I'll assign you a writer."

"So, I'm a producer?"

"Just as soon as you can replace yourself."

"I can do that today. Tom Terry was a big help on the Stampano thing. I think he'd do a great job for us."

"Then hire him. Offer him a little less than you're making and let him pick out a car for himself. When can he start?"

"Right away, I should think. I'll call him today."

"Then today, you are a producer, my son. Here's what I have in mind."

Rick listened as Eddie sketched out a production deal, and he liked what he heard.

"But, Rick, you've got to remember that in this business you're only as good as your last movie."

"I'll keep that in mind."

"I'll find you an office in this building and a new secretary."

"I'd like to bring Jenny with me, if that's all right."

"Okay, I'll find Tom Terry a new secretary."

"And if you'd still like him to move into your guest house, I think he'd like that."

"Absolutely. Suzanne will like him."

The two men shook hands, and Rick walked out of the building on a large cloud. He headed back to the soundstage to tell Glenna the news.

56

The next months went briskly and happily for Rick and Glenna. He finished shooting on *Caper* and simultaneously worked on the post-production for that film and the pre-production for *Ready to Go*. He discovered that he loved editing and spent many hours in a darkened room with an editing machine and an editor.

They went out often, to Ciro's and Mocambo, or dined at Chasen's and the Brown Derby. The columnists, particularly Hedda Hopper, were kind to them, and Rick's new sobriquet — the Prince of Beverly Hills — stuck, and was referred to whenever they were mentioned in the press. He also got good ink on his elevation to producer. He had become a player.

They were taking Rick's dad to dinner a couple of times a month, and Jack and Glenna were practically in love with each other. Jack had never been one for dining out a lot, and Rick was happy to have more time with him.

Glenna's musical came out in the spring, and they attended a gala Hollywood premiere at

Grauman's Chinese Theater. She got spectacular reviews in the papers, and fan mail began to come in, first a trickle, then a torrent. Rick looked forward to the premiere of *Caper*, which would have huge momentum following the success of the musical, and he hoped for an Academy Award nomination for Glenna's performance

Rick continued to receive letters from Clete Barrow, usually through Montreal, but sometimes through Gander, Newfoundland. Clete had found friends among pilots who were traveling to Canada in order to ferry bombers back across the sea, and who would transport his letters that far, then mail them, avoiding the hazards of mail sent via the North Atlantic, where the submarine war was in full force.

Clete exhibited a boyish enthusiasm for everything he was learning in the Royal Marines, and especially for commando tactics, which had yet to be used in the war. Clark Gable passed on a couple of letters from David Niven, too, which were hilariously funny.

In early May a letter came from Clete, describing his regiment's "foray into Norway," as he called it, in which they fought bravely, but received "a bloody nose" and had to be evacuated. "It is the first time we've seen action," Clete said, "and as badly as it turned out, we learnt what it was like to fight and gained experience that will be valuable to us in days to come. My men were all pleasantly surprised to find that they were still alive, and that did wonders for morale."

At the end of May, the Battle of Dunkirk ensued, during which more than 300,000 British troops were taken off the beaches of France in a flotilla of ships, big and small, and returned to England to fight again.

In early June, another letter came from Clete, written before Dunkirk, enthusing that Churchill had been made prime minister, after Chamberlain had gone through a vote of confidence in Parliament that he had won, but in which so many Tories had voted against him or had abstained that his position as prime minister was no longer tenable. "There's a whole new attitude here, now that we have a real leader in command," Clete said. "We'll be off to France soon, is my guess."

The next day, Rick was at his desk, having completed shooting on *Ready to Go*, and working on the budget for his next film, when Jenny came in with a telegram from London. Rick ripped it open and read the short message:

BARROW KILLED AT DUNKIRK
STOP LETTER TO FOLLOW.
NIVEN

Rick felt as if he had been standing in surf and hit by a very large wave. The breath was taken from him and he seemed to tumble, head over heels, through a montage of dinners out with

Clete, of fishing on the Rogue River, of laughing at anything and everything.

He remembered what Clete had said that night at Jimmy's, that half the young men in the place were going to die in the coming war. It had never occurred to Rick that Clete would be among them, let alone among the first.

After a few frozen minutes, Rick got up and walked down the hall to Eddie Harris's office, where a meeting was in progress. He walked into the room without knocking. Someone was in the middle of a budget presentation, but Eddie took one look at Rick's face and held up a hand for silence. "What is it, Rick?" he asked.

Rick handed him the telegram. Eddie read it and reacted as though he had been slapped across the face. Apparently unable to speak, he passed the cable around the table, which was filled with people who had worked with Clete over the years.

"We'll resume this later," Eddie finally said to the group. When they had left, he motioned for Rick to sit down, then buzzed his secretary. "Clete Barrow is dead," he said. "Have maintenance lower the flag in front of the building to half mast, then come in here with your pad."

"I don't think I would have believed it if the telegram hadn't come from Niven," Rick said.

Eddie's secretary came in, looking shocked, and sat down. "Yes, sir?"

"Take this down," Eddie said. " 'The studio has received reliable word that Clete Barrow died in the Battle of Dunkirk.

" 'When war broke out in Europe, Clete did not hesitate. He went home at the first opportunity and rejoined the regiment with which he had served some years ago. We hated losing him, but it was no less than we would have expected of him.

" 'A patriot has died and a brilliant career has been cut short. Everyone at Centurion Studios mourns his loss.'

"Messenger that to the columnists, wait an hour, then call the AP and UP and read it to them. Then run off some copies and post it on every bulletin board on the lot. Get some help and call all the soundstages and shops and tell everybody to shut down — the studio is closed for the rest of the day."

The woman left in tears.

"I never had a brother," Rick said, "but I feel as though I've lost one."

"Same here," Eddie said, then stood up. "I can't work anymore. I'm going home. I suggest you do the same."

Rick went back to his office, broke the news to Jenny and told her to go home, then he sat in his office, alone, for a few minutes and tried to compose himself. Then he got into an electric cart and began looking for Glenna, stopping whenever he saw someone he knew to break the news. Everywhere he went, people were holding each other and weeping. Clete would be astonished, he thought.

He found Glenna in the costume shop, being fitted for a dress. He told her what had happened.

Glenna sat down heavily in a nearby chair, ripping a seam. "God, but that takes the wind out of your sails, doesn't it?"

Rick nodded.

She stood up and shed the dress, then came and sat in his lap. "I hardly knew him," she said, "and I can only guess how you feel. But he was the most charming man I ever met."

Rick buried his face in Glenna's breasts and cried like a child, while she held his head.

57

It was the first of July before David Niven's letter arrived, postmarked Gander, Newfoundland. Rick saved it until he had a quiet moment alone, then opened it and unfolded the onionskin airmail paper.

My Dear Rick,

I trust that you received my telegram, telling of Clete's death at Dunkirk. I am sorry to have been so blunt, but getting a telegram out of London in wartime can take a while, so brevity is encouraged. The following is what I have put together after speaking with two old chums who served with Clete.

In mid-May, Clete's regiment was sent to Belgium to bolster defenses there. Almost before they could take up positions the Germans attacked the Benelux and low countries, driving them north and toward the French beaches. Clete's regiment fought, if personal accounts can be believed, a brilliant rear-guard action against tanks and over-whelming numbers, taking many casualties, until they finished up at Dunkirk.

The battle there raged for more than a week, as British ships came to take troops off, and they were constantly being strafed by German fighters, as well as bombed. Un-accountably, the Germans withdrew their tanks from action, leaving the battle to their infantry, and this break gave our people time to evacuate many more troops than might have otherwise been possible.

Finally, with what seemed like every small boat from the south coast of England massed off the beaches, something like 320,000 had been taken off, and the figure may have been higher. Clete's company, their numbers re-duced by a third by casualties, were among the last groups off the beach. As Clete, his exec and one other officer were wading out to a small motor cruiser, a Messerschmidt made a low pass, guns ablaze, and Clete took a single round in the neck.

The other two officers got him aboard, and a medic attended him, but he was losing blood rapidly, and the flow could not be stanched. His exec told me that during this time, Clete looked down at his feet and said, 'Damn, these boots were new a month ago.' Those turned out to be his last words. He died before the boat reached England.

His body will be interred on the Duke of

Kensington's estate in a few days, and I will be there to bid him farewell from both you and me.

One final irony: Clete's father, who had been Duke of Kensington for only a few months, died in a motor accident in London at almost precisely the moment when Clete was being taken off the beach at Dunkirk, so Clete was Duke for an hour or so and will be buried as such, next to his father and uncle.

I can hear the old boy laughing now.

With kind regards,
David

Rick laughed, too, through his tears. He sent a copy of the letter to Hedda Hopper, who called him and said she would run it as her column the following day.

That afternoon, Rick heard the news on the car radio: Congress had passed a new Selective Service Act that day, by one vote. All men between nineteen and thirty would have to register for the draft immediately, and inductions would start in the fall.

Rick was driving past the intersection of Hollywood and Vine, and while stopped at the traffic light, he saw a Navy recruiting office with a poster featuring an aircraft carrier landing by a Navy fighter. Impulsively, he parked his car and walked into the office. A dozen young men were filling out forms.

The yeoman at the front desk looked up as he walked in. "Can I help you, sir?" he asked.

"I'd like to speak to someone about flying for the Navy."

"Just a moment, please, sir." The young sailor left his desk, walked to an office at the rear, knocked and stuck his head through the open door. Then he looked at Rick and waved him back. "This is Lieutenant Commander Chelton," the yeoman said, then went back to his desk.

The officer, who appeared to be in his fifties, waved Rick to a chair and offered his hand. "What can I do for you?" he asked.

"I'm Rick Barron." He noted the wings on the man's tunic. "I've read in the papers about this new program you've got for training Navy pilots," Rick said. "I'm interested."

Chelton leaned back in his chair and regarded Rick. "How old are you?" he asked.

"Twenty-nine."

"You look older."

"It's the suit."

"Most of the boys entering the program are nineteen to twenty-two," Chelton said.

"I've got over three thousand hours in about fifteen types," Rick said, "including about two hundred hours of aerobatics."

The officer looked more interested. "We need instructors," he said.

"I'm a lousy instructor. Tried it, was no good at it, don't want to do it again."

"What's your educational background?"

"BA from UCLA and a year of law school."

"What have you been doing since then?"

"I was a cop for eight years. Now I'm a movie producer."

Chelton laughed and shook his head. "Only in LA," he said. "You could land something cushy with the Navy, making training films."

Rick shook his head. "I'm only interested in combat flying."

"Well, I guess maturity is a qualification for the program," he said. "You healthy?"

"Perfectly."

"Think you can keep up with a bunch of kids in physical training?"

"Yep."

"Married?"

"Not yet, but planning to."

"When do you want to go? We've got a new class starting the first of every month."

"Consisting of what?"

"Six months at the naval air station in Pensacola, Florida. If you live through it and don't bust out, you get your wings and a commission, then back to San Diego for advanced instruction and gunnery training and eventual assignment to a carrier."

"I'm not ready yet, but . . ."

Chelton grinned. "But you'll get drafted anyway, right?"

"Right. I heard the news on the radio."

Chelton took a sheaf of papers from his desk.

"Fill these out. I'll keep them in my desk drawer. I'll schedule a physical for later this week, and I'll keep that in my desk drawer, too. We won't mention your flying experience. The instructor's corps would grab you immediately." He handed Rick a card. "Call me when you're ready, and don't wait until you get your draft notice."

Rick filled out the application, made an appointment for the physical and left the recruiting office, feeling better than when he had come in.

58

When Rick got home, he was greeted by Glenna, who was in tears. She threw her arms around him. "I heard the news on the radio," she said. "That's you they're talking about."

"We can't worry about that now. We don't know what's going to happen."

"Let's get married now," Glenna said. They had been talking about this for weeks.

"I don't think that's a good idea," Rick said.

"You thought it was a good idea as recently as yesterday," she said, obviously stung.

He led her to the living room sofa and took her into his arms. "Of course I want to get married," he said. "But we're headed into uncharted waters, here. We don't know what's going to happen, and I think we ought to get a better handle on it before we make that decision."

She pushed back and looked at him. "You're afraid you'll get killed, like Clete, aren't you?"

"No, but it's a possibility. Thousands and thousands of people are going to have to face it."

"I don't want you to talk about even the possibility of your getting killed," she said. "I want to marry you, no matter what, and if you don't tell me right now that's what you want, too, then I'll just go right out and find myself another fella."

Rick laughed. "All right, all right, we'll do it whenever you like."

"Let me finish my picture — that's next month. How about September?"

"Whatever you say. What kind of wedding do you want?"

"I'd just as soon run off to Reno or someplace and do it in the dark," she said, "but Eddie Harris would kill us both."

"You're right about that. He's going to want to do it up for the fan magazines, lots of guests and pictures."

"If he makes us do that, then let's make him pay for the wedding."

"I like the way you think. Eddie's due back from New York tomorrow. I'll talk to him about it."

He didn't tell her about his visit to the Navy recruiting office.

The following morning, before Rick could go to see him, Eddie called him in and told him to sit down.

"How was your flight?" Rick asked. It was the first time Eddie had been coast to coast in the studio's new DC-3.

"Best flight I ever had," Eddie replied. "Good

weather both ways; headwinds weren't too bad coming back."

"I'm glad to hear it. Did you get a lot done?"

"Yes, including seeing Luciano."

"No kidding?"

"I know somebody in New York, never mind who, who knows Meyer Lansky. Lansky arranged a meeting up at Sing-Sing. We met in his cell."

"And what was that like?"

"Big enough for four men, maybe eight. Table and chairs, a real bed, not a bunk. A couple of Italian landscapes on the wall."

"Did he have a phone in the cell?"

"If he did, I didn't see it, but the guards were deferential. They called him 'Mr. Luciano.'"

"And what did you two talk about?"

"You know what we talked about. I ran down our list of grievances about Stampano, but of course he wanted something, too."

"What did he want?"

"He wanted to buy into the studio. He'd been talking to Ben Siegel, of course."

"I hope to God you didn't —"

"Of course not. I'm already dealing with Siegel more than I like, since he's gotten his hooks into the extras' union. I'm not about to take him on as a partner, no matter how legitimate they want to make the deal."

"What did Luciano have to say about Stampano?"

"Oh, he's a bad boy, sometimes, but he's a

good kid at heart. He's the son of a woman Luciano knew when he was younger, dead now. You want my opinion, he's Luciano's bastard. Anyway, he promised her he'd look out for the boy. I suggested he could look out for him better if he was closer to home; say, in New York."

"How'd that go down?"

"He says Siegel needs him on the coast. I don't believe that for a moment. I think Ben would be happy to be rid of him."

"Did you mention that?"

"I sort of alluded to it, but I didn't want to go too far."

"I can understand that. No need to piss him off. Luciano would make a bad enemy."

"He did make one friendly gesture," Eddie said.

"What was that?"

"He said you should watch your ass."

"No kidding?"

"His very words. 'Your boy should watch his ass,' he said."

Rick didn't like that much. "Well, I guess he's a pretty authoritative source."

"Yeah. My impression was, it wasn't coming from him, it was Stampano's personal score to settle. He said he couldn't interfere with that. 'A matter of honor,' as he put it. And another thing: Since some of those photos were found in Siegel's safe, he's got to be involved in the black-mail scheme. And he's not going to like the fact that you sent somebody into his safe."

"Well, I'll just have to deal with it," Rick said. "I'll speak to Al."

"No, at least not yet. I'm not prepared to go that far."

"You going to sit around and wait for Stampano to make the first move? That could be fatal."

Rick shrugged.

"You're at a disadvantage, Rick, waiting for him to move. You won't know where or when; he'll just be there."

"I still go around armed, when I'm not at the studio."

"I think that's the very least you should do. You've got to think about Glenna, too."

"Oh, there was something else I wanted to tell you: Glenna and I are going to be married in September, after she finishes her picture."

Eddie smiled broadly. "That's wonderful news, Rick. Now, I know Glenna's dad is dead, so I want to play father of the bride."

"Right, you can give the bride away."

"More than that, the wedding's on me."

"That's very generous of you, Eddie, but it's not necessary."

"It's necessary for me. Now let's not say any more about it. We'll get Glenna and Suzanne together and have them work it out. I'd suggest having it at our house. It's perfect for a big party."

"Whatever Glenna and Suzanne work out is fine with me. I'm just going to be along for the ride."

"You thought about a honeymoon?"

"Not yet."

"Sol Weinman has a very nice house down in Acapulco that's yours for the asking, and you won't have to ask. We'll send you down there in our new airplane."

"If it's okay with Glenna."

"You get out of here and go talk to her," Eddie said. "Leave the rest to Suzanne and me."

"Eddie, something else I need to talk to you about."

"Shoot."

"You heard about the new draft."

"Yeah, I knew it was coming, I guess."

"I'm not going to let myself get drafted."

Eddie looked alarmed. "You're not going to enlist now, are you?"

"No, but I stopped by a Navy recruiting office today and investigated their flight program. When the draft board starts sniffing around me, that's what I'm going to do."

"I might be able to help with the draft board."

"No. Thank you, but no."

"I understand," Eddie said, sounding resigned.

"I just wanted you to know what's coming."

"I appreciate that. Have you said anything to Glenna?"

"She knows I'm going to have to go. We talked about that, but she doesn't know I've talked to the Navy."

"If you have any trouble getting into the program you want, I know a couple of senators and a few congressmen."

"I don't think that will be necessary, with my flying experience. The only thing that might work against me is my age."

"Your age!"

"Yeah, the Navy thinks I'm pretty old."

They had a good laugh over that.

Rick shook Eddie's hand and went back to his office. He called Glenna and reported on his conversation with Eddie. "What do you think?"

"I think he's right. Leave it to Suzanne and me," she said.

"Just tell me when and where to show up."

"I'll give you at least an hour's notice."

Rick tried to go back to work, but he couldn't think of anything but Stampano. He called Ben Morrison and told him what Luciano had said.

"This is not a good development, Rick," Morrison replied.

"Gee, I didn't think so, either. Have you been keeping an eye on Stampano?"

"Sort of. I'm going to put two guys on him today. In the meantime, you watch your ass."

Rick certainly intended to do that.

59

The summer passed quickly. Glenna finished her picture and was spending nearly all her time with Suzanne Harris, planning the wedding. Rick tried to stay out of the way.

In late August, with the wedding only a couple of weeks away, Rick finished shooting on his film. He called Glenna. "You want to come to a wrap party?" he asked.

"Thanks, but no thanks," she said. "I've got to work on the seating chart for dinner, so I'm sticking close to home."

"I'm going to have to be there," he said. "It's my duty."

"Yeah, sure. Don't tie one on. I don't want to worry about you driving drunk."

"I'll take it easy, don't worry." He hung up and began working through the pile of stuff on his desk. He wouldn't be starting another film until after the honeymoon, but there were still dozens of post-production details to take care of, and he was at his desk until nearly eight o'clock.

He was on his way to the party, locking his office door behind him, when he heard the telephone ring. He ignored it. Whoever it was could wait until tomorrow. He drove over to the soundstage where the party was on and plunged into the merriment.

It was nearly eleven when an assistant director found him. "The studio operator has an important call for you," he said. "I told her to put it on the phone in your production office."

"Thanks." Rick walked across the soundstage to the office he used when shooting and picked up the phone.

"Mr. Barron?"

"Yes."

"I have a call from a Mr. Ben Morrison. May I put it through?"

"Yes, please."

There was a click. "Hello?"

"Rick?"

"Yes, Ben, what's up?"

"I've been trying to find you all evening."

"Ben, what's up?"

"We've lost Stampano."

"What do you mean you've lost him?"

"I've had a man on him ever since he got back to LA, but earlier this evening he went into Schwab's Drugstore and apparently left by the back door, got into another car and disappeared."

"I don't like the sound of that," Rick said. "Can you get a man over to my house right away? Glenna's there alone. I'll start home now."

"I'll have somebody there in ten minutes."

"Thanks, Ben. Call me at home if you hear anything else." He hung up.

"Rick?"

He turned to find the director of his film standing in the doorway.

"Some of us are going over to the Trocadero. Durante's opening tonight, and we can make the midnight show. You want to come?"

"No thanks, Harvey. I've got to get home." He went back to his office in the administration building for something he had forgotten. He slipped into his shoulder holster, checked the .45 and stuck it under his arm.

It was eleven-thirty before he turned into his driveway, and the first thing he saw was a flashing red light illuminating the trees. He sped up and nearly ran into an ambulance parked next to Glenna's car. Two men were bringing a stretcher down the front stairs, led by a police detective.

Rick ran up to him. "What's happened?" he demanded.

"Mr. Barron, I got here half an hour ago and found Miss Gleason on the floor in the living room."

"Is she all right?"

"She's been badly beaten," the man said, "and she's unconscious."

Rick ran to the stretcher and walked alongside

it, taking Glenna's hand. Her face was covered with gauze patches and an ice pack, and a young doctor walked on the other side of the stretcher. "I'm going to the hospital with her," Rick said.

"All right, there's room," the doctor replied.

Rick turned back to the cop. "Call the Judson Clinic. Have them find Dr. Judson and have him meet us at Cedars-Sinai."

"Yes, sir."

Rick got into the ambulance and sat next to the doctor. "How badly hurt is she?" he asked.

"She's had blunt force trauma to the face and the upper body. She has a couple of broken ribs. She's unconscious, but I think she'll come to soon. Don't worry, she's not going to die."

"What was she beaten with? Did you find a weapon?"

"No. My guess is fists."

Rick held Glenna's hand all the way to the hospital, and he wouldn't let go of it until they made him, when they took her in for treatment. He didn't want her to wake up without his being there.

Dr. Judson showed up a few minutes after they arrived at Cedars-Sinai and had a word with the attending physician, then he came to Rick.

"We're going to sedate her, keep her under for at least twenty-four hours."

"Whatever you say, Jim," Rick replied.

"She's stable and doesn't have any life-threatening injuries, so you needn't concern yourself about that."

"I'm glad to hear it."

"You should go home and get some rest, Rick. She's in good hands, and she won't wake up, so there's nothing you can do here."

"I want to see her face," Rick said.

"No, you don't."

"All right, I'll go home." Somebody called a taxi for him, and as soon as he was through the front door he picked up the phone and called Ben Morrison. "It's Rick. Have you found Stampano?"

"No, not yet. I'm sorry, Rick. My man was there in a hurry, but —"

"It's not your fault, Ben. Just find Stampano."

"I'll call you when I do."

"I'll be by the phone." He hung up and looked around. A lamp had been knocked over, and so had the coffee table. He went around straightening up, willing the phone to ring with news of Stampano's location.

Then, suddenly, he knew exactly where to find him. He looked at his watch: just after one a.m. He ran down the stairs to his car, then decided not to take the cream convertible. He'd drive Glenna's black coupe, instead.

He thought of calling Tom Terry, but he wanted to do this alone.

60

Rick sat half a block up Sunset from the Trocadero, waiting. A floodlit sign proclaimed the opening of Jimmy Durante's show. Rick knew that Stampano would not miss an opening at the Trocadero.

Shortly past one o'clock in the morning, a trickle of customers began leaving the club, then a flood, and by one-thirty the crowd had become a trickle again. Then a waiter came out onto the sidewalk and gave the parking attendant a ticket, and a black Cadillac was brought to the door. A moment later, Chick Stampano emerged, escorting a beautiful girl in a sparkling evening gown. They got into the car and drove west on Sunset.

Rick let a couple of cars get between them, then followed. After a few blocks, Stampano turned right, into the Hollywood Hills, and Rick turned, too, switching off his headlights. He could drive into the hills following Stampano's taillights and not be noticed in the rearview mirror.

The Cadillac made a couple more turns, then entered a driveway and drove behind some trees. Rick stopped a hundred yards away, then made a U-turn and parked facing down the steep street. He got out and walked back toward the driveway, looking around for other cars. There were none. The street was deserted at this hour.

He walked up the driveway in time to see the living room lights go on in the house. The Cadillac was parked just outside the garage. Stampano was apparently looking forward to a night in the company of the young woman.

Rick gave him ten minutes, then found a twig and opened the driver's door of the Cadillac. He pressed the horn button, jammed it with the twig, then stepped into the shadows. The horn pierced the desert night, and through the trees Rick could see the lights of another house come on. The neighbors were annoyed.

A moment later, Stampano appeared at the front door in a dressing gown, a gun in his hand. He looked around the property and, seeing no one, ran quickly down the front steps to the open door of the car. Holding the gun in front of him, he inspected both the front and rear seats before checking the horn. The noise stopped, and the man could be heard swearing to himself. He turned to start back to the house, and Rick stepped out of the shadows.

"You were warned," Rick said.

Stampano's gun hung at his side in his hand,

but Rick's .45 was pointed at his head. "You haven't got the balls," Stampano said.

Rick fired a single shot at Stampano's face. He staggered against the Cadillac, then fell, the gun clattering across the pavement. Rick took a quick look at him. The top of his head was gone. Satisfied, he ran lightly down the driveway and looked both ways up and down the street. Lights were going on; he had only a moment. He ran to Glenna's car, leaped inside and released the hand brake. The car began to roll silently down the hill. Not until he was around the next corner did he start the engine, and he drove another block before turning on the headlights.

Rick drove aimlessly around for ten minutes to be sure none of Stampano's colleagues were following him, then headed home. He parked Glenna's car in the driveway next to his own and went into the house. He quickly dismantled and cleaned the .45 and reloaded it, to have it ready for any inspection. He was washing his hands in the bathroom when the doorbell rang.

Rick retrieved the gun and, holding it behind him, walked cautiously to the door, checking windows. He peeked through the sidelight at the front door and saw Ben Morrison standing there.

Rick opened the door. "Good evening, Ben," he said.

Ben stepped inside without being invited. "So it's done," he said. It wasn't a question.

"What's done?"

"Don't play dumb with me, Rick. The hood is still warm on Glenna's car, and I smell gun oil."

"I don't have the faintest idea what you're talking about," Rick replied.

"Here's how this is going to go," Ben said. "I came here and got you out of bed. Both cars were cold. Your gun was clean. I went away. When I came back to talk to you the following morning, you were gone. Asking around, I discovered that you had left for Canada to join the RAF in Montreal. No way to track you down. Got that?"

"You really think this is necessary, Ben?"

"You're suspect number one, Rick, and you have shit for an alibi, so don't even start with me. You've got motive and opportunity, and a comparison of the bullet we dig out of Stampano is probably going to match your gun. Jesus, you know the drill."

"I guess I do."

"And we're not going to be the only people looking for you," Ben said. "When Bugsy Siegel hears about this, goons all over Beverly Hills will be hunting you."

"Could be."

"The Canada story sound all right to you?"

"I guess so. How much time do I have?"

"I'll give you until nine a.m. I'll get Stampano's body taken to the morgue as a John Doe, and I'll see that the story doesn't get to the press before then. Is that enough time for you to get clear of the city?"

379

"I'd rather have a day."

Ben shook his head. "You'd be in jail or dead by noon."

Rick nodded. "I'd appreciate every minute you can give me."

"By ten o'clock it'll be out of my hands."

"I understand. Thanks for your help, Ben."

"Take care of yourself, Rick. Don't come home for a long time, and check with me before you do."

"I will." The two men shook hands, and Ben left.

Rick went into the house and called Eddie Harris at home.

"Hello?" Eddie sounded sleepy and annoyed.

"It's Rick."

"God, man, I've been trying to call you. I heard about Glenna from Judson. Where are you?"

"At home, but not for long. I have to leave town."

There was a moment's silence. "I gather our boy is not going to be a problem anymore?"

"Not the kind of problem he was before. Eddie, I'm going to have to depend on you for a few things."

"Anything I can do. Name it."

"The story is going to circulate that I went to Canada to enlist in the RAF, motivated by Clete's death. You can foster that idea without leaning on it too heavily."

"Sure."

380

"Glenna is going to need your help, and you'll have to explain to her why I had to leave at this moment."

"Of course I will. I'll be there when she wakes up."

"You're going to have to assign somebody to complete postproduction on the film, and I don't know what the hell you're going to tell people about the wedding — the invitations have already been mailed."

"I'll work up a story. You went to Canada, and Glenna went to see you off, something like that. She thought it was more important that you fight than get married, and now she's taking a long rest. I'll get her out of town, send her down to my place in Palm Springs to recuperate."

"I'll leave that to you."

"Are you going to be able to get into the Navy right away?"

"I hope so. There's a class starting the first of every month. That's next week, and I've already had my physical."

"Let me know if you have a problem getting accepted, and I'll make some calls."

"Will do."

"You need any money?"

"No, I've got a couple of thousand in the safe here."

"You're still on the payroll, pal."

"That's more than generous, Eddie. You're a good friend."

"Call me when you can, and send me an address when you get one."

"I will. Tell Glenna I'll call her tomorrow at the clinic and that I love her more than ever."

"Will do."

"Goodbye, Eddie."

"Goodbye, my friend."

Rick hung up and went to put a few things in a bag.

At eight a.m. Rick was parked at Hollywood and Vine, outside the Navy recruiting office. He saw Lieutenant Commander Chelton park his car and open the front door, and he followed the naval officer inside.

"Well, Mr. Barron," Chelton said, offering his hand. "You thinking of joining the Navy?"

Rick shook his hand. "Is right now too soon?"

Chelton smiled. "Come into my office. Let me see what I can do."

61

Fifteen months passed. Rick had been sent to San Diego by bus for induction, then he traveled by train to Pensacola, Florida, where he was introduced to Navy flying. The training was in Boeing Stearmans, which Rick had flown before, and his only difficulties were in hiding his previous experience from his instructors so that he would not have to join their number, and in flying the Navy way, instead of his own.

Rick got a letter every week from Eddie Harris, and the first one was disturbing. Eddie had been with Glenna at the Judson Clinic when she awakened after her ordeal, but three days later someone came for her in a car, and she walked out of the clinic and disappeared. Rick worried about her, pined for her, but not even Eddie Harris had been able to find her.

Subsequent letters kept Rick posted on studio production and passed on gossip. The killing of Stampano had made front-page news in LA, but as time passed without a resolution of the case, the story had faded from the news. Word from

Ben Morrison, though, was that Ben Siegel was livid and that his boys were still looking for Rick. The story of his trip to Canada to join the RAF and the cancellation of the wedding had made the papers and had apparently been accepted, as had the news of Glenna's taking time off from work. There had been some speculation in the columns that she might have gone to England to be with Rick.

Rick, who had immediately been pinned with the nickname "Dad" by the younger pilots, had received his wings and commission and had been sent back to San Diego for four months of gunnery and bombing training. He had been so proficient that he had been unable to avoid becoming an instructor, but after months at this, and with Eddie Harris's help, he had finally gotten a carrier assignment. Still, neither he nor Eddie had heard from Glenna.

So it was that, on a Sunday morning in early December '41, Rick had stood on a quay in San Diego and watched his new ship, the *Saratoga*, sail into the harbor. Then a car had driven onto the quay, and people had begun to gather around it to listen to the radio. Their excitement and shock attracted Rick, and he walked over to hear the first reports of the attack on Pearl Harbor. He sailed for Hawaii on the *Saratoga* the following day.

They had arrived at Pearl on the fifteenth of December, when there was still smoke rising from the ruined ships scattered about the harbor, and everyone who stood on the flight deck, staring, had been appalled by the carnage — huge ships capsized, beached, or on the bottom of the harbor, only their superstructures showing above water.

There had been no liberty, just a quick refueling, and word was they were on their way to relieve embattled Wake Island. They were delayed by their slow oiler, and when word was received that Wake had been overrun, they turned back. Rick's squadron had been thirsty for action, and there was much disappointment.

Their luck failed again when the *Saratoga* was torpedoed by a Japanese submarine and had to return to the States for repairs, thus missing the Battle of Midway.

During their stay in San Diego, Eddie Harris came down from LA for dinner with Rick at the Hotel del Coronado, where he was quartered. They sat down to dinner in the dining room.

"The Army Air Corps requisitioned our DC-3," Eddie said sadly, "so I had to drive down. They say we'll get it back, but I don't believe them. I think some general is flying around in it."

"Have you heard anything at all from Glenna?" Rick asked.

"Only secondhand," Eddie said. "Barbara Kane told me that she was in New York having surgery on her face, but that now she's in Wisconsin."

"Back home. She still has relatives there."

"She's worried about Siegel, I think. She called Ben Morrison last week, and he told her to stay where she was."

"I don't blame her."

"The good news is, Luciano is going to be deported to Italy when the war's over."

"I thought he was doing thirty years."

"He was, but apparently after the burning of the *Normandie* in the New York docks, he was helpful to the government in getting the dockers unions to help with harbor security, so they're going to ship him back to the land of his birth at the first opportunity. I think this is a good development for us, having him out of the country. It seems clear that Stampano's protection came from Luciano, not Siegel."

"I hope you're right. I always had the feeling that Siegel didn't like Stampano all that much, anyway. What set Siegel off was my getting into his safe, then killing one of his people."

Eddie dug into a pocket and retrieved a fat envelope and handed it to Rick. "This came for you at the studio," he said. "It's postmarked London, July of 'forty."

"Well, that took a long time, didn't it?" Rick looked at the envelope. "It seems to have gotten wet somewhere along the way." He ripped it open and read the first page. "Good God!" he said.

"What is it?"

"It's from a firm of solicitors in London, and

there's a copy of Clete Barrow's will. Apparently he bequeathed me all his assets in LA."

"You mean his house?"

"His house, car, clothes and whatever he had in the bank. There's an LA law firm handling that part of his estate."

"You want me to look into it for you?"

"Yes, thanks. I'll give you a letter authorizing you to represent me."

"The house is closed up. I heard that the Filipino couple who worked for Clete have opened a little restaurant in West Hollywood."

"Good for them."

"Clete's car is still in our transportation department. Hiram told me he got the parts he needed in what must have been the last shipment from Germany before war was declared. He's determined to rebuild it."

"How's business?"

"We're doing great with war-related movies and comedies. *Caper* did well, and Glenna got a nomination but didn't win."

"I read about it in the papers."

"We're making some training films, which have to be shot quickly and cheaply, and we're picking up some techniques that will come in handy when we get into television."

"You're getting into television?"

"Well, not until after the war, but I think there'll be an explosion of sets as soon as they can start making them again, so there'll be money to be made. You heard about Carole

Lombard, of course."

"Yes, I wrote Clark a letter but didn't hear back from him. He must have been inundated with mail after she died."

"He took it very hard. He volunteered for the draft, you know; got a commission and trained as a gunner in bombers."

"I read something about it."

"They'll never let him fly missions, you know. If he got killed, it wouldn't be good for morale, but he's in England." Eddie cleared his throat. "Listen, Rick, I apologize for bringing this up, but I just want you to think about it."

"What?"

"I can get you transferred back to LA. You can make training films for us."

"No chance, Eddie. I haven't even seen combat yet."

"I figured I'd try. I can understand why you want combat."

"We're sailing — well, I can't tell you when, but soon — and I think we'll be in it before long."

"I'm glad for you, and sorry at the same time. I don't want to lose you."

"I don't want to lose me, either," Rick replied. He looked at his watch. "Well, I have some packing to do." They got up and he walked Eddie to the parking lot.

"There's going to be plenty for you to do when this is over, kid," Eddie said. "I'm going to need you. You remember that."

"I will," Rick replied. "Eddie, will you see if you can find Glenna in Milwaukee? I'm sure that's where she is."

"Right away."

"Tell her I love her, and give her my APO number, so she can write." Rick handed Eddie a card with the address.

They shook hands and hugged, and Rick walked back to his room. The *Saratoga* would sail the following morning.

62

Early August 1942. Rick launched from the *Saratoga* and circled while his squadron fell in with him. He was a lieutenant now, and a squadron commander, the fruits of his age and rapid wartime promotion.

The aircraft formed up and followed Rick toward the beaches of Guadalcanal. He could see the wakes of hundreds of landing craft circling, waiting for the artillery barrage on the beaches to cease so they could land their Marines.

The barrage ended as Rick's squadron approached, and he led his airplanes down to the beach. They made two runs, dropping bombs just inland from the beach and strafing any Japanese positions they could see, then returned to the *Saratoga* for fuel and rearming. Four more times that day they made the run, bombing and strafing targets farther inland, as the Marines progressed. Rick rarely knew if they hit anything, since the Japanese positions were carefully concealed. They made another dozen runs the following day, and at the end of the second day, Rick counted thirty-one bullet holes in his airplane, small-arms fire, fortunately. On the third day they withdrew toward a rendezvous with an oiler for refueling the *Saratoga*, and they took on ammunition and supplies from other ships.

They took on mail, too, and Rick waited in vain for the mail clerk to bring him something. He had still not heard from Glenna, and Eddie Harris had not been able to find her. His only theory was that her face was ruined, and she didn't want him to see her ever again. His heart ached whenever he thought about it. He was determined that the first stateside leave he got, he would go to Milwaukee and find her himself.

Rick was taking a nap the following evening in the small cabin he shared with another officer when an announcement came over the squawk box:

"THIS IS THE CAPTAIN SPEAKING. ALL OFF-DUTY PERSONNEL WILL REPORT IMMEDIATELY TO THE HANGAR DECK FOR SPECIAL TRAINING." The announcement was repeated.

"What the hell?" his cabinmate said from the upper bunk. "What kind of training?"

"Beats me," Rick said wearily, getting to his feet and stretching.

"You think he meant officers, too?"

"He said 'all off-duty personnel,' " Rick reminded him. "The old man is always specific. Come on, get your ass in gear."

Half an hour later, Rick found himself sitting on the deck among a group of flyers, waiting for he knew not what. Then the lights dimmed and total blackness ensued. A moment later, he heard a whir of machinery, and then a hauntingly familiar sound, one he had not heard for nearly three years: the Artie Shaw Orchestra playing "Nightmare." Then the lights came on, illuminating the giant elevator used to lift aircraft between the hangar and the deck. It was descending, and the band was riding it.

A gigantic cheer went up from the three thousand men assembled there, drowning out the music for the moment. Then the elevator reached the hangar deck, and the band broke into "Traffic Jam," and the men went wild.

Rick was carried along with the moment, until they finished the number and began to play "Begin the Beguine." At that he was overwhelmed with memories of Ciro's and the Shaw band and Glenna singing "Stardust." He got up and, choking back tears, made his way back to his cabin and threw himself on his bunk. From down the companionway, he could hear the band on the squawk box, and he pulled a pillow around his ears to blot it out. Soon he was asleep, until he found himself being shaken by a yeoman.

"Mr. Barron," the man said, "the air officer

wants you in the briefing room on the double!"

Rick shook himself awake. The music could no longer be heard. He checked his watch: after eleven. He splashed some water on his face and made his way to the briefing room. A night mission? What was going on?

He entered the briefing room, only to find it empty, its lights dimmed. A large-scale map of Guadalcanal was up on the board, showing their most recent targets. They would be going back tomorrow. He took a seat in the front row, then he heard the door open and close behind him.

"Rick?" A woman's voice. There were no women on the *Saratoga*. He got up and turned around. She was standing in the shadows by the door, and he began walking toward her. "Glenna?" he said, though he knew it couldn't be.

"I found you," she said.

He swept her up in his arms and held her off the floor, kissing the tears from her face. "Am I dreaming?" he finally managed to ask. "How did you get here?"

"Artie brought me," she said. "I've been touring the Pacific with the band."

He held her back and looked at her. The face was nearly, but not quite, the same. "You're beautiful," he said.

"If I am, you can thank a doctor in New York."

He led her to a chair and sat down beside her. "Tell me everything."

She took a deep breath. "First of all, I'm so sorry I haven't been in touch."

"That's all right, you're here now. Just tell me what's happened."

"I woke up in the Judson Clinic, and Eddie Harris was there. I didn't — still don't — remember what happened. Eddie told me that Stampano was dead and that Bugsy Siegel was looking for you, and that you'd had to leave LA. He told me you were joining the Navy. I had known something like that was coming, of course, but I hadn't expected it so soon."

"Neither had I," Rick said.

"After the swelling went down on my face, a few days later, Barbara came to get me, and I took the train to New York and moved in with a girlfriend, another actress I'd known at home in Wisconsin. I found a doctor and had three operations to repair the damage."

"You look wonderful."

"Oh, I'll never be quite the same again, but he did a good job with what he had to work with."

"You look wonderful to me."

"When my doctor was satisfied that he'd done all he could, he said all I needed was time to heal, so I went back to Wisconsin and stayed with an aunt. An agent I'd met in New York wrote me and said that Artie had joined the Navy and formed a band. He knew that I'd sung with Artie on occasion, and he sent Artie a telegram asking if he might want me for a tour. And, three months later, here I am. Did you hear me sing 'Stardust' for you?"

"No, I went back to my cabin as soon as Artie began playing the familiar stuff. The memories were a little too much."

"I thought you'd find me, but when you didn't, I asked one of the ship's officers and he took me to the air officer, and he sent me here. Now tell me about what's been happening to you."

Rick told her about his training and his assignment to the *Saratoga*, about his letters from Eddie, too. "You should write to Eddie," he said. "He's worried about you."

"Oh, Eddie will just want me to come back to work."

"No, not yet. Not until he knows you'll be safe."

"I won't feel safe in LA again until you're there with me. Oh, and neither of us should go back there. Ben Morrison told me before we sailed for the Pacific that Siegel is still determined to get you."

"Well, it may be a while before I get stateside again. I'm here for the duration. How long can you stay?"

"Only until they come for me. The band's instruments are being loaded on launches right now. We're sleeping on a hospital ship tonight and giving a show there tomorrow." There was a knock on the door.

"Go away!" Rick yelled.

The door opened and the air officer came in.

"Sorry, Miss Gleason, but you're needed at the gangway immediately. The boat is ready to leave. Rick, let go of that girl."

They stood up and embraced. "I want to hear from you often," she said, pressing her address into his hand. He gave her his APO number and kissed her once more, then she was gone.

He sank back into his seat, trying to remember every moment of their short time together.

63

In late August, Rick and his squadron were summoned to the briefing room and told that there were reports of a large force of escorted troop transports approaching Guadalcanal, in an attempt to reinforce the Japanese presence on the island.

Rick led his squadron in search of the convoy, but they failed to find it and returned to the *Saratoga*, short of fuel. As they were landing, another report came in of a contact report on enemy carriers, and as soon as they were refueled, Rick's squadron launched again.

Shortly after midafternoon, Rick spotted a carrier dead ahead and mustered his group for a bombing run. As he dived on the carrier, Rick could see that aircraft were being readied for launch, and he wanted badly to put one into the deck to prevent them from taking off. His angle of attack was steep, and he cut loose his bombs at five hundred feet, then pulled away in a climbing right turn, looking over his shoulder for results. He saw one of his bombs strike the carrier's deck amidships and another, not his, farther aft, and he identified the carrier as the *Ryujo,* as he had been trained to do.

As he continued his turn, he heard a loud bang and felt something shake his airplane and, simultaneously, severe pain, as if someone had kicked him in the right knee. He continued his climbing turn away from the carrier and set a rough course for the *Saratoga.* Then he saw that his instrument panel was spattered with blood and, looking down, found a hole six inches across in the fuselage, through which he could see the leading edge of his wing. His ass felt warm and wet, and he knew he was losing blood rapidly.

He yanked the scarf from around his neck, tucked it under his thigh and made a tourniquet, while flying the airplane left-handed.

"Skipper, one more run?" his number two called on the radio.

"Affirmative," Rick replied, "but I've been hit, and I'm heading for home. The squadron is yours."

"I'm with you, Skipper," he heard his wingman say, and he looked out to see the airplane flying formation with him.

"They didn't have a chance to launch before we bombed," Rick said, "but they could've gotten something up before we got there. Keep a sharp eye out."

"Wilco. Are you hurt?"

"I took something in my right knee, but I'm

controlling the bleeding. How's your fuel?"

"Nearly half full; no sweat."

Rick felt a wave of nausea and fought it off. He took a long swig from his canteen and began looking for the *Saratoga*.

"We've got an undercast ahead, three miles, looks like tops at one thousand," his wingman said.

"Roger, let's get under it now," Rick replied and pushed the stick forward while retarding the throttle. The tops were at seven hundred feet, not a thousand, and he wasn't under the clouds until two hundred feet. He leveled off. "*Saratoga*, Sparrow One, coming in damaged but controllable. Give me your heading and a short transmit."

"Sparrow One, read you loud and clear. Heading is three, zero, zero. Did you get my transmit?"

Rick had already watched the radio direction–finding needle swing left fifteen degrees, and he adjusted his heading. "Roger."

"We have a three-hundred-foot overcast here. Are you on top?"

"Negative, Sparrow One and Two level at two hundred. We'll be straight in."

"Roger, Sparrow One. We're painting you at twelve miles with numerous aircraft eight miles behind you on your heading. Is that your squadron?"

"Negative. My group is making a second run. Those will be bandits, but they'll have a hard time finding you, what with the overcast."

"Roger, Sparrow One, continue your approach. Call deck in sight."

Rick saw the *Saratoga* ten miles away and turned slightly to line up on the deck. "*Saratoga* in sight, nine miles, straight in. Sparrow Two is behind me." He saw his wingman drop back to line up behind him and kept his speed up for a moment longer to allow him spacing.

"Roger, Sparrow One. Will you require assistance?"

"Affirmative, leg wound."

"Do you want to ditch?"

"Negative, airplane is controllable." Rick dropped the gear, put in a notch of flaps and retarded the throttle.

"You're hot and low, Sparrow One."

"Roger, slowing." He put in another notch of flaps and watched his airspeed come down, then, two miles out, the final notch of flaps.

"You're still hot, Sparrow One."

"I may need the net," Rick said. "Sparrow Two, you read that?"

"Roger."

"If I need the net, go around."

"Roger."

Rick was still ten knots hot at five hundred feet, and he wasn't going to get any slower. He watched the deck man with his paddles and hoped to God he didn't get a waveoff. He was a little light-headed now. The deck rushed up at him, and the deck man waved him in. He touched down and felt the hook grab, then he fainted.

He felt people clawing at his clothing as he came to. He didn't have a left sleeve anymore, and he saw a medic standing above him, holding a pint of blood, which was draining into his arm.

"Easy there, Lieutenant," the man said. "We're cutting your clothes off."

"Do I still have two legs?" Rick managed to ask.

"So far," the man replied.

Rick fainted again.

He woke up two days later. A doctor came and looked into his eyes with a flashlight. "Can you talk to me, Lieutenant?" the man asked.

"What would you like to talk about?" Rick muttered.

"You're on a hospital ship, bound for Pearl," the man said. "You're going to need knee surgery, and we don't want to do it here. There's a good man at Pearl, though."

"I'm thirsty," Rick said.

"Scotch or bourbon?"

"As long as it's wet." A straw was stuck in his mouth and he sucked on it greedily. "It doesn't hurt," he said when he could.

"That's the beauty of morphine," the doctor said.

Six weeks later, he was wheeled aboard a

supply ship returning to San Diego. Two weeks after that, he was in Cedars-Sinai in Los Angeles, being examined by the best knee man on the West Coast, courtesy of Eddie Harris.

Three weeks after that, he was home. So was Glenna. He was a civilian now. Two studio cops were guarding the house at all times.

In March of '43, assisted by a cane, he hobbled down the aisle next to Glenna at Eddie and Suzanne Harris's house. Among the ton of flowers, Rick had seen a large horseshoe of roses with a card reading, *I wish you both every happiness. Ben Siegel.*

Rick didn't believe it for a moment, but he had been awarded a Distinguished Flying Cross for his squadron's sinking of the Japanese carrier, and Siegel wouldn't want to mess with a war hero. Not yet, anyway. He would bide his time, and Rick would just have to be ready.

64

June 1947. Eddie Harris sat in Sol Weinman's old office, going over the plans for a new soundstage. Weinman had been dead for a year, and Eddie was now chairman and CEO of the studio. Rick was head of production and working in Eddie's old office.

Building materials had been in short supply since the beginning of the war, but lumber was starting to become available again, and Eddie was thinking about starting construction on a new soundstage. He was going to need it, if his plans for a television production department were going to develop on schedule.

Eddie's phone buzzed, and he pressed a key. "Yes?"

"A Lieutenant Ben Morrison for you. He says you know him."

"I know him. Put him through." He picked up the phone. "Ben?" He had spoken to Morrison often over the past seven years.

"Yes, Mr. Harris."

"Congratulations on your promotion."

"Thank you, sir."

"What can I do for you?"

"I hoped I wouldn't have to make this call, but you told me if it became necessary, to call you and not Rick Barron."

"Yes, I did, Ben. Tell me about it."

"This is for your ears only."

"Of course."

"My people arrested a medium-level mob guy a couple of days ago."

"He works for . . . ?"

"He's out of New York, the Genovese family. They were looking at him hard for two murders back East, and he came out here to reduce the heat."

"I see. And this affects us how?"

"We've been sweating him, and he's starting to play ball a little. He wants to go to Mexico, but we're in his way, so we have some leverage with the guy."

"Go on."

"This guy has just come back from Naples, where he took a vacation, and where he spent a fair amount of time with Charlie Luciano."

"That's interesting."

"Yeah, it is. He says that during this time, he and Charlie Lucky fell into conversation about West Coast activities, and Charlie tells him, in the way of an anecdote, about a blackmail thing that Ben Siegel was running out here."

Eddie froze. "Are we talking about . . ."

"We are."

"And Luciano said *Ben Siegel* was running it?"

"That's what he said."

"Did Stampano's name come up?"

"It did. Luciano said that Siegel was using Stampano for the legwork, the setting up of the girls."

"Holy shit."

"My sentiments exactly."

"How much credence do you place in this guy's story?"

"I sat in on the interrogation and we went through this backward and forward, and I can't see that this guy has any particular ax to grind with Siegel or anybody else out here. He's just looking to get out from under. I think the subject came up because he was looking to entertain us a little."

"I see."

"There's more. He says Siegel sent Rick and Glenna some flowers on their wedding day, with a message. You know anything about that?"

"Yes, I saw them and the message myself."

"This guy says Siegel did that to get them to relax. Then, in due course he would get around to them. This guy says Siegel is still deeply angry about the busting up of his plans and the killing of his guy."

"I haven't heard much about Siegel lately."

"He's been spending his time up in Las Vegas. He bought this hotel and casino, and he's expanding it — word is, with mob money."

"Yeah, I did hear something about that."

"We've had reports that Siegel has given up all his mob activity except this casino, but our guy says that's not entirely true."

"What is true?"

"Siegel flies back and forth to LA in a private airplane, makes him hard to keep track of at times. This guy says that soon, on one of his trips back, he's going to personally settle the score for Stampano. Siegel has always been known to be a guy who holds a grudge forever."

"Personally?"

"That's what this guy says."

"And you think he's credible?"

"There's no way to check this, of course, unless it's finding Rick with a bullet in his head, but this guy has given us other stuff that's been verifiable. I tend to believe him."

"Where is Siegel now?"

"I hear he's coming back to LA today, to meet with some people from New York. Seems he's into a lot of cost overruns with the casino, and it's not going down well with the boys putting up the money."

"Does Siegel still live in that house he made Lawrence Tibbet sell him?"

"No, he had to sell the place to raise money for the casino. He lives at Virginia Hill's house now, when he's in LA."

"I know the place. Well, Ben, thank you very much for the information. I'll see that you get a little something in the mail very soon."

"My pleasure, Mr. Harris."

Eddie hung up and sat thinking for a moment, then he rooted around in his desk drawer for a slip of paper he knew was there somewhere. He found it and dialed the number. It rang several times then was finally answered.

"This is Al," a voice said.

65

Rick, dressed in tennis clothes, lay on a blanket in the backyard of his newly built house, watching, fascinated, as his two-year-old daughter ran through the grass chasing a retriever puppy. Both of them seemed to be enjoying themselves immensely, he thought.

He could see Glenna leaving the house with a tray of glasses, heading his way. She was past playing tennis now, being due for another child in a month, but Eddie and Suzanne Harris were expected, and they had said they were bringing a fourth.

He loosened the brace on his knee a notch. He didn't want it too tight, it would cut off the circulation. He'd been playing again for a month or so, and he was getting around the court quite well.

Glenna set the tray on a nearby table. "They should be here soon, shouldn't they?"

"Soon."

"Your dad is coming at one, for lunch."

"Great."

Rick looked back toward the house and saw

408

the Harrises and another couple coming. As they got closer, he saw that the man was David Niven. They had not seen each other since the war. He got to his feet.

"Rick, my dear fellow," Niven cried, smiling broadly. They pumped hands and Niven introduced Rick to his wife.

"I gave David the new script this morning," Eddie said. Suzanne and Mrs. Niven went to greet the little girl. "You seen the paper yet?"

"Not this morning."

Eddie handed Rick the Los Angeles *Times*. "I thought you'd be interested in this."

Rick took the paper and was greeted by a photograph of a man in a suit, sprawled on a sofa. Some of his face was missing. The headline read: "Ben 'Bugsy' Siegel Dead in Apparent Mob Slaying."

"Holy shit," Rick said.

"My sentiments exactly," Eddie said. "Word is, Ben spent way too much of some other people's money on this casino thing of his in Nevada; made his investors unhappy. Other people have already taken over the project."

Rick looked at the text of the story. "30–06 rifle, many shots fired. Sounds like a BAR."

"All sorts of war surplus stuff available these days," Niven said.

"Yes," Rick agreed, glancing at Eddie, who seemed to be avoiding his gaze.

"Well," Eddie said, "that's that. Tennis, anyone?"

Rick went and handed the paper to Glenna. "Read that when you get a chance."

"How's the knee?" Eddie asked as they walked down to the court.

"Never better," Rick said. "Funny about Ben Siegel getting it that way."

"I don't think it was a mob hit," Eddie said.

"No?"

"Nah, I think Virginia Hill had him blasted. Probably caught him with another woman. Ben always liked the girls."

"Maybe a little too much."

"Yeah," Eddie said, "maybe a little too much."

"I like the mob hit theory better, though."

"That works for me, too," Eddie said. "You serve. Cripples first."

"That remark is going to cost you, pal," Rick said.

Acknowledgments

I want, once again, to express my thanks to my editor, David Highfill, and all the people at Putnam who work so hard to get my work to its readers.

I'd also like to thank my literary agents, Morton Janklow and Anne Sibbald for their continuing attention to my career over the past twenty-three years. Where would I be without them?

I'm grateful to the master gunsmith, Terry Tussey, who makes .45s very much like Rick Barron's, for his patient tutorials on firearms.

Author's Note

I am happy to hear from readers, but you should know that if you write to me in care of my publisher, three to six months will pass before I receive your letter, and when it finally arrives it will be one among many, and I will not be able to reply.

However, if you have access to the Internet, you may visit my Web site at www.stuartwoods. com, where there is a button for sending me e-mail. So far, I have been able to reply to all of my e-mail, and I will continue to try to do so.

If you send me an e-mail and do not receive a reply, it is because you are among an alarming number of people who have entered their e-mail address incorrectly in their mail software. I have many of my replies returned as undeliverable.

Remember: e-mail, reply; snail mail, no reply.

When you e-mail, please do not send attachments, as I *never* open these. They can take twenty minutes to download, and they often contain viruses.

Please do not place me on your mailing lists

for funny stories, prayers, political causes, charitable fund-raising, petitions, or sentimental claptrap. I get enough of that from people I already know. Generally speaking, when I get e-mail addressed to a large number of people, I immediately delete it without reading it.

Please do not send me your ideas for a book, as I have a policy of writing only what I myself invent. If you send me story ideas, I will immediately delete them without reading them. If you have a good idea for a book, write it yourself, but I will not be able to advise you on how to get it published. Buy a copy of *Writer's Market* at any bookstore; that will tell you how.

Anyone with a request concerning events or appearances may e-mail it to me or send it to: Publicity Department, G. P. Putnam's Sons, 375 Hudson Street, New York, NY 10014.

Those ambitious folk who wish to buy film, dramatic, or television rights to my books should contact Matthew Snyder, Creative Artists Agency, 9830 Wilshire Boulevard, Beverly Hills, CA 90212–1825.

Those who wish to conduct business of a more literary nature should contact Anne Sibbald, Janklow & Nesbit, 445 Park Avenue, New York, NY 10022.

If you want to know if I will be signing books in your city, please visit my Web site, www. stuartwoods.com, where the tour schedule will be published a month or so in advance. If you wish me to do a book signing in your locality, ask your favorite bookseller to contact his Putnam representative or the G. P. Putnam's Sons publicity department with the request.

If you find typographical or editorial errors in my book and feel an irresistible urge to tell someone, please write to David Highfill at Putnam, address above. Do not e-mail your discoveries to me, as I will already have learned about them from others.

A list of all my published works appears in the front of this book. All the novels are still in print in paperback and can be found at or ordered from any bookstore. If you wish to obtain hardcover copies of earlier novels or of the two non-fiction books, a good used-book store or one of the online bookstores can help you find them. Otherwise, you will have to go to a great many garage sales.